M000032868

Love Sick

Autumn J. Bright

A
LIGHT
BULB
Publishing

North Carolina

Love Sick is a work of fiction. All of the characters, organizations, and events portrayed in this novel are either products of the author's imagination or are used fictitiously.

Copyright © 2014 by Autumn J. Bright
Excerpt from *Lovely* Copyright © 2015 by Autumn J. Bright

All rights reserved.

No part of the this book may be reproduced in any form or by any electronic or mechanical means, including information storage and retrieval systems, without permission in writing from the publisher except by a reviewer who may quote brief passages in a review.

This book contains a preview from the forthcoming novel *Lovely* by Autumn J. Bright. The excerpt was set for this edition only and may not reflect the content of the forthcoming edition.

Library of Congress Control Number: 2015902636

ISBN: 978-0-9861923-1-9
eBook ISBN: 978-0-9861923-0-2

Printed in the United States of America

Cover design by Damonza
Photography by Jennifer Wolfe

First Edition

www.autumnjbright.com

www.alightbulbpublishing.com

Dedicated to Mother

Love is a mysterious force.

Love Sick

Prologue

From the corners of my heavy eyes, I see bright flashing lights. I hear indistinct voices everywhere. My body is weightless, and I am traveling fast.

I feel pain. I'm afraid.

What about my children?

Now darkness surrounds me, and it's getting cold.

I'm fading.

So, this is death…

Toni

Part One

Chapter 1
Saturday, August 9, 1986 11:43 PM

She paced up and down the living room floor multiple times and then stopped to pull back the curtains and peek out of the window. While waiting anxiously for someone to pick up the line, she wiped her snotty nose with a wad of toilet tissue. She couldn't believe the horrible thing she just witnessed. A second later, a woman answered.

"911, what is your emergency?"

"Please, ma'am. I need help! He's hurting Mrs. Jones," she said over the telephone, her young voice taking on an even higher pitch. The girl was frantic.

"Who's hurting Mrs. Jones?" the operator asked.

"It's her husband. He's beating her up right now. Please hurry up. Please send help!"

"Okay, now listen to me," said the operator. "I know you're scared, but I need you to slow down and give me some information. Can you do that for me?"

The girl closed her eyes and inhaled deeply to settle her nerves. "Yes ma'am," she answered, twirling the telephone cord around her skinny fingers.

"What is your name?"

"Janette Simmons."

"How old are you, Janette?"

"I'm sixteen."

"And are you calling me from a safe place?"

Janette nervously scanned the room to make sure her surroundings were still secured. It had taken her all of one minute, with the assistance of a baseball bat, to lock all windows and doors before dialing 911.

"Yes, I'm fine," she answered. "I'm home, and my mom should be on her way."

"Good. Now tell me what happened."

Janette took another deep breath, rubbed her swollen red-strained eyes, and began to tell her story. "I was baby-sitting at the Jones' and around eleven o'clock, I heard arguing outside. So, I looked out the window and saw him. It was kinda dark, but I could see Mr. Jones on top of Ms. Toni. He was beating her. "

"Ms. Toni is the wife, right? That's her first name?"

"Yes ma'am," she whimpered.

"Okay, go on. What happened next?"

"Well, somehow he knew I was watching because he stopped hitting her, turned around, and headed straight for me. I was so afraid. But, as soon as he got in the house, I found the nerve to ask him what was going on. But, he didn't answer. Instead he just grabbed me by the arm and threw me into the room with the kids. Then he said, 'Don't think about coming out!' And—"

"Hold on Janette, stop right there," the operator interrupted. "How many children do the Joneses have and where are they right now?"

"They have two," she sniffled. "But I had to leave them behind."

"Okay Janette, go ahead and give me their address. Do you know it by heart?"

"Yes ma'am, it's 1711 Lackman Road. They live in the brown house at the end of the street."

"Okay, sweetie, I've got it. Help is on the way."

"Oh, thank God!" the girl said, feeling somewhat relieved. But then a silence came over her as images of Mr. Jones started to reemerge in her head. The phone drifted from her ear as she stood in place and started looking around.

"Are you still there, Janette?" the operator asked, waiting for a reply.

"Janette, are you there?" she sternly asked again.

"Yes, I'm here," the girl finally answered. "I'm sorry. My mind kinda wandered off. It's just that I keep seeing his face. I mean, I've watched their kids several times before, and I've never seen him like that. And when I saw blood on his shirt, I just knew I had to get help."

"There was blood on his shirt?"

"Yes, ma'am," Janette murmured with a low moan. "That's why I hid those kids in the closet. I needed to crawl out the window and get help fast. I don't know what he's done to her, but I think she's hurt real bad."

Immediately after speaking those words, the unthinkable crept into her mind. Fear took over and Janette yelled out, "She could be dead! Oh, please hurry up. Please help them!" She began to sob uncontrollably.

"Alright, honey, calm down," the operator said, using a soothing voice like she'd done in so many other emergency calls. "I know it's difficult, but you have to relax. The police are almost there. And I promise you, I will stay on this phone until they arrive."

Janette flopped on the couch, wiped her tear-stained face, then breathed in deeply to console herself. She tried being strong but couldn't stop the tears from pooling up in the corners of her eyes. Janette clutched a throw pillow and started thinking about the children.

"I just hope those kids listened to me. I told them to stay in the closet and keep quiet until someone came to get them out."

"It's okay, Janette. You did the right thing. Let's just pray everything will turn out fine."

Janette lowered her head as though the weight of the world had been placed upon her boney shoulders. She didn't share the woman's optimism at all. She knew something bad had happened. There was too much blood on his shirt.

Chapter 2

Creeping up the steps in the humid night air, three police officers kept their guns pulled as they approached the front door. The dispatcher informed them that the assailant may have caused serious physical injuries and precautions should be taken.

"Mr. Jones, this is Sergeant Bryant from the Charleston County Sheriff's Office. I need you to open this door right now, sir." Sergeant Bryant sounded like a dominant figure with a deep Southern accent and looked to be in his mid to late thirties. He was white, stood around 6 feet 3 inches tall, had a bald head that shined like a brand new bowling ball, and weighed in at about 215 pounds of pure muscle and attitude.

"We got a complaint regarding a domestic dispute from here. Sir, you've got about thirty seconds to open this door."

Time elapsed. He already had probable cause.

"Cover me," the sergeant ordered.

The door cracked open after a few hard kicks and the officers strategically filed in to search the premises. Blood trail on the floor. *Eerie silence in the house.* The officers looked at each other with a heightened sense of alertness. Quickly, they followed the red droplets and found him—Mr. Jones crouched over his wife on the bed in a pool of blood. He was saturated. Blood was all over his hands, shirt and in the corners of his mouth.

This is one sick son-of-a bitch, the sergeant thought to himself as he aimed with precision.

"Back off, Mr. Jones. Back off," he commanded.

A burst of adrenaline rushed in the moment the sergeant re-holstered his gun. It seemed like it took him one swift move to snatch the perpetrator off the bed, slam him up against the wall, and handcuff him while the other officers stood guard with their service weapons ready to be used if necessary.

"What the hell are you doing?" Mr. Jones shouted with his cheek pressed against the wood paneled wall. He started to resist by tensing his muscles and jerking around. "Why are you arresting me?" he asked, breathing heavily. He got no response and tried jerking one last time…still no match for the sergeant.

An officer leaned over and felt for a pulse. "She's unconscious but still alive. I'm getting the paramedics. You got this, Sergeant?"

Sergeant Bryant nodded and flashed an okay sign with his fingers while he caught his breath and wiped beads of sweat from his red face.

"Thomas," he instructed the other officer standing next to him, "go to the bedroom and get those kids out of that closet. And for heaven's sake, please don't bring them out this way. Use the back door. Those kids don't need to see their mama like this."

The entire ordeal made Sergeant Bryant sick to his stomach thinking about the woman lying on the bed. He had a wife. He had children. And he knew all too well from experience that only a dangerous, cold-hearted man could commit such a horrendous crime against a mother with her children in the next room. His attention went back to the suspect as the paramedic rushed in.

"Mr. Jones, you have the right to remain silent. Anything you say can and will be used against you in a court of law."

"Look man, I didn't do this shit!" he protested while being escorted out the door. "I found her that way. You've got it all wrong. I was trying to help her."

As Sergeant Bryant continued to recite the Miranda rights and proceed to the cruiser, he heard a paramedic announce, "She's been stabbed and is losing too much blood. Her pressure's getting low. We're running out of time. We need to get her to the hospital now."

Chapter 3

She ran down the hallway, and could barely catch her breath. Being forty-one years old and physically inactive, she couldn't remember the last time she ran so hard. It seemed like it was taking Thelma a lifetime to reach the ICU at Roper Hospital.

When she finally found the unit, she approached the receptionist and asked her about the location of Toni Jones and if she knew the whereabouts of the family members. The plus-sized lady behind the desk looked at Thelma with such sympathy, as though she knew something but wasn't allowed to tell. She pointed her finger toward the double doors. Thelma turned, feeling like her heart was in her stomach and its beat was the only sound she could hear. With great caution, bracing herself for whatever lay ahead, she entered the waiting room.

Thelma looked left and right to find a familiar face among the crowd. But she saw no one, making her anxiety worse. She had only been given the slightest details over the phone: Toni had been seriously hurt, and her children were being taken care of by the neighbors.

"Mama!" she desperately called out across the large room.

"Over here," a recognizable voice shouted back.

Thelma turned her head and there they were: her mother huddled between her two siblings sitting behind a row of tall tropical plants. "Mama, I got here as fast as I could. What happened to Toni? What did he do now?" Thelma fell into her mother's arms with a steady stream of tears flowing down her face.

"Thelma, your sister is hanging on to life by a thread, but we can't lose faith. We have got to believe *God* will pull her through this," her mother said with glassy eyes.

The news rendered Thelma speechless and her skinny legs too weak to stand on their own. Her knees buckled. Thelma's brother Charles and youngest sister Stephanie rushed over to catch her limp body and guided her to rest on a couch. Mama, also known as Pat by most, sat next to Thelma and latched on to her eldest daughter's hand. Her head lowered and eyes closed as she began a silent prayer.

Mama Pat was a reserved woman, the type who didn't cry often in front of people or show too much affection. But she loved and had a strong belief in faith. And she raised her children to be the same way: strong and enduring.

Pat raised her head.

"Like I said, we need to stay in prayer and be strong for your sister," Pat said, trying hard to push through her anguish as a mother while remaining the pillar of strength for her family. "Even though Toni survived the surgery, the doctor told us her condition is still critical because she's lost so much blood. The situation could go either way. It's just too early to tell."

Pat pulled out some tissue from her purse then continued to talk. "But I don't care what the doctor says. I believe she's going to make it. You know, she flatlined on that table tonight."

Thelma's eyes grew big.

"That's right, sure did. The doctor said it took them almost two minutes to resuscitate her. Thelma, your sister was at Heaven's door. But, with the grace of God, she came back to us and that tells me she's a fighter and wants to live."

"Resuscitation!" Thelma exclaimed. "Mama, what happened? What exactly did he do to her?

Pat tightened her lips and looked off into the distance while shaking her head. Thelma glanced at her siblings. Everyone had the same blank expression on their faces.

Something's not right. What the hell is going on?

"What are y'all not telling me?" she demanded.

Pat looked at Thelma and with a trembling voice said, "Chile, Toni was stabbed in the chest and a lung got punctured. The lung was so damaged, they had to remove it. She only has one now."

Thelma lost her breath—it felt just like the time when she fell out of a tree as a kid and got the wind knocked out of her sail. "What?" she managed to get out. "Oh my *God*, how did this happen?"

"What do you mean how did this happen?" Charles angrily jumped in. "You know exactly what happened. We all do."

Charles shot up out of his seat and stood in front of his mother in a stern manner. He knew all too well she didn't want to hear it, but it had to be said. This was no time to just pray, to let the *Lord* work it out and turn a blind eye.

"Now Mama, I've got something to say and I want you to listen to me. And I say this with all due respect, but you can't let Toni cover this one up. Marvin has been kicking her ass for way too long, and look where it's gotten her—on a hospital bed half dead."

"You better watch your tongue, Charles Jr.," Pat warned, giving her son an intense stare. "I told you, she's not going to die. So, don't talk like that and speak things into existence."

"Mama, that's not what I meant," he said in a more humble tone. "I'm just saying she's never done anything about that man before, and I'm damn sure she ain't gonna do anything about him now."

"Charles, I hear you," Pat replied. "But what am I supposed to do? I have begged and pleaded with her to leave that man. Toni never listens to me. We'll just have to pray this will turn her around." Pat wiped her wet eyes and nose again. "It just has to."

"That's right, Charles," Stephanie said, gripping her mother's hand while flashing her brother a hard, disapproving look. "You can't expect mama to fix this? She's already got enough on her plate as it is. And I agree. Surely you don't think Toni's going to let this one slide and take him back? Don't be so negative."

"*Shiit!*" He sighed. "You all can sit here and believe what you want…I know my sister."

Charles was the second of Pat's four children. He used to be a straight-up thug before he settled down, took on responsibility, and got a real job at the Ports Authority, so he knew a hoodlum when he saw one. As a teenager, he hung around the wrong crowds doing the wrong things and knew Marvin's reputation from the streets.

"But, you know, I warned Toni about him," he continued to preach. "Didn't I, Mama?"

Pat simply nodded her head, too tired to think or utter words to respond.

"Toni is so damn hard-headed." Charles sat back down and stopped talking long enough to take a swig of his Pepsi Cola. "If Toni had only listened to me, none of this would have never happened. I know one damn thing: they better lock his ass up for good, because I might just get my gun and shoot the mutha…"

Charles caught himself and took a swift look at his mother. "Mama, I'm sorry for my language. You know I don't mean any disrespect, but I wanna kill that bastard."

Charles Jr. was no prized fighter nor did he have any real combat skills. But, for a short man with a stout stature, he sure had a firecracker temper with a short fuse just like his father. And even though Charles' bark was almost always mightier than his bite, that never stopped him from backing down from a good fight. "And who got him anyway, the city or the county?" he asked.

In a weary voice, Pat replied, "The Charleston County Jail."

Chapter 4

Detective Sergeant Wade Anderson entered the interrogation room nonchalantly as he headed for the long steel table. The room was unusually cold. Cold enough to make one think the temperature had been deliberately set low to torment detainees. Only a single lamp shined brightly overhead to keep a person warm. The sergeant placed a folder and a cup of steaming coffee on the table. He sat down, sipped, then started reading the folder's contents. After finishing a couple paragraphs and flipping through photographs, he glanced at Marvin, shook his head in disgust, and then resumed going over evidence from the crime scene. They were the only ones in the room, and it was too damn early in the morning.

"Hey man, what's wrong with you? It's freezing in here!" Marvin complained as he rubbed his hands together and blew warm breath over them. He'd been in a holding cell for hours with only a thin orange inmates' jumper to keep him warm. They took his clothing and personal belongings for processing, leaving him soiled with traces of dried blood on his body and still demanding answers.

"What took you so damn long?" he asked, irate.

Sergeant Anderson didn't respond. He had over fifteen years of service under his belt: threats, pleads, tantrums, and curse words no longer ruffled his feathers. As far as he was concerned, this was just another day at the office and Marvin was just another coward beating up his wife.

"Are you listening to me?" Marvin asked louder, making sure he was heard. "So that's what you're going to do? You're just gonna sit right there like a fucking mute?"

Marvin paused for a response, but waited in vain. "Hey," he shouted. "Are you going to answer any of my damn questions?"

The sergeant steadily ignored him, still unperturbed by his temper. Marvin leaned into the table and stared straight ahead at the man while he continued to press questions.

"Why am I being kept in this cold ass room when my wife is in the hospital? Is she even alive? Can you at least tell me that?"

Marvin couldn't get an answer or reaction from the stone-faced investigator. Out of sheer frustration, he slammed his handcuffed wrists on the table. His eyes were strained red and the little veins in the middle of his forehead were protruding. "I told you. I didn't do this. I found her that way." He continued to rant loudly.

The sergeant calmly took a deep breath, closed the folder, and was finally ready to respond. "Mr. Jones, my name is Detective Sergeant Anderson and your case has been transferred over to me. I will first conduct an interview with you and this is how the interview will go. I will ask the questions and you will answer them. It's that simple. So, you can save your outbursts and theatrics for someone else. Do we have an agreement?"

Marvin scowled then grudgingly nodded in agreement.

"Good," Sergeant Anderson said. "Now that we have an understanding, let's move on to the first question: What is your full birth name for the record?"

Marvin looked confused. "You know my damn name. What kind of question is that?"

"Mr. Jones, our record shows you have two aliases: Antwon Jones and CJ Jones. So, why don't you go ahead and clear that up for me and not make this difficult."

Marvin knew the detective was a hard-ass and dealing with this SOB required a different approach. He relaxed, leaned back in his chair, and decided to play ball.

"My name is Marvin Terrell Jones."

Just when the sergeant started writing on his notepad, Marvin tried pleading his innocence again but this time with a lot more composure. "Listen Detective Anderson, I know what you people are thinking. You bust all up in my house and see me on top of my wife. I got blood all over me. I can imagine what that looked like. But I am telling you, it wasn't me. And while y'all got me in here, the fool that stabbed my wife is still out there on the goddam streets."

Sergeant Anderson dropped his pen and looked Marvin evenly in the eyes. "Mr. Jones, I'm sure you are aware of your history. You have a criminal record that runs a mile long. This is not the first time the police have had to intervene in a domestic dispute between you and your wife. In the last three years, we've collected over five reports of domestic violence on you. If you ask me, I'm pretty sure there were plenty more incidents that went unreported. But, I've got to stick with the facts. And the facts are we've received calls on you beating your wife from your neighbors, family members, and now the babysitter. Hell, two years ago, we got an anonymous call claiming you sliced your wife's hand with a box cutter. Do you remember that, Mr. Jones?"

Marvin didn't flinch. He just looked and listened.

"Right," the sergeant sarcastically said, pulling out photographs of Toni's bloody body and spreading them out in front of the suspect. Marvin stared at the pictures in complete silence. Toni looked stone dead with her eyes closed, bare chest open and blood scattered everywhere. Marvin pushed the photos away.

"Is she dead, man?" His nostrils flared and eyes watered. "Is she dead?"

"Mr. Jones, at this very moment, your wife is in the hospital fighting for her life."

Marvin lowered his head and went silent again as he wept. Sergeant Anderson watched his emotional meltdown, but didn't buy the act. It was a good performance, but it was all just a well-played act he'd seen many times before.

"Come on, Mr. Jones, how stupid do you think I am?" He chuckled. "You have a history of beating and cutting your wife. And you want me to believe you had nothing to do with this?"

Marvin jumped forward. "Fuck you!" he shouted. "I didn't cut my wife. That was an accident, and I never got charged for it. You can't connect that to this."

The investigator stood up.

"Sit down, Mr. Jones," the sergeant ordered through clenched teeth. "You jump frog at me one more time, and I'll make you regret it."

The door sprung open.

"Is everything alright in here, Sergeant Anderson?" asked an eager officer with a nightstick in hand.

"Yeah, we're fine," he answered, never taking his eyes off the perp.

Marvin sat back down. Sergeant Anderson moved in closer to his prime suspect. He saw rage growing in Marvin's eyes. "You want to hit me, don't you?" he whispered. "Come on, I want you to try me. Why don't you try somebody your own size for a change?"

Marvin wiped his mouth, revealing a slight smirk.

"No sir, Detective Anderson. Everything's cool." He snickered. "I know what you're trying to do, but it ain't gonna work on me."

"Smart man," the sergeant replied.

The detective got back in his seat and crossed his legs. "But getting back to your file, Mr. Jones, you're absolutely right. You weren't charged. Just like in that incident and every other time we showed up to arrest your sorry ass, you got off. Your wife never pressed charges against you. It seems like she always came up with a clever accident excuse. I don't know why." He shrugged. "And maybe it's not meant for me to understand…. That's not my concern. My business is getting people like you off the streets. Mr. Jones, you will get caught someday, one way or the other. Because, let's face it: You've been in trouble with the law ever since you were a boy. You've been arrested for street fighting, domestic abuse, theft, and even tax evasion; the list goes on and on. In 1984 you pleaded guilty on a misdemeanor assault charge you committed against your wife and got off with a simple fine. But I found an earlier conviction more interesting: you actually served eighteen months in juvenile jail. And what was that for?"

The sergeant re-opened the folder and pushed his finger across words as he read.

"Robbing a convenience store and hitting the cashier...who happened to be a defenseless woman. You should be glad it wasn't armed robbery, because you would have served much more time for that regardless of good behavior."

"I was a kid and I served my time," Marvin said.

"Yes, you did your time, Mr. Jones. But that case told me something about you. It told me you have a pattern. You're a violent man who likes to beat up women."

He waited for a response but got nothing. Marvin remained quiet and kept on looking right through the investigator.

"That's alright, Mr. Jones. You don't have to say anything. Obviously, you know you have rights. But I've got enough evidence against you to keep your butt in one of those jail cells until the magistrate arrives on Monday. You see, I don't need your wife's testimony, because I've got something better, something more reliable and consistent."

Sergeant Anderson flaunted a smile like the joke was on Marvin.

"I've got an eye witness who has given us a written statement, stating that you were indeed beating on your wife last night. You don't believe me? Well, it's all right in here." The sergeant gloated as he patted his fingers on the folder. "So you got anything to say to me now, because I know you stabbed your wife?"

Sergeant Anderson studied Marvin's face and body movements for any signs of breaking down. He hoped the pressure would forfeit a confession and save everybody time and taxpayers' money. But it failed to work. Marvin gazed angrily at the sergeant and said, "I want a damn lawyer."

Chapter 5

Sister Lula Mae raised her head and arms to the sky and began to glorify God. "This is the day that the *Lord* has given. Knowing it was You, *Lord God*, and not man that brought this child out of the wilderness. *Jesus*, I want to thank You for Your grace and mercy." She bowed her head, placed her finger on Toni's forehead, and began to paint the symbol of the Cross. Passionately, she continued to preach.

"*Lord*, I ask You to anoint this oil and allow Your power to manifest through this young lady's body. In the name of *the Father, the Son, and the Holy Spirit*, Amen."

"Amen," everyone in the hospital room repeated in chorus.

Sister Lula Mae Ellis, sometimes called Sister Lu for short, was a woman of faith who almost never missed a shut-in visit for church members or friends. In her mid-sixties, Sister Lula Mae's light-brown skin complexion had limited wrinkles, and she was still full of energy to spread the good word. Always well groomed and known for her sharp sense of fashion, she wore a royal blue suit with shoes to match and a small gold angel pin on her lapel. Today her silver long hair, normally worn in tight spiral curls, was placed neatly in a French roll, and her manicured fingernails were polished red. The sister was not a nun but an evangelist and had been successful in the Baptist ministries for over forty years.

"Chile, the *Lord* has been good to you. Has He not?"

"Yes, he has," Thelma mumbled under her breath, sitting at the opposite side of the bed. The sister placed Toni's hand into her palms. "You were in the presence of the *Father,* and it was by His grace alone that brought you back to us."

An overwhelming feeling came over Sister Lula Mae and made her jump to her feet and shout to the heavens again. "Ooh, yes Lord, speak to me," she said, with her arms stretched out wide, head tilted back, and eyes shut. Sister Lula Mae had just caught the *Holy Ghost* and moved around the room with a soul-stirring power.

"Toni, *God* is good," she declared after settling down. From her purse, she located a signature-embroidered handkerchief and used it to dab the sides of her mouth and her forehead. "Even though the enemy wanted you dead, *God* let you live to see another day."

"Yes, He did. Thank you, Jesus," Pat said, rocking slowly back and forth in a chair and trying hard to control her emotions. But her child was alive and a few tears of joy managed to escape her weathered eyes and trickle down her cheeks.

Toni gently turned her head toward Sister Lula Mae and tried her best to utter a thank you. But the mere task of breathing out words appeared too difficult. She raised her hand a little and smiled instead.

"I know, baby. I know what you're trying to say," Sister Lula Mae said while stroking Toni's head. "But you shouldn't do much talking. Just concentrate on saving your strength so you can get well and back to those precious children of yours."

Pat smiled at the evangelist. "Lula Mae, I wanna thank you for coming down. You've always been good to me and my family over the years."

"Now Patricia, you know you are welcome." Sister Lula Mae reached over and hugged her old friend. "That's what I've been put on this Earth for, to help people. If there's anything else I can do for you or any of y'all, please don't hesitate to ask me." Pat nodded and smiled, then embraced her friend again.

"So Pat, what's Toni's status?" Sister Lula Mae asked. "The child has been hospitalized for nearly a week. How much longer will she be here?"

"Well, the doctor said she's coming along fine, but they plan to keep her a little longer for observation. Maybe another week, we're not sure. And as far as having one lung, it should function properly as long as she exercises and stops smoking."

"One lung, Pat." Sister Lula Mae shivered at the thought and clutched her chest as though she had just been stabbed and could feel the pain from a piercing blade. "Well, at least the child is not on a ventilator and can breathe on her own," she added, trying to look on the brighter side of a dark situation.

The room became still and somber again. The family knew Sister Lula Mae was working her way to questions most people wanted to know.

"So what's going to happen to Marvin? Have they scheduled a court date yet?"

The tension in the room was thick. When Toni got stabbed, the news hit the streets faster than the morning paper. Everybody knew Marvin was being held as the only suspect.

Thelma folded her arms in a defensive manner.

"No ma'am, there's no trial date yet," she answered with a hint of pessimism in her voice. "He's been arraigned, though. And can you believe the judge actually granted him bail?"

"Say what?" Sister Lula Mae blurted, like she was about to lose her religion. She couldn't believe what she just heard.

"Yes, ma'am," Thelma nodded. "But I heard he's still in jail, because he can't afford to post bail. At least that's some good news."

"Bail?" Sister Lula Mae said, giving Thelma a baffled squint. "What kind of legal system do we have in this country where dangerous, ruthless people are let out onto the streets so easily?"

"Oh, it gets better than that, Sister Lu," Thelma said. "I spoke with a detective on the phone yesterday, and he told me it was going to be tough to get Marvin convicted on Janette's statement alone. Marvin's got some lawyer who's trying to get the case thrown out based on the lack of evidence. They can't find the knife and something about hearsay."

"Now that's astonishing." Sister Lula Mae shook her head. "You mean to tell me they just can't take the babysitter's word? But the child saw everything. That ain't enough?"

"Evidently not," Thelma replied.

No one in the room understood the injustice. They all felt powerless and nauseated over the situation and sat with frustrated expressions on their faces. Sister Lula Mae let out a disappointed sigh and looked at everybody.

"Well, have the police tried to talk to Toni yet?" She continued to probe. "She can tell them everything that happened."

Thelma shook her head. "No, but I wish they could. The doctor doesn't want Toni talking to anybody about the incident for a few more days. He said re-living something so traumatic too soon can cause a major stroke, and we don't need that. All we have right now is Janette's statement. And to make things worse, Janette's parents really don't want her more involved than she already is because of her age. We may lose her as a witness."

"So, Thelma, what happens if Janette can't testify?" Stephanie asked.

"I really don't know." She shrugged. "It would probably cause the whole case to unravel. That's why I hope and pray the prosecutor will consider everything: the statement, Marvin's criminal background and go after that sick bastard."

"Well, that won't be a problem," Sister Lula Mae assured. "Because I believe Marvin will get charged and put on trial. As soon as Toni becomes strong enough to testify, I'm sure she will be more than willing to send that evil man to jail."

The sister started wagging her finger in the air. "Let me tell y'all something. The *Lord* will prevail. Let Him handle this. Whatsoever goes on in the dark shall and must be seen in the light. Hallelujah!" Their heads turned and all eyes fell on Toni.

Chapter 6

The neatly dressed man stood still in his khaki pants, shirt, and overworn navy blue blazer while the officer waved the metal detector from his torso to the bottom of his feet. "You're all clear, Mr. Harris," the detention officer said. He opened the door and escorted the gentleman to his client.

Jim Harris was a black, fairly young attorney who'd been paying his dues by circulating through the county courts for the last five years. And like the majority of lawyers employed by the Office of Public Defenders who were underpaid, overworked, and assigned to revolving clients who all said the same thing—"I didn't do it"—his attitude toward domestic abuse cases was indifferent at best.

"Hello, Mr. Jones. How are you holding up today?" he asked, giving a half-smile to a client who he already knew from their first encounter was going to be difficult and impatient.

"How the hell do you think I am? I've been locked up for six days," Marvin snapped, skipping all niceties. "You got any news for me?"

"Well, yes, I actually do," Mr. Harris said, having a seat.

"Okay, let's hear it."

"Alright, I have two updates. First, the prosecutor hasn't filed the complaint yet. When I met with the assistant district attorney for a pre-preliminary hearing, we laid out all the evidence against you on this case. I challenged him on the point you made regarding the reliability of Miss Simmons' sight on the night of question. As you requested, I went to your house and took photos of the area in which she claimed to have seen you beating your wife, and it does get rather dark around there. Your babysitter acknowledged that fact both during the emergency call and in her written statement. Besides, the knife is still missing and that's needed for forensic analysis such as fingerprints."

Marvin bitterly nodded his head in agreement, focused on his lawyer's every word. "That's right. That's what I've been saying all along. Why isn't anyone listening to me?"

Mr. Harris watched his client while slowly flipping his pen until Marvin stopped talking.

"Right," he said, putting down his pen. "Well, Mr. Jones, I made my case and the assistant DA did not seem interested at all. Matter of fact, he didn't even offer a plea bargain. So we can interpret that in two ways: maybe he feels this case is already in the bag or maybe he doesn't have enough to go on to prove you committed this crime. Here's what I think. The prosecutor still has a few more days left until it's mandatory to file formal charges. My guess is he's stalling to get your wife's statement so it can be presented at the preliminary hearing. The DA's office is going to want that evidence to build a stronger case against you and get you indicted on assault and battery with intent to kill. And if convicted, that's a Class A felony punishable up to twenty years in prison."

Mr. Harris gave Marvin a sobering look and nodded his head to make sure his client got the point. "This is some serious stuff, Mr. Jones. And with that being said, let's get to the second update. I just learned your wife will be able to receive visits from investigators sometime next week."

Marvin's eyeballs seemed to pop out of their sockets the moment he heard those words.

"I need to talk to her. I've got to get out of here," he excitedly said.

"Mr. Jones, I can understand why you're so anxious, but you have got to find some patience to get through this process. Now, the magistrate has already lowered your bail, so it's up to you to get the money. And remember, Mr. Jones, because of this case and your alleged history of domestic violence, you are not to make any contact with your wife. If you do, that would be a violation of the bail agreement. And in doing so, you will lose your freedom."

Marvin let out a heavy sigh, like the whole world was against him. "Mr. Harris, I know the evidence looks bad.

And yes, I've been guilty of a lot of things in the past, but this I did not do. I love my wife. I just want to see her."

Mr. Harris stayed neutral, not showing any signs of belief or disbelief. He opened his briefcase and retrieved his pad and tape recorder. "Mr. Jones, I want to go over your version of what happened one last time to clear up any loose ends. If there's anything, and I mean anything you haven't told me, the time is now to bring it to the table. We don't need any surprises."

The lawyer put on his glasses and began to read.

"Now, you said you were at an award ceremony with your wife on Saturday night, August the ninth of this year. Is that correct?"

"Yes, that's correct," Marvin said. "Toni was being honored as Charleston's Black Woman of the Year at the Radisson Hotel for her works in the media and community service. Anyway, we got there a little late—around 7:18 PM. We were supposed to be there at 7:00 PM, but you know 'CPT'—color people time." Marvin chuckled.

Mr. Harris wasn't amused and ignored his remark. "So you said after your wife received her award, you decided to leave. Why?"

"Yeah, I wasn't feeling well at all. My stomach was turning upside down. It had to been something I ate, because I only had one glass of champagne."

"You and your wife went to the ceremony in the same car, correct?"

"Yes, I was going to take a taxi cab home, but she insisted that I take the car. She said I would get home faster."

"So why didn't your wife leave with you?"

"Well, you know, it was her night. I told her to stay, have a good time, and enjoy herself. Toni agreed. She said one of her girlfriends would bring her home. And that was that."

"What time did you get home, and what did you do when you got there?"

"Well, I got home around 10:00 PM. I remember being quiet going in because I didn't want to wake the kids. It wasn't often, but Janette would sometimes spend the night when she babysat for us, especially if we were returning home really late. Um, then I took some Ibuprofen and fell asleep on the bed. I was so tired; I didn't even change my clothes."

"Alright Mr. Jones, let's get to when your wife came home. How did you discover her?"

"Right." Marvin bobbed his head up and down. "So, I'm a light sleeper. And I remember waking up because I heard noises. It sounded like someone was crying from outside. I went to investigate, but I really couldn't see anything at first. And like I said earlier, we have this tall tree near our driveway that blocks out the streetlight. Well, I got closer and there she was lying on the ground. That's how I discovered her, Mr. Harris, alone and on the ground."

Marvin inhaled deeply then exhaled.

"So what did you do after that?" the lawyer asked.

"Toni was pale and looking up at me with her arms partially stretched out. So, I put my arms around her and started to lift her. But then she yelped from being in so much pain. It scared me. There was blood all over her."

Marvin choked up and couldn't get his words out. He took a momentary break with his head tilted back and then he wiped his eyes and mouth with his collar before resuming his story.

"Then all of sudden"—he shrugged—"she started coughing up blood and gasping for air. It was crazy. Man, I thought she was going to die right there in my arms. So, yes, I yelled at her. I told her to get up. Stay awake. You can do it. Just try, dammit!" Marvin blew out a long sigh. "I just kept thinking: *Get her in the house. Get her on the bed.* I needed to keep her warm, right? The cold air would have made her go into shock, right?"

"I'm not sure, Mr. Jones," Mr. Harris said. "What about the girl?"

"Who? Janette?" Marvin sharply replied. "Yeah, she saw me outside with Toni, but it wasn't what she thought. I didn't want her or my kids to see Toni like that, so I quickly put her back into the room with the kids and told her not to come out. And yes, I was angry. Wouldn't you be if some punk walked up to your wife and stabbed her? You'd probably kill."

Marvin leaned over and put his hands on the back of his neck. The stress was unbearable.

"Look man, I was trying to save her life any way I could. When I finally got her into the house, Toni wasn't talking or making any noises. I thought she stopped breathing, so I started mouth-to-mouth on her, just like they do on television. Did I know what I was doing? Absolutely not, but I knew had to try something."

"Mr. Jones, do you know anyone who would want to harm your wife? Did she have any enemies? Did she complain of crazy radio fans? Did she ever mention a stalker?"

"No." He shook his head. "Everybody loved her."

Mr. Harris took off his glasses and massaged his eye sockets while taking everything in. The story sounded believable, but he also knew from experience his client could be a clever liar. "Mr. Jones, I have one last question."

A look of puzzlement flashed across Marvin's face.

"Why didn't you simply call 911 when you first discovered your wife?"

Marvin hesitated then sucked his teeth.

"Man, I don't know." He shrugged. "I panicked. It all happened so fast."

The public defender wrote Marvin's words on a notepad. He felt confident if the case ended up in front of a grand jury, his client would have an answer for any question thrown at him. Mr. Harris was certain he had a fair defense. There was nothing more he could do except wait to hear Mrs. Jones' testimony and let the evidence play out.

"I believe Detective Sgt. Anderson will be interviewing your wife soon, and when that's done, it should be easier to get you out of here and back with your family," Mr. Harris said as he packed up. "All she needs to do is back up your story."

Marvin got caught up on his lawyer's last words.

Toni just needs to tell them I'm innocent and this will all be over, he told himself.

"Mr. Jones," the lawyer called out, interrupting his client's concentration. "I have all the information I need from you today. Unless the DA's office has a sudden change of heart with your case, the preliminary hearing will still go forward as scheduled. Is there anything else I can do for you? If not, I'll be on my way."

"Yes, Mr. Harris. There is something you could do for me. I need to make a very important call to one of my relatives. Could you make sure I get my phone call today?"

Mr. Harris nodded and shook Marvin's hand before leaving. "Yeah, I can do that."

Chapter 7

The day he was arraigned, Marvin called the only person he could think of to help. He told his disabled, stage II emphysema-stricken father about the entire mess he was in. Knowing his father was tightfisted with his fixed monthly income, Marvin begged him to make some phone calls and do whatever necessary to get him out.

The bail amount had been set too high. Even after the magistrate lowered the bail from five thousand dollars to one thousand, it still seemed impossible to pay. But several days of waiting paid off. Marvin's father finally got in touch with his drug-dealing nephew to raise the money. And on the seventh day of waking up in jail, Marvin posted bail.

Now Marvin was at Roper Hospital violating his bail agreement. Mr. Harris' strong warnings were heard loud and clear back at the county's detention center, but Marvin's need to contact his wife was urgent and worth the risk of getting caught.

He stepped into the lobby trying to look incognito wearing dark sunglasses, a ball cap, and a navy blue sweat suit. His eyes shifted to the gift shop with an idea in mind. He purchased a five-dollar bouquet of pink carnations and held a sealed letter along the side of the glass vase.

It was early in the day. Marvin cautiously walked down the ICU hallway looking out for security guards and any of Toni's family members who could point him out, cause a scene, and ultimately derail his plan. He came upon an attractive woman sitting alone behind a desk. Her nametag said *Rhonda*.

Marvin took off the shades, leaned into the waist-high desk, and turned on the charm. "Hi Rhonda," he said with a glowing grin, greeting the woman as though he knew her for years.

"Hello," she replied, looking up and returning a radiant smile. "How may I help you?"

"Yes, my name is Steve and I'm here for Toni Jones."

"Okay, sir. Are you an immediate family member? I ask only because Mrs. Jones has a restriction on visitors. But, if you are family, you can simply sign the visitor's log book right over there next to you, and I can find out when she's available." The woman extended an ink pen along with another bushy-tailed smile.

"Oh, that won't be necessary," Marvin quickly replied. "She doesn't actually know me. The radio station where she works sent me here to drop this off. Hey, listen. You seem like a reliable person who just happens to have one the most beautiful smiles I've seen in a long time."

"Why, thank you, sir." Rhonda grinned wide, showing off her deep dimples and a lot of teeth. Her eyelashes started to flutter lightly. "I don't believe anyone has ever said that to me before."

"Well, it's very true."

Marvin leaned in closer and spoke low, making sure his voice wouldn't carry down the hall. "So Rhonda, could you do me a favor? Could you personally give this to Mrs. Jones while I'm still here? I want to make sure she gets this. It's very important to her boss and co-workers." He added a persuasive touch by giving her a flirty one-sided smile and seductive stare.

"Sure. That's not a problem. Wait right here."

He watched the woman bounce out of her chair and swish toward the end of the corridor then step into a room and come out empty-handed. Now that he knew exactly which room belonged to Toni, he considered returning at night to see her. *But would that be wise? Would that be pushing it too much under the circumstances?* He wanted more than anything to touch his wife again, and wished he had been the one who delivered those flowers and letter to her bedside. *Dammit!* He lamented inside. Toni was only a few feet away.

Rhonda happily raised her thumb in the air while walking up the hallway, clearly feeling like she just accomplished a mission for a possible new love interest. Marvin returned the gesture with a phony, quick smile then turned and promptly left.

Toni's Story

Chapter 8

"Oh, look at you. You're doing so well today," the nurse informed me with a cheerful smile. I was alone in the room exercising my lung with a blow machine. The object was to blow hard enough to lift the blue balls to the top of the box. I was told this exhaustive daily feat is necessary to help prevent blood clots.

"You've done about five minutes' worth," the nurse said. "You can stop for now." She removed the tube from my mouth and grabbed my hand to help me sit up in bed. I pushed too hard too fast. "Shit!" I grunted. Those damn stitches stung like hot needles poking my chest.

"Ooh. Be careful, Mrs. Jones," she said with a grimace while adjusting my pillows. "You don't want to hurt yourself and cause a lot of pain."

Pain! Did she just say that? The young, bubbly woman looked like she had no idea what real pain felt like. Compared to the feeling of being stabbed, I really didn't care about a little soreness from stitches. I was just glad to be alive and on my way out of this hospital. Almost two weeks on a hard hospital bed would drive anybody crazy, maybe even insane.

"I almost forgot. Look at what I've got," she said, dangling a small plastic bag. "While you were asleep, your mother told me to give you this. Looks like more mail. You sure are one popular woman. Rhonda just stepped in to deliver those pretty flowers. I wonder what else you're going to get today."

"Yes, I know. Aren't they wonderful?" I said with excitement, reaching for the bag eagerly like a child waiting for Halloween candy at somebody's doorstep. I placed the mail on my lap and leaned toward the nightstand to sniff the flowers once again. They smelled good, just like the others that decorated the room. Words alone could not express how I appreciated getting these well wishes from family members, close friends, or co-workers. Last week, I received numerous cards and flowers from people I hadn't seen or heard from in a dirt-long time. I guess the old saying is true: *It always takes a tragedy to bring people together.* Lord knows I was blessed to have so many people in my life to pray and care for me. I drew strength from them, and that helped me get through the pain and fight each day.

I flipped through the stack of letters. I got cards from my girlfriend Brenda Carter, some church members I shamefully couldn't remember due to my poor church attendance, and my job at the radio station. Among them was a card from Janette. I opened hers first. Inside was a folded good-bye note expressing her sympathy while letting me know she was no longer available to babysit. I wasn't shocked. Who could blame the girl for not wanting to put another foot in my house or even look at my face again? I'm sure Janette wanted to get on with her life and forget the entire experience as much as I did. That night was traumatic enough for all of us. I just hope and pray someday she would heal and forgive me for putting her in such a dangerous situation.

But I'd miss her after-school visits. I enjoyed her sharp mind and bubbly personality, and looking at her cute face. I used to tease about how she looked like a teenage Diana Ross with her caramel skin, big round eyes, and big smile. This coming school year she would be a senior in high school, and I knew I was going to see a lot less of her anyway, especially since she was preparing for college next year. She'd mentioned maintaining a high GPA was going to be priority number one to reach her future goals. Janette told me after earning a bachelor's degree she planned on becoming a lawyer. And there was no doubt in my mind she would become just that.

Feeling a little down after reading Janette's letter, I took comfort in looking at the picture a nurse taped on the wall for me. It was a drawing from my children: Justine, age nine, and Adrian, age two. They drew a picture of us holding hands in a field of yellow and purple flowers. It was a beautiful reminder of what I had at home and always brought a smile on my face.

Justine came from a short-lived relationship, and I had Andre with Marvin. I missed them, but I was adamant about not letting them see me in the hospital with machines and tubes hooked up to my body. The whole mess would have scared them even more, and they'd already seen too much horror in their young lives.

Mama told me how they were asking about my whereabouts and what happened to Marvin when the police officers came to take him away. They were smart kids, especially Justine. For her young age, she understood a lot and had no problems asking questions. Mama told me when she picked them up from Ms. Gertie's house, little Miss Justine walked up to her and asked, "How bad is Mama hurt, and is she going to die?" Mama explained that I was in a very bad accident, but I was all right and the police officers took their daddy to the police department to find out what happened. I can only hope they believed Mama and were content with her answers.

As I reached for the letter from the radio station, I noticed the envelope was plain and handwritten. This was a little noticeable because most stationary was computer generated with the station's emblem on it. Not thinking too much about it, I opened the envelope and discovered its true identity. It was a letter from Marvin. I took short shallow breaths, closed my watering eyes, held the letter close to my stapled chest for a few minutes, and then began to read:

To my dearest wife; the love of my life and mother of my only child. I am so sorry for the pain and suffering you are in right now. Most of all, I regret that I am not by your side feeling your pain with you. For all the bad times I've put you through in the past, Lord knows I deserve to experience what you're feeling. Toni, I wish I could trade places with you. I wish I could trade my health for yours. Baby, the love I have for you is so intense; sometimes I feel I am going to explode when I'm not near you! Sitting in jail day after day being away from your loving arms really reminded me how good I have it. My children, a beautiful wife who has stuck by my side through thick and thin, in sickness and in health, for better or for worse. And baby, this is our worst. God has brought you back to me. He has given us another chance together to honor our vows. To raise our children and live right.

This is a new day…God is forgiveness!

While locked up, I sat in that jail cell and often remembered the good times we've shared. Do you remember our third date at the Earth, Wind & Fire concert? Oh man, were you beautiful. Every man in the auditorium wanted your phone number, even Philip Bailey. He had his eyes on you. But was I jealous? No. I didn't care, because I knew you were with me. Damn, was I proud to be with you! You could've had any cat you wanted that night, but you chose me. Do you remember how we danced all night long? Your feet were hurting, but we sure had a good time. I knew right then you were and still are the only woman for me.

Toni, I want more times like that. That's why I can't wait until this mess is over with the police. They're still trying to indict me on Janette's statement. The lawyer said that her claim could be dismissed just as soon as you tell them that I am innocent. Baby, I think the police are coming to see you this week. And as soon as you give them your statement, I will be free. I can't wait to see you. I heard the doctor said you can go home in a matter of days. I wish I could go home. Baby, I love you so much. I'm missing you and the children. I can't wait to put this behind us. You know, when you almost lose someone is when you truly realize how much you love them.

I love you. Sincerely, Marvin.

My cheeks were sore from the constant wiping of tears. I returned the wet letter back into the envelope and hid it underneath the mattress. Then I slid back down into the sheets and folded my body into a fetal position. I became hypnotized by the off-white wall while thoughts ran wildly through my mind. My body and spirit grew weary quickly. I needed sweet peace. So, I pumped the morphine drip. And there I was, again, almost dead to the world.

Chapter 9

Have you ever been involved with someone or something you knew was bad for you, but you just couldn't let it go because you had to see it through until the end? They say your greatest strength can also be your greatest weakness. For me, that would be perseverance.

I'd had a lot to think about the last twenty-four hours since receiving that letter from Marvin. The investigator would be there any minute and, still, I didn't know what to tell him. I hadn't talked about that night with anyone, not even my mother. But I knew she knew. I knew they all knew. The truth was Marvin stabbed me. I remember almost every excruciating detail. And even though I should be mad as hell and want to lock his ass up for good, I still had love in my heart for my husband.

Love is indeed a strange, mysterious force. If you think about it for a second, love can be downright illogical regarding the people it makes us fall in love with. How did an ambitious woman like me, with so much potential, get involved and stay with a man like Marvin?

Throughout my life, I had always been courageous, strong-willed, and confident. Attributes hard learned to survive on the streets and in the entertainment business. Back in the day, you could have easily described me as one tough cookie, the type of female who didn't bow down to intimidation or let anything distract my mental focus. I took crap from no one and was ready to fight—either man or woman—to the death should anyone try to harm my family or me. But, with Marvin, it was different.

"God is forgiveness," he wrote. That was his manipulative, clever way of telling me he was sorry without implicating himself of wrongdoing. For a man who didn't have a lick of an education except for a trade he learned while in jail, he was very intelligent. During his incarceration, he spent a lot of time reading books about business and the law. "I'm a self-taught man," he'd often boast. Ironically, this is one of the many reasons why I fell in love with him.

As I lay on my hospital bed, my mind flashed back to the first time we met. It was seven years ago in 1979. I was doing a live broadcast from a new club called The Palladium. The club had only been open for a few weeks and was already gaining accolades for its size and sound system. Formally a 6,000 square feet furniture store, it was transformed into Charleston's premier disco tech. So, when I got the invitation to do my show on location, I jumped at the chance and was eager to meet the masterminds and money behind the whole business venture. From what I heard, they were three good-looking fellas in their thirties: Isaac Heyward, Donald Mack, and—yes, Mr. Marvin Terrell Jones.

Doing live broadcasts was a normal routine for me on Friday nights. I had been with Q-101.5 for about two years and had a popular show called "Toni's Night Life." Back then, the show was broadcasted live three nights a week via my home phone or from another remote area. I rarely was obligated to work from the radio station. The show focused on entertainment news. If there was something going on in the music world, I knew about it and so did my listeners. I also wrote a column for a local black-owned newspaper called *The Black Chronicles*. Now, I wasn't making a whole lot of money at the radio station or with the newspaper— maybe $250 a week combined, if even that. But none of that mattered. No one got into the radio business for the money starting out. You did it because you loved it. Besides, with my constant on-air exposure, I was always landing freelance jobs to host events or do some type of advertisement to help supplement my income.

Being a well-known air personality in the black community gave me access to a lot of people and a lot of places. Funny, I could have only one dollar to my name but, in my black book, you would find the addresses and phone numbers of *who's who* in the music biz. I definitely had the gift of gab and wanted to use it for the masses. Not bad for a college dropout. I hustled my tail off to get my FCC license back in 1977 and build a name for myself and had no intentions of settling for less—and that included the men I dated.

After finishing my show, I went to the bar to get a quick drink for my dry mouth. I pulled out a Marlboro and asked the bartender for a glass of orange juice. Alcohol was never my thing. As soon as I was about to light my cigarette, Marvin walked up to me and introduced himself.

"Allow me to light that for you. Derrick." He snapped his fingers. "Whatever she wants tonight, it's on the house."

"Yes sir, Mr. Jones." The bartender hustled.

"Hello, Ms. Toni Williams," Marvin said slyly. "I don't think we've met, but my name is Marvin Jones. I'm the co-owner of this establishment."

Marvin's smile was as bright as the sun. He had perfectly shaped teeth with an open-faced gold crown decorating a tooth, well-defined lips that were thick but not too big, and seductive eyes that could evoke a smile from the coldest heart. He was at least a six-footer, medium built, brown skin, and dressed to impress.

Oh, the brotha was coordinated. He had on a beige two-piece pleated suit, beige alligator shoes, real gold on his neck and fingers, and his voice was oh-so-silky smooth. Old Spice never smelled better on a man. Marvin was absolutely fine as wine.

Playing it cool, I told him thank you and gave compliments on his new club as I sipped my juice.

"Oh, please, don't thank me." He chuckled and then modestly said, "I should be thanking you. We've pulled in over three hundred people tonight just by you being here. You're a real celebrity here in Charleston."

I raised my glass and gave him a gracious smile.

Michael Jackson's "Don't Stop 'til You Get Enough" was the new jam playing loudly in the background. I began to feel the groove and my shoulders started swaying back and forth.

"Would you like to dance?" he asked.

I quickly jumped off the stool. "Ooh yes, this is my song!"

We danced the night away under the multi-colored disco ball. And man, could he get down. Marvin had me spinning, twirling, and dipping all over room in my peach sundress like a *Soul Train* dancer. Hell, we dominated the floor. I knew we looked good together; we had to be the envy of every couple in the club that night.

Finally, after exhaustion caught up with us, we left the dance floor for a quiet table in the back of the club. The VIP section, he called it. We had a stimulating conversation that lasted well over two hours and discovered we had many mutual interests, like music and working within the entertainment industry. I told him about my dream of hosting my very own national radio show, and he shared how he wanted to get into managing R&B groups and eventually start his own record label. We were young, ambitious, and excited for each other's aspirations. It made the chemistry between us all the more obvious and unavoidable.

"Toni, I have to say you are a very special lady. You're smart, talented, and classy. You are everything a man dreams of," he said while fondling my hand and staring deeply into my dark brown eyes. "You're so captivating, absolutely beautiful."

And according to most, he wasn't lying. Not only was I known for my shows and/or talents, I was also famous for my Coca-Cola bottle figure many men swore could stop traffic. At the age of twenty-seven, I was a brick house. Foxy Brown didn't have shit on me! My other natural assets included thick black hair that reached the middle of my back, smooth flawless ebony skin, and a winning smile. I took pride in myself and never left the house without being properly dressed. And to add to my repertoire, I could sing. Jazz was my specialty. It was nothing for me to get up on stage and sing a tune with best of them.

Marvin continued to flirt. "Toni, I don't want this night to end. I am really enjoying myself with you. Are you in a relationship? Lady, I hope not, because I definitely want to see you more of you."

Blushing everywhere, I replied without hesitation. "No, sir, I'm not in a relationship," I said flirtatiously while cooking up an idea in my head. "So, I'm guessing you already know Heatwave is coming to town, right?"

"Yeah, I know about that. Hopefully, with the right contact we can score an after party right here at the Palladium." He smiled, then nudged my arm, making sure I got the hint.

"Well, I'm going to be co-hosting that show at the Gaillard Auditorium next weekend. So things are going to get pretty hectic for me very fast. But, if you like, you're more than welcome to join me as my guest."

I was drawn by Marvin's allure. There was something about his confidence I found extremely attractive. And although I enjoyed being a single woman, I was digging homeboy and more than willing to take his application for the position of becoming a permanent lover. What can I say? He was good looking, a go-getter, and making money. The Perfect Catch.

That was many moons ago.

Chapter 10

I gazed out the open window from my hospital bed. The sky looked bluer than usual in mid-August. The mild breeze felt good on my skin, and the sounds of people and cars hustling and bustling outside seemed to engulf my room. Those sounds of life only made me want to break free even more and be a part of society once again.

It was lunchtime and the investigator still hadn't arrived. Mama, Stephanie, and Thelma had just walked in for a visit and to treat me with my favorite dish: baked turkey wings over white rice, cornbread, and sweet tea. My appetite was back in full force, and I wanted to throw down.

"Mmm, this is going to hit the spot," I said with glee while opening the warm take-out tray. No one rolled a pot like Pat Williams. She was known for superior dishes and Sunday night dinners. "I married you for your cooking first and your looks second," Daddy used to tease.

"How are you feeling today, baby?" she asked.

"I'm okay Mama, much better than before." I took a hearty bite out of the turkey wing. The rich savory flavors burst in my mouth and provided instant comfort. *Heavenly*, I thought to myself as the food slid down my throat. *Will I ever master her cooking skills?*

"You've got to give *God* His praise, baby," Mama said. "Praise Him for your health and strength. And praise Him for your second chance on this Earth."

Mama and Stephanie pulled chairs next to me and sat down. "Hey pretty girl," I said, looking at Stephanie and still chomping on food. "When are you going back to school?"

She was going into her second year in college. My goodness, had time flown. It was just two summers ago when my baby sister was crowned Miss Black Charleston and won a first year free-ride scholarship to Allen University in Columbia, South Carolina.

"Oh, I go back this week," she said. "But you know I couldn't leave without seeing you first. Toni, you know I love you, right?" Stephanie reached over to hug me with tears falling down her olive-toned face.

"Hey, I love you too, baby," I said, pulling away. She looked so much like Mama staring back at me with her beautiful deep-set eyes, warm complexion, and thin nose. I took my napkin and dried her face, then kissed her cheek.

"Now, you listen to me, girlfriend," I said with some pep in my voice, trying to avoid an emotional scene. "I don't want you up in that school just partying and giving your stuff away to boys. I want you to study hard and get good grades, okay? You're going to be the first in our family to earn a bachelor's degree. You're going to do good in life, alright, sweetie?"

I squeezed her shoulders. Stephanie nodded and smiled, unable to speak through her light tears. I wiped and then kissed her face again.

"So Toni, have you spoken with the detective yet?" Thelma asked forcefully, standing at the foot of the bed with her hands on her waist. She seemed agitated.

Thelma was always considered the responsible one. The one who got her associate's degree in accounting and held the same job for over ten years. I loved my sister, but she could be self-righteous at times and that got on my nerves.

"When Thelma makes a mistake, she takes responsibility and tries to fix it. Y'all need to learn from your sister," Mama used to say to us when we were kids.

But, Thelma wasn't perfect. Ever since she divorced George three years ago, Mama had no idea how a lonely night could make big sister smoke a whole bag of reefer and drink like a fish. We all had our vices, and Thelma was no different.

"No," I said quickly, scanning her up and down. "And I don't know when he's coming."

A nurse walked in.

"Mrs. Jones," she said, looking serious.

"Yes."

"Ah, there's a Detective Sergeant Anderson here from the County Sheriff's Office wanting to see you. Would you like to speak with him now?"

Instantly, the room became still. And again, all eyes fell on me.

Chapter 11

Plain *nervous* couldn't sum up my feelings. I was confused and felt my vitals quicken the moment I told the nurse to let the detective in. Mama picked up her purse as though she was going to leave.

"Oh, no Mama, we're not going anywhere," Thelma said, standing guard like a correctional officer.

The tall blue-eyed detective, with white hair and who appeared to be in his forties, walked in and stood next to my bedside.

"Good afternoon, ladies." He smiled and made eye contact with everyone in the room. "Mrs. Jones, my name is Sergeant Anderson, and I'm with the Charleston County Sheriff's office. I sure am glad to see you're recovering well."

"Thank you." I said.

"Well, ma'am, I'm here because I'm investigating your case and would like to ask you some questions about the night you were stabbed."

The investigator took a backward glance. "Mrs. Jones, are you comfortable with these ladies here or do you need privacy to answer the questions?"

I looked at my family and then shrugged my shoulders. "They can stay."

"I understand you're still healing," he said. "So, I gotta be clear. If you start to become too stressed and don't feel like completing this interview, please let me know. Also, I want to tape record this conversation. Do I have your permission?"

I looked up at him and nodded while he pulled out his recorder.

"Could you verbally answer yes or no for the record?" he asked.

"Oh, yes, you have my permission to record me," I replied.

"Mrs. Jones, on August 9th, we received a complaint from your babysitter stating that your husband was beating you. Do you remember what happened that night?"

Everyone looked at me with great anticipation, waiting for me to say what they already knew to be true. My body tensed up. I wasn't able to decide even then. All I could do was think about how much I loved Marvin and our family.

In his letter, he said we had the chance to start anew. Maybe he was right; maybe this is why God allowed me to live—to honor our vows: *in sickness and in health, for better or for worse.* Surely, I realized, this had to be our worst and our marriage could only get better from this point on. The more I fantasized about the possibilities, the faster my anger toward him started to dissipate. I hated him, but I loved him at the same time.

Sergeant Anderson's friendly expression turned into a confused stare. Apparently my long hesitation to answer perplexed him. And by the sound of his tone, I could tell he was getting impatient.

"Mrs. Jones, did you hear me? Would you like for me to repeat the question, or do you just need more time to answer?" he asked with furrowed brows.

Thelma's eyes widened, waiting for my response. She knew what I was going to say. I could already feel the heat radiating from her body.

"I don't know," I blurted out, looking down at the white blanket draped across my legs.

"I don't understand, Mrs. Jones. What do you not know?" The sergeant's eyes reduced to a squint. My heart raced, and I needed a cigarette now more than ever.

"I don't remember!" I snapped. "That night is a blur, okay? I don't know what happened after I was stabbed." I took a deep burning breath and let a few tears drop.

"So that means you remember who stabbed you, correct? Was it your husband?"

"My husband?" I said, giving him a scowl and acted dumbfounded by the accusation.

"Yes, Mrs. Jones. Your husband has been arrested on the suspicion of assault and battery with a dangerous weapon. I thought you already knew." The investigator peered at me, waiting for me to say something. "Well, Mrs. Jones? Did your husband stab you or not?"

My head started to throb from the pressure, and before I knew it I said, "No! My husband did not stab me. It was a young black man who jumped me for my purse."

Mother covered her face and moaned in agony. "Why, *Lord*?" she mumbled into her palms.

My heart pumped faster, expecting more outbursts. Here they come…

"What the hell is wrong with you?" Thelma yelled, taking her turn to scold me. "You know that bastard stabbed you!"

"Toni, why are you doing this again?" Stephanie shouted as she ran out the door.

"Stephanie!" Mama hollered, trying to stop her.

"Can you blame her, Mama?" Thelma said, pounding her clenched fist into her hand. "You know, every time I get a phone call about Toni being beaten up, half-dead somewhere, I want to run away too. Toni's not the only one who's hurting here, Mama. So just let Stephanie go. Let her be by herself." Thelma picked up Stephanie's handbag.

"Mama, I'm leaving. Are you coming?"

"Please don't leave, Thelma," Mama said softly. "Just wait a few more minutes. I want to hear what Toni has to say."

Thelma rolled her eyes and sighed heavily with frustration. She made another protest, but this time directly to the investigator. "Mr. Anderson, this is some bullshit. I don't know what's wrong with my sister, but you can't listen to a word she says. She's always lying for her husband. He's the devil, and I know that crazy fool stabbed her. We all know the truth!"

I sat speechless. Never had I ever seen Thelma lose her temper like that before. I couldn't even look her in the face.

"Ma'am, I can understand your feelings, but I can only take your sister's word," Sergeant Anderson said. "If you could please calm down, have a seat, and let me finish the interview, I would greatly appreciate it. Thank you."

Thelma sat next to Mama, her leg bouncing rapidly. They both looked disgusted as they listened in.

"Mrs. Jones, can you please tell me what happened after you left the ceremony?"

Somehow I found the courage to focus and continue the lie. "I told you. I remember very little about that night. I only remember being attacked by a young black man who was short, maybe around eighteen years old and 5'5 in height. We got into a struggle. He punched me, gagged me with a cloth, and then stabbed me. The man assaulted me for nothing. I only had twenty-two dollars in cash in that purse."

"Jesus," Mama cried out.

I took a second to close my eyes and swallow hard and then kept on talking.

"I'm sorry, but I have no more details to give you. But what I know for sure is this: It wasn't my husband who stabbed me. So, all charges against him need to be dropped immediately."

The investigator paused and stared at me for a moment then muttered, "Ah- huh" under his breath. I knew he didn't believe me.

"Mrs. Jones, did you get a good enough look at your attacker to describe his features?"

"No." I shook my head. "It was dark and everything happened so fast. I only got a glimpse of his physical description."

I scanned the faces of my mother and sister—such pain, such anger. I was sincerely sorry, but they would have never understood.

"Are you sure this is all that happened, Mrs. Jones? Do realize with the information you've given me, it may be near to impossible to catch the man you described as your attacker. Not only that, we haven't located the knife that was used on you. And your neighbors claim they didn't hear or see anything that night either. Are you sure that's all you can remember?"

The investigator waited for my reaction, but I didn't have anything else to say. I avoided eye contact with him and only nodded my head. He switched off the tape recorder.

"Alright, Mrs. Jones, I guess your statement will help clear your husband's name. If you say your husband didn't do it…." He shrugged. "Then he didn't do it. But if you start to remember anything about that short black man or even want to change your story, please let me know. I'm leaving my card on this nightstand for you."

I looked up and gave Sergeant Anderson a quick smile and a curt nod. The investigator gathered his paperwork. He knew I was lying to protect my husband, but there wasn't a damn thing he could do about it. I learned a long time ago that a wife didn't have to testify against her husband.

"Thank you, Mrs. Jones. I'll get this report submitted to the district attorney's office today, and I hope you continue to have a speedy recovery." Sergeant Anderson gave Mama and Thelma a nod before leaving the hospital room.

Thelma walked up to the side of my bed and leaned in close to confront me. "After all that man put you through, you just had to let him off the hook again. Do you know you almost died on that operating table? Toni, I am so sick of you covering up for him. I will never understand you…"

I drifted off in my head while Thelma continued to gripe. She didn't understand me? Well, there were some things I didn't understand myself. Like what went wrong between Marvin and me? And at what point did our relationship go downhill?

Chapter 12

Thelma had every right to be mad at me…they all did. I put the family through a lot of changes in being married to Marvin. If, before we got married, someone would have told me our life together would consist of violent battles and us going from plentiful-to-poor, I would have never believed it. I think I actually would have accused that person of being on crack right in their face. But in life, never say never because all things are possible.

We had a whirlwind affair and married in the winter of 1980. The first three years of our marriage were pure bliss. We had very little problems and didn't want for a damn thing. If we desired something, money was available. I drove a mint condition 1970 red Corvette LT-1 and Marvin rolled around in a Cadillac Seville with a cabriolet roof. We lived in a nice neighborhood and had a lease-to-own arrangement on a three-bedroom townhouse, which was fabulously furnished in the latest decor.

Our careers were on a fast track as well and going in the right direction. I was in rising demand for live appearances and often spent my Friday nights split between broadcasting from The Palladium and hosting events at other venues. Marvin was making headway with his aspirations too. In addition to running a successful club and maintaining a small barbershop on the side, he found a talented male singing group to manage and had them performing in the club sometimes.

On the home front, things were wonderful. I couldn't have been happier. Marvin treated my daughter as though she were his very own. Plus, we had an amazing sex life. The sex was so incredible, we had our hands on each other almost daily. Like sex addicts, we just couldn't get enough. For a young black family in the South, we were living large and were socially known as the power couple on the move. But with more money, you get more attention and more problems.

It all started in the early spring of 1983 with the increase of gang fights in the club followed by a federal drug raid. In a short span of time, The Palladium underwent a drastic change to match the current trend. Disco music was out and rap was all the rage. I didn't care for it too much. Some of the beats from the songs were catchy, but the style of music promoted an undesirable atmosphere in the club. The rap scene attracted younger people, gang bangers, and constant suspicion from the local police and the FBI.

The raid that spring caused rampant rumors. There was a lot of talk about Marvin and his partners being big time drug dealers, and the Palladium was just a front for illegal activity. Those rumors weren't new; I had heard them all before. For years, people speculated drug money was how three black men were able to start a lucrative business. But I felt all that slanderous gossip only intensified the law enforcement's aggressive tactics toward the partners. Even when the federal interrogation stopped, a few local police officers would randomly show up to inspect them on proper alcohol licensure, underage admission, and any probable violation that would lead to the discovery of drug trafficking in the club.

Marvin was no drug lord and neither were Donald and Isaac. But, like most people, they weren't angels. Back in the day, Marvin and Isaac sold reefa and did some number running to survive on the streets as kids. I heard Donald dabbled in moonshining with his uncle years ago. But those days were long behind them, and they became legitimate businessmen through hard work.

Eventually, Marvin took that trade he learned and went on to get his barber's license at the age of eighteen. He used the money he saved from hustling and cutting hair to invest in Donald's grand idea of opening a nightclub.

He didn't know Donald Mack very well, but he trusted Isaac. And when Isaac assured Marvin his forty-five-year-old brother-in-law was solid and trustworthy, Marvin jumped on the business opportunity. Now, the guys weren't equal partners. A small twenty-five percent of the shares belonged to Marvin, which paid out an average $5,800 a month after business expenses. Donald Mack owned the majority of the club with his money coming from years of working as a longshoreman at the Charleston Ports Authority. I couldn't verify the information, but I also heard Donald made money on the side from other undisclosed investments.

The bottom line...no one in the partnership was innocent. They all had something a little shady in their background. The cops used that and hearsay as excuses to stalk their business. And after several months of not finding any incriminating evidence, the scrutiny finally died down. But that's when the real drama unfolded. Out of the blue, the IRS came to audit.

Apparently, Donald's accountant had been skimming the books for years and not properly filing annual returns. The partners owed over $200,000 in back taxes, and the Internal Revenue Service was out for blood. Till this day, I still blame Donald for the shakedown and ultimately the loss of the business. I believe he knew more about the tax scandal than he claimed. Donald had a very controlling personality and insisted he would be responsible for maintaining cash flow and the business' paperwork while Marvin and Isaac handled entertainment, public relations, and the liquor vendors.

When it was all said and done, it took lawyers almost a month to settle the case and broker a plea bargain. The outcome was predictable. The partners were forced to shut down The Palladium and liquidate whatever they could. Marvin lost everything: his investments, our home, our cars, his longtime friendship with Isaac, and worst of all, his freedom. Marvin, Donald, and James pleaded guilty on tax evasion charges. They were fined and each served four months in jail. The accountant got off easy with serving only one. By the time Marvin was released, I had already moved out of Mama's house into a cheap rental I found near the projects. Before he reported to jail, Marvin gave me $3,500 wrapped up tight in plastic for safeguarding. It was his last bit of money in the world he kept hidden at his father's house in an old wood shed in the backyard. He told me to spend what I needed to keep the family afloat but save as much as possible. With his last words in mind, I put our situation in perspective and placed our finances on a strict budget for his return.

As we shifted into our downgraded lifestyle, I knew it would be a challenge for Marvin to find employment. He had another mark on his criminal record and renewing his barber's license would be impossible. I remained optimistic—but Marvin, not so much. Prison changed him. He used to be ambitious and upbeat. When he came back, he seemed hopeless and became more irritable and negative with each passing day, always sensitive to whatever I had to say.

But being the supportive wife, I assured him that everything would be fine. After all, this was not our first time seeing hardship. We both came from humble beginnings, so I had faith we would make it through somehow and Marvin would find his way. With the leftover savings, the money I was making from the radio station and newspaper, plus the extra income from hosting events, we could manage temporarily. But he didn't want to hear that and kept on saying, "I'm the man of this house. I'm supposed to be holding you up." And to add fuel to the fire, I was three weeks pregnant with Adrian.

Now, there was never a doubt in my mind he wasn't happy about the baby, especially since it was his first child. Still, the pressures of having another mouth to feed played horribly on his masculinity. From that point on, he started to reveal his dark side and became abusive.

By the time 1984 rolled in, Marvin still had no luck finding work. He claimed there were several reasons why he couldn't find a job: "employers ain't hiring black men with criminal backgrounds," he didn't have a high school diploma or any other vocational skills, and the hourly wages were too low. The fact was he couldn't let go of his old life and being his own boss. He had a major chip on his shoulder and his pride was definitely not allowing him to do anything manual like sanitary work. I knew what Marvin wanted, and I told him we could make plans on setting up a new business later on down the road. It was time to forget about the entertainment world and the barbershop. Our funds were depleting rapidly and I needed immediate help.

Looking back at that conversation, I think when I asked him to take any job, he felt I lacked confidence in his abilities and was blocking him from reaching his goals. What if he never forgave me for that? Maybe that's when things started to change and the trouble began.

Marvin landed a few hustle jobs here and there but nothing steady. It was such a sad time for our marriage, and all communication between us stopped. He ignored me in every way possible and quickly developed a daily drinking routine: Budweiser in the morning and Crown Royal by night. He also became unusually obsessed with martial arts. Every damn day, he'd watch kung-fu videos and imitate moves. When discussions came up about expenses for the coming baby or the household, he would get angry and take his frustrations out on me.

At first there were only screaming matches, but then we upgraded to hand-to-hand combat. He would slap me around then I'd scratch him. He would twist my arm, and I'd kick him. This went back and forth. It was a miracle little Adrian wasn't aborted or born with any birth defects. But as soon as he was born, Marvin's beatings became more intense. There was no way I could fight back. Marvin fought me as if I were a man.

Chapter 13

I remember the first time he viciously attacked me. It was on a Saturday evening. I had just returned home from grocery shopping and found Marvin sleeping on the recliner. The smell of alcohol was strong, and beer cans were collected on the sides of the chair. It looked like he had been passed out for hours. I continued to the bedroom to put Adrian in his crib and when I returned to start dinner, he was up and waiting on me. His eyes were red and face wrinkled from sleeping, and I could tell he hadn't washed all day. By the looks of it, he was still drunk. And as usual, I paid him no attention when he was in his funky mood. So I proceeded with my task and worked around him.

"Oh so, you can't speak this morning," he muttered.

"Marvin, it's nearly 5 o'clock in the evening."

He opened the blinds. "Shit, it is almost dark."

He turned around and pointed his finger at me. "See. That's what I'm talking about. You always got something smart to say. Well then, where the hell you been all day? And don't tell me at work, because I know you got today off."

"Marvin, you can remember today is my day off, but you can't remember me telling you that Adrian and I were leaving early this morning to shop for the house? You really need to slow down your damn drinking," I said, rolling my eyes and putting away meat in the freezer. Within seconds, he turned into another person.

"What!" he shouted, sounding vexed. "Woman, who do you think you're talking to like that?"

I ignored him and avoided eye contact. Marvin walked up behind me and leaned in close to my ear. His breath was hot and rank.

"Do you think I'm no longer the man of this house because you make more money than me? Is that what you think?"

"Marvin, I never said that." I turned around and looked him straight in the eyes. "But if you want be the man of the house, fine! Get a real job instead of bringing home only fifty dollars every other week, if even that," I snapped.

Marvin yanked my arm like a rag doll and threw me into the living room. I landed on the couch and braced myself as he approached me.

"Do you see a child around here?" he asked, fixating his gaze on me like a snake about to strike. "Do you? Answer my goddam question, Toni."

"No, Marvin. I'm just..."

Before I could get my sentence out, he dragged me off the sofa by my hair and jabbed me in my face. I was shocked. That was the first time he hit me extremely hard. Not even my father had ever hit me so hard when I used to intervene between him and Mama. I staggered around to get to my feet and regain my senses.

"What the fuck is your problem hitting me like that?" I shrieked. Furiously, I mustered all the strength I had left in my body and threw a punch to his chest. No effect. It felt like hitting a brick wall. Marvin returned the same gesture but in the form of a karate kick to my stomach. That was it; I was out. I lay there on floor in agony, unable to move.

"That's right! Now you know not to play with me," he said proudly, like he'd just won a kickboxing tournament. "I'm not your fucking child."

Apparently Marvin wasn't completely satisfied with the last blow delivered, because he reached for the small brass clock on the end table and chucked it across my back.

"Bitch!" he yelled. "Now get your ass in the kitchen and start cooking."

Not another word was spoken between us that night.

Chapter 14

The next morning, Marvin came in the bedroom and crawled up next to me. He slowly peeled away the blanket I held throughout the night for comfort and placed his hand on my arm. The warm touch immediately made my pupils dilate and body tremble, as I wondered if he was the drunken Marvin looking to do more damage, or the Marvin I loved and married. I hadn't an ounce of fight left in me, so without any objections, I let him have his way.

Gently, he pulled my nightgown strap off my shoulder, exposing the purple wound on my back. He began to kiss it while tears streamed down my swollen, discolored face.

"Toni, are you up?" he asked in a whisper. I kept my back facing him and moved my legs to answer his question. I couldn't bear looking at him.

"Toni, I'm so sorry. You know I love you. That was not me yesterday, baby. That was the alcohol. And you're right, I need to stop drinking so much. But it gets so hard sometimes, you know? I'm supposed to be taking care of you and not the other way around. I just don't know what's happening to my life, but I need you."

I heard him crying. It sounded genuine. And just like that, without a word, I forgave him.

When Thelma dropped off Justine the next day, she questioned me about my face. I told her I accidentally fell while exercising, and of course, she drove off not believing a word I said. I guess I took him back because I felt bad for him. While his business failed, my show continued to do well. I was still working toward my dreams, and he was still unemployed.

We were still fighting over many things even after that incident. If it wasn't over financial problems, it was about his jealousy issues. *Why are you coming home so late and why are you talking on the phone with your boss so long?* He constantly asked these types of questions.

After several more karate fights and Marvin sporadically working some mysterious job he would never tell me about, Brenda persuaded me to take the children and run away to a place called My Daughter's House, a shelter for battered women.

I had always been a closed book when it came to my marriage and intimate feelings. It took a lot of courage for me to go there with my children. At first I felt reluctance because of the fear of someone recognizing me. And worst of all, I worried about my co-workers finding out. I didn't want anyone's pity or be the subject of a late-night gossip call. So when I registered, I used an alias: Wanda Hamilton.

I really tried to give it a chance and follow the program, but our stay there was very short-lived. After one week, the children and I got put out of the shelter because I broke the first and last rule. Never, under any circumstances, tell your abuser where you are. At the time, listening to those women, I just didn't think my problems were as bad as theirs. I sat in a circle and listened to repeated stories of never-ending fights with no mention of love. It seemed like my situation was different, triggered by temporary unemployment and depression. My man only hit me when he was drunk. He didn't mean it. Being abusive hadn't always been a part of Marvin's nature. In a twisted sort of way, I actually felt lucky compared to those women.

And that's how I justified it. For the sake of my marriage, I refused to give up on my husband. I knew about his troublesome past. He told me about his harsh childhood, the drug dealing and his jail time. All those skeletons in his closet weren't secret from me, and I believed him when he said those days were over. Not one time did I ever think Marvin would let the ghosts of his past come back to haunt us. I guess I thought wrong.

In the end, love and my determination to help him always overpowered me. So I stayed and endured. Most of the time, I would just take his beatings and not ask anyone for help. But when a fight got really bad, I can't deny running off to call Mama and have her enlist the cavalry: Charles Jr. and Big Willie from around the corner. They would show up to either whip his ass or scare him off. Then I'd have a change of heart and beg them not to call the police. Normally, I'd get my way. There was even one time when Mama went against my wishes, and Marvin got arrested. But I found a way to get the charges dropped. He always knew what to say.

Chapter 15

Back in the hospital room, Mother stood up and scolded me. "Tonnetta Marie Williams, I am tired and getting too old for this. My heart can't take much more."

I knew I had Mama really upset when she used my full birth name. I felt terrible and torn at the same time. The last thing I wanted to do was hurt anybody, but I loved my husband. What was I supposed to do?

"I love you all and appreciate what you've done for me, but I'm a grown woman," I said. "And I have to make my own decisions for me and my family. Marvin did not stab me. Please, you've got to trust me on this one."

"Trust you?" Thelma seethed. "You crazy heifer! Do you even hear yourself?"

"Thelma, stop it," Mama yelled.

Ignoring Mama, Thelma continued to read me. "Who in the hell are you trying to convince? Mama used to lay black and blue where you are right now. And do you remember my first marriage? We know the script!"

I almost forgot how Thelma's first husband used to fight her. Nothing major like Marvin and me. Thelma never knew how to forgive—that was the difference between us. Oh, no. After three slaps on the face, she left her husband and two teenage boys along with all of her belongings in that house and never looked back. But Thelma could do that. She had a good paying job and could afford to buy everything from scratch. I never had that luxury.

"Are you listening?" She got close to my ear and reprimanded me like a child. I turned and gave Thelma a glare through my narrowed, damp eyes. She was really tap-dancing on my last nerve with her constant fussing. It annoyed me just like a dog barking through the night.

"Yes, I'm listening!" I snapped and pounded my fist on the bed railing. "I don't know what the hell you want me to say. I'm so sorry for causing you so much grief, Thelma. But, the truth is, you've never liked Marvin from day one. And yes, we've had our problems in the past, but I've forgiven him for that. Now, for the last time, I told you. He didn't do it! Marvin is not the one who stabbed me!"

The lies became easier the more I said them. I even started to believe them myself. But there was some shame. Not only had I lied to the people I loved, but deep down inside I knew they were right. Like my sister said, I was crazy in love and I didn't care about alienating myself from my entire family. I loved my man. He had my heart, and I would have done anything to make our relationship work. Thelma turned away from me and picked up the handbags again.

"Mama, let's just go. I'm done talking to this woman."

Mama walked up and kissed my forehead then softly said, "Toni, I am your mother. And no matter what happens, I will always love you. But I promise you, nothing good will come from this. You'll only get heartache and regrets. "

Mama always had the gift of saying so much with so little words. Tears welled and overflowed. As they were walking out the door, Thelma turned around and just had to put in her last two cents.

"Go ahead. You need to cry, because he's going to kill you someday. Not only are you laid up in that hospital bed sick in your body, you are really sick in your head. Don't get it confused."

Determined on not changing my mind, I stood my ground and searched the room for a comfortable place to rest my eyes until they left.

Part Two

Chapter 16

Springtime rolled around in full bloom this April. I could smell the strong mixtures of azaleas and sweet magnolias in the warm air as I sat on a bench at the historic Battery Park looking out at the water. I loved living minutes away from downtown Charleston, South Carolina. The aroma of seawater and the beautiful harbor scenery were therapeutic for me. I had a deep appreciation and connection to this city.

There's an old maritime folklore. They say if you're born and raised on the coast, the ocean is in your blood. And like a sea lion to the shores of a beach, I was drawn to the waterfront. Maybe that's why I preferred to come here when I have a little me-time to relax, read, and get away while the kids were off at school.

I got up to walk through the park, passing war relics of the past and an old gazebo on my way to the promenade. The view of Fort Sumter was clear. As I continued to breathe in the surroundings and take notice of the seasonal change, I thought about the changes made in my life over the last two and half years.

It was 1989, and after leaving the hospital and being out for two months, returning to work proved to be much more stressful than I had ever anticipated. Due to budget cuts, I no longer had a column with the newspaper and the radio station was suddenly under new management and heading for a total makeover.

"Appealing to a younger demographic requires younger, hipper air personalities," a co-worker told me she overheard the new program director tell someone over the telephone. I wasn't surprised. I felt the change coming when they cut my hours with no real reason; that action alone triggered me to start looking for another job.

Fallen ratings and two hard-hitting competitors made it clear Q-101.5 no longer controlled the airwaves. The slip in numbers created a lot of friction and finger pointing that unfortunately resulted in the firing of Mr. Davis, the man who gave me my first job and had been managing the station for over twenty years. That's when the big shots decided to hire Donna Matthews as his replacement, a twenty-nine-year-old executive with a curvy figure, a college degree, and a reputation of having a stab-you-in-the-back personality. And to make matters worse, the word around the office was the bitch had been fucking the station's owner for some time now—the same owner who just turned sixty-three years old last week and recently celebrated his twenty-fifth wedding anniversary last month.

It became obvious to me how *Ms. Thing* landed that position at such a young age with only five years of radio experience on her resume. The change caused an uproar in the office. There were several more qualified people, including myself, who wanted the job and had been at the radio station much longer. I didn't have time for the drama nor the patience to work my way into her good graces. My dues were paid, and I had already made a name for myself.

Besides, I got tired of all the stares and chatter going on about Marvin and me. If I heard Lisa whisper, just one more time, "and she didn't even press charges" to somebody in the office and act like she wasn't talking about me when I walked by, somebody would have called the police on me for snatching that tired-ass looking weave off her head. So, before anybody could piss me off even more, I decided to leave Q-101.5 and join a new station called Foxy 100.

It was a good move. Paul Goodwin, the general manager, had been following my career for years and felt I could contribute to his vision of formatting the station to exclusively urban adult contemporary and oldies music. It was more my speed rather than all that hip-hop stuff. He offered me seventy-five cents more from my last hourly wage as well as a better schedule to spend more time with my family. Noon to 4:30 PM was my new shift, where I hosted

The Midday Cafe Thursdays through Saturdays—and maybe some Sundays if we were short-staffed.

The hours weren't prime like I hoped, but it was a blessing because I no longer had to get dressed up and do live broadcasts from nightclubs. Instead, I did my entertainment news shows and disc-jockeying from the radio station. The change was exactly what I needed: more studio time and nobody in my business.

Things were also improved with my home life. Marvin and I decided to leave the old neighborhood and bad memories behind and head for the suburbs of Summerville, a small town just outside of Charleston County. We needed a fresh start and scored a small three-bedroom house near a noisy railroad track. The train came mostly in the mornings and a few times late at night. The noise didn't bother us; that's what kept the rent so low.

It took Mama almost a month to speak to me again after the charges against Marvin were dropped. I wasn't back at work yet, and when she found out that we were catching hell financially, she offered me $400 to sustain us until we got back on our feet. This was done in secrecy, of course; the family had declared they wouldn't contribute a single dime to me that would benefit Marvin. But Mama, she was always a forgiving woman…through her tribulations and mine.

"As long as I have life in my body, I just can't sit by and watch you and my grandbabies go without," she said, shoving an envelope into my purse. "This is between me and you."

I knew Mama gave me all of her emergency money she had hidden away in the pocket of her forty-year-old winter coat. The same worn-out black coat she stored deep in the back of the closet and thought nobody knew about. But I knew her secret. On many occasions, I used to sneak and watch Mama through a hole in the door reach down into that pocket, pull out a roll of money and, with tears gushing down her face, contemplate leaving Daddy after a fight.

With Mama giving us her last, Marvin and I knew we had to do some serious hustling. He finally realized we needed to put our dreams on the back burner and focus more on our family. We made a commitment to each other: no more chain smoking for me and no more drinking for him. With all of the medical bills and other living expenses looming over our heads, Marvin understood we needed some money.

It took some time to track him down, but when I got a hold of him, it sure was a blessing. James Franklin, a childhood friend, was now an instructor for PJ Trucking School. And after reminiscing about old times and catching-up on each other's lives, I boldly asked him to help my husband get his CDL and secure a job. When James agreed, Marvin wasted no time taking advantage of the opportunity. He became a commercial truck driver and, despite our numerous critics, for the last few years, we'd been stable, happy, and living in peace.

Chapter 17

While driving home from the harbor in my cream Ford Escort, I came up with the most sensual idea. It was a Friday evening, and I had been expecting Marvin to return home from a grueling five-day workweek up and down the East Coast. I was feeling sexier than ever and wanted to give my man a relaxing treat. So I called Brenda, told her my plans, and begged her to keep the kids for the weekend. When that was all taken care of, I went to work on transforming our bathroom into a private spa, just for two. Candles outlining the bathtub, rose petals floating on top of bubbled water, the scent of white linen in the air, and Sade playing softly in the background. I created the perfect ambience for romance.

It was 8:45 PM and about forty minutes since I last talked to Marvin. He called to let me know he was less than an hour away from home. Speaking to him took all the composure I had to hide my excitement and not give a clue to what was in store for him at home. Knowing very little time was left, I scurried around trying to place notecards and rose petals systematically around the house. After putting on my diva makeup and brushing my shoulder-length hair into a curly updo, I stood in front of a cherry wood full-length mirror to critique myself while rubbing shimmering lotion all over my chocolate body. For a woman thirty-seven years of age and going on thirty-eight next month in May, I was still young and fine. Even with the weight I had packed on. I wore a curvaceous 155 pounds very well.

I heard the truck door slam. My mind instantly recalled that song, "Tonight is the Night" by Betty Wright. I chuckled inside. This was not, by far, the first time for Marvin and me, but the anticipation felt the same. I raced over to the window and saw my man climbing out of his black tractor-trailer truck parked at the dead end of the street. My pulse jumped. He would be in the house in less than one minute.

"Toni, I'm home," he called out. "Baby, why is it so dark in here?" And just when he was about to say my name once again, he stopped. Marvin must have noticed the rose petals on the ground, the music, and the smell of sweet perfume in the air. He knew something was up. He found the first card and read it out loud.

Follow The Rose Petals!

"Okay Toni, I'll play your game," he said, snickering. He found the second card on the bedroom floor. He picked it up.

Take Off Your Clothes. Leave Nothing On!

"Damn girl, you on fire tonight," he murmured, sounding aroused and more serious. He did exactly what he was told and stripped then continued to follow the rose petals. He saw the last card at the bottom of the bathroom door. He picked it up.

Open The Door & Claim Your Prize!

Marvin walked in with a crooked smile as I stood there posing in my red stilettos and matching red satin robe.

"Come here," I demanded while giving him my best bedroom eyes. I had him revved up and rising. Lust took over and he pulled my body close to his. I could feel his big manhood pulsating against my stomach. My nipples grew hard and I tingled everywhere. Finding no more use for words, we kissed like we hadn't seen each other in years. After bathing each other quickly, we moved to our bed and started to make love. His tongue navigated my curves and wet spot. Then he parted my thighs wider and laid his muscular body on top of my mine. Marvin's strokes were so strong. He wanted me to feel every thrust. Consumed by desire, I flipped him over and straddled his hips. Vigorously, I slid up and down his thick shaft. Moments later, we climaxed together and lay there with our limbs intertwined. It was amazing. The older we got, the better our lovemaking became.

In the middle of the night, I got up to cover my naked body with a blanket. And just before I turned completely around and returned to sleep, I noticed the moonlight shining slightly on Marvin's face. He was gorgeous and getting finer with time. At the age of forty, his body was broader and face more chiseled. And his well-groomed beard had sprinkles of gray. Marvin could have had any woman he wanted, but he was mine. I marveled at the sight of my husband and thanked God for his changed ways, and our second chance together.

Chapter 18

I **woke up** early the next morning feeling energized and good all over. "Wake up, honey. It's time to get up," I said while rubbing Marvin's chest, trying to bring him back to consciousness. Slowly, he opened his eyes and looked up at me.

"Hey baby, what time is it?" he asked, struggling to get up.

"It's about twenty-five minutes after six."

When I leaned over to kiss his mouth, I slipped in my tongue.

"Whoa! There you go again." He flashed a smirk. "Toni, I don't have time for that."

"Why not?" I whined like a child.

"Girl, you're going to kill me. You know I have to get on the road and make a special run for my boss."

"C'mon, Marvin." I nudged his arm. "I promise it won't take more than five minutes."

"That's a lie, Toni. And you know it." He laughed. On his way to the bathroom, he leaned over and kissed me on the cheek.

"Anyway, you know your stuff will have me stretched out. I'd be asleep for hours."

"My stuff will have you stretched out?" I jokingly repeated. "You better remember that when you're on road and some young thing tries to hit on you. I bet there are plenty of hoochie-mamas around those truck stop stores always on the lookout for sugar daddies."

He spit out the toothpaste and rinsed.

"You know you need to stop."

"Hey, I'm just saying. Remember what you just said when a big-butt opportunity comes your way." I walked up behind him with hands on my hips and wearing a devilish grin.

He looked at me in the mirror. "Now Toni, you know I only have eyes for you."

"Really, you love me that much?" I smiled like a schoolgirl getting her first love letter in class. Marvin turned and wrapped his arms around me.

"Yes woman, I love you that much," he replied. "Besides, I've never seen another woman with a bigger ass than yours." He smacked my butt then we laughed together.

"But seriously, are you happy?" I asked.

"Of course I am." He pulled away and gave me a suspicious look. "What kind of question is that? You're the only person who's ever believed in me. Toni, you're my best friend." Marvin placed his hands on my shoulders and gazed lovingly into my eyes.

"What about you? Are you happy?" he asked, sounding concerned. My eyes watered slightly thinking about all the pain I went through with this man, and now I was on top. We weren't perfect people or wealthy, but we loved and understood each other.

"Yes baby," I said without a doubt in mind. "You have no idea how happy I am."

Marvin gave me a deep passionate kiss, then pulled off my panties and gave me a quickie before leaving.

Chapter 19

Brenda pulled into my driveway wearing a big Kool-Aid smile on her face. She lived less than fifteen minutes away from me and called to let me know she was on her way. Brenda got out of the car and got close. "Give me the juice," she demanded.

"Brenda, what are you talking about? There's really nothing much to tell. We had a beautiful night and that's all," I said in a prim and proper way as I bypassed her to help the kids get their bags out of the car. Justine and Adrian jumped out and went straight for the front door without saying a word to anyone.

"Hey, where are your manners?" I shouted. "Y'all better say something to Ms. Brenda."

"Oh, bye, Ms. Brenda," Justine replied. "Thanks for the weekend."

"Yes, thank you for the pizza," Adrian followed.

Brenda smiled and waved back and then returned her attention to me. She rolled her eyes then gave me a *get-real* look. "Toni, don't play with me."

"Okay, shit, I can barely walk," I laughed. "My thighs are that sore."

"Alright," she said, snapping her fingers up and down. "I am glad to hear you put it on him, because I was getting so tired of hearing you complain about Marvin's long hours on the road. 'I miss my man; I need my man.' That's all you talked about. So where's *Mr. Man* now? I don't see his truck anywhere."

"Girl, you are too much," I said. "But Marvin actually left for Maryland yesterday morning. His boss asked him to do another weekend delivery. He's getting overtime for it, so I don't press the issue."

"Damn, I know he has got to be tired." Brenda winced. "How many hours can a truck driver spend on the road anyway?"

Brenda was a longtime friend, my partner in some serious clubbing crime during our younger years. Lord knows I didn't have many female friends in my life, but I trusted her. No matter what mess I got myself into, Brenda was there, right or wrong.

"Girl, I don't know." I brushed off her question. "Besides, I'd rather have him out there making money than not making any at all. You know what I mean?"

"I know that's right," Brenda said while getting back into her Toyota.

"Well, let me go so I can get these kids situated for school tomorrow," I said. "I'll call you later, and thanks again for watching the kids this weekend."

As I waved goodbye, Brenda's question got me wondering. I thought truck drivers could only work a certain amount of hours during the day mandated by law. But, Marvin's boss had him pushing extra hours on the road every week since March.

Chapter 20

"You're lying!" I exclaimed in a hushed voice. Listening to Stephanie over the telephone almost caused me to pee my pants. What she was telling me, I knew would happen someday. But I wasn't mentally ready for that someday to be today.

I juggled turning off the pot of lima beans and neck bones I was cooking for dinner with holding the phone between my ear and shoulder. "Hang on a second," I told Stephanie, dragging the long telephone cord behind me and looking around the corner to make sure all the bedroom doors were shut and I had complete privacy. I dropped on the couch in disbelief.

"Lewis Taylor told you to tell me hello and to call him," I repeated, making sure I heard my sister correctly.

"Yes, that's what he said," Stephanie replied.

"Stephanie, how do you know Lewis Taylor?"

"Well, I don't know him. He approached me on my job today."

"He approached you?" I asked, raising an eyebrow.

"Ah yeah," she responded in a slightly sarcastic way. "Listen, he came up to me while I was folding jeans and said I was a very attractive young woman. I said thank you. And just in case he was trying to hit on me, I gave him one of those I'm-not-interested looks."

"Why did you do that? Did he look bad?" I pressed, curious.

"Oh no, he didn't look bad. The man just wasn't my cup of tea. That's all. But anyway, I guess he got the hint because he quickly apologized then said he had a son around my age."

"Really, so how did I get into the conversation?"

"Well, let me finish," Stephanie said, getting all excited. "He went on to explain how my resemblance to someone he knew long ago was so remarkable, it couldn't have been a coincidence. There was something about my eyes and smile. And that's when I mentioned your name and told him how a lot of people say I look like the light-skinned version of you. Man, was he surprised. So Toni, what's up with all the mystery? Who is this guy?"

I threw my head back, looking up at the popcorn ceiling and sighed from stress. "Girl, Lewis Taylor is Justine's real father, and he doesn't even know it."

Chapter 21

I sat in the Waffle House rapidly stirring my coffee waiting on Lewis' arrival. It took me a whole day to call him. I had no idea how I was going to break the news to him about Justine, but I knew I couldn't do it over the telephone. I told him that old friends deserve a better reunion, and he agreed to meet this Thursday morning. This would be the first time I'd laid eyes on Lewis Taylor in almost thirteen years.

I pulled out my mirror to make sure my hair and makeup was on point. I was no longer in my twenties or available, but I wanted him to see that time had been kind to me. No more than five minutes later, he walked through the door wearing a blue and green windbreaker jump suit.... Still cute, still a jock, and still one of the best fucks of my life.

"Hey Toni," he said with his forever charming smile and arms stretched wide open. "You better get up and hug me girl." At 6'5, Lewis had the arm span of an eagle. I returned the gesture and leaned in. He smelled good and felt even better.

"Toni, you look great!" he said as he checked me over with a mischievous grin, obviously pleased with my appearance. "How could anyone forget you?"

"Thank you," I said, smiling brightly. "You look damn good yourself."

It seemed like time hadn't changed Lewis' spirit a bit. He still had a sparkle in his light brown eyes and a warm, inviting personality to match.

"Well, you know. I try," he joked, stroking the bottom of his chin with his thumb.

We laughed out loud then our eyes locked. The room became still. No doubt the same intense memories that were racing through my mind had to be coursing through his. I needed to clear the air.

"Are you still playing basketball?" I asked.

Lewis was a professional basketball player who played for teams overseas. Not a famous man, he was just a guy who played for the love of the game. I met him at a New Year Eve's party back in 1976 over a punch bowl. We hit it off right from the start. We talked and danced the entire night. After the countdown, we ended up back at his hotel room and had mind-blowing sex. The kind of sex you never forget. The next day, he left for Europe. And a month later, I found out I was pregnant.

Back then an abortion was not an option. Mama always warned, "If you're grown enough to lay for it, then you're grown enough to raise it."

"Yeah, I'm still playing a little," he said, "but actually, I'm getting ready to retire and return to the States. My son is here. My family is here. I think it's time for me to come home. Who knows, maybe I'll get a job coaching at my old high school."

"That's right, I remember you telling me about your son. How old is he? He should be all grown up by now, maybe even married."

"Yeah, Brandon is nineteen and going into his sophomore year at Clemson. And no, he's not married, too young for that. Time goes by fast, doesn't it?" He wagged his head side to side.

"You're telling me," I agreed, drifting my eyes to his left hand. There was no wedding band. But I still wanted to know. "So did you ever get married?"

"Yes, I was once married, but I got divorced." He shrugged then grinned. "Hey, let's just say she couldn't get used to my nomadic lifestyle."

"Oh, I'm sorry," I said.

"Don't be. I'm not."

I nodded and thought of another question. "So tell me something, Lewis. Does Brandon have your impeccable b-ball skills? Is he playing for Clemson?"

"Nah." He shook his head. "That boy's knee deep into football."

"Oh, I see," I said, nodding again.

I noticed Lewis watching my hand as I raised my coffee cup. "I see you're hitched. I'm not surprised," he said. I flung my hand up and dangled my ring finger while I swallowed.

"Good for you," he replied, showing off his dimples. At that very moment, I saw Justine.

"And do you have any children?" he went on to ask.

"Yeah, I have two, Justine and Adrian," I answered, trying hard to maintain a slight smile. And there it was, the purpose of our meeting coming into view. My smile faded into nothing. He noticed it.

"Toni, what's wrong?"

I froze for a few seconds. My stomach churned.

"Toni, is everything alright?" he asked again, looking baffled by my instant mood change. There was no easy way of telling him.

"Justine is your child," I blurted. "She's your daughter." I waited for a response but got nothing. He sat there speechless and still like petrified wood. *What did I expect?*

"Lewis, I know you're shocked," I said nervously. "And I know you'll probably want a paternity test, but I'm telling you Justine is really yours. She looks just like you. See!"

I whipped out Justine's school picture and pushed it across the table. Lewis finally took his gaze off me and looked down at the photograph. He studied her face. They had the same eyes, the same round-shaped face, and the same dimples. It was undeniable and he knew it. A paternity test would just be a formality.

"Toni, why didn't you tell me about her?" he asked, wide eyed. "Why spring this on me now after all these years?"

"Lewis, I lost your number. I had no way of finding you. I'm sorry." I started to tear up.

"Well, does she even know about me?"

"No," I said looking down and drying my eyes with a napkin.

"No!" he exclaimed, raising his voice a notch. A waitress and an old man at the bar turned around and stared at us.

"Listen," I whispered. "We had a one-night stand. How was I supposed to tell a child about that? I wanted to wait until she got a little older."

Suddenly, his pager went off. *How convenient.*

"Look, I've got to go." He stood and dropped a ten-dollar bill on the table.

"Call me tonight, Toni. We've got to fix this."

Lewis walked off hard and fast. I got up and went to the pay phone to call my boss and ask for the day off. He accepted my made-up excuse. I needed some time and clearly today would be a long day. I sat back down at a table and for another hour, I thought about how I was going to make this right.

Chapter 22

Mama was the first person I called when I returned home that afternoon. I told her the meeting with Lewis went as well as it could have under the circumstances. At least the man didn't deny the girl outright, and it seemed like he wanted to get involved. That was a start. But throughout the day, I had moments where I wished I had just thrown out Lewis' number. It would have been much easier. And even though Justine already knew Marvin was not her biological father and didn't have his last name, she always knew him as daddy ever since she was three years old.

Not this time, I thought to myself. Too many mistakes had been made in the past. Lewis and Justine had a right to know each other. Besides, if Justine ever found out that I turned down a chance for her to meet her real father, she would only hate my guts for the rest of her life.

"The truth needs to be told," Mama said. "Every child deserves to know who their daddy is and where they come from. She can handle it."

Mama had a point. Justine was smart and very mature for her age. If anybody could absorb a shock like this, it would be her. I planned on telling her everything the moment she got back from school.

I heard Justine fumbling around in her bedroom.

"Justine," I shouted, "could you please come to my room?"

She walked in looking like her father now more than ever: slim, brown-skinned with almond-shaped eyes and a beautiful smile. My daughter was becoming an attractive young lady and at the age where boys would soon come sniffing around. Justine sat on my bed. I didn't bother closing the door. Marvin was on the road and Adrian would find out soon enough.

"What's up, Mama?" she asked.

"I need to tell you something important." When I sat next to her, Justine gave me a serious look. The kind of look someone gives when they think something is wrong or someone is dead.

"Oh no, honey. Nothing's wrong," I said, grabbing her hand with a warm smile. "It's actually a good thing."

"Okay." She breathed a sigh of relief. I'd never been the type of woman to sugarcoat anything. So I came right out with it.

"Justine, your dad is in town and he wants to meet you. I'm talking about your real father."

Justine jumped up and folded her arms over.

"Well, I don't want to see him," she snapped.

"You don't mean that, Justine."

"Why not? He left us!" A tear slid down her cheek. She tried putting up a brave front, but I could see the hurt in her eye as her lips quivered. "He didn't want me before. So, why does he want to meet me now?"

And there it was. The dreaded question I knew I had to answer one day. The tension in my neck started to tighten like a noose. I rubbed it.

"Justine, your father didn't leave us. And by the way, his name is Lewis Taylor."

She sucked it up and began drying her face with her sleeve. She gave me a puzzled stare.

"What do you mean he didn't leave us?"

I lowered my head and nodded.

"He didn't abandon you because he never knew you existed. Lewis and I were together for a very short time. We separated and I discovered I was pregnant with you after he left for Europe. I lost contact with him."

"Europe!" Justine exclaimed, sharply rolling her eyes and neck. "Are you trying to tell me I'm half white?"

"No girl, nothing like that." I snickered a little. "Your father is black and he's a professional basketball player who plays overseas."

Justine's eyes became big.

"Yeah," I said, nodding my head. "He's been playing over there for more than, I wanna say, eighteen years now. That's where he's been."

"But Mama, why didn't you tell me about him before? I always thought he was a no-good jerk who bailed out on us. You never said a thing." Justine tried hard to fight away her tears, but the battle was lost. She looked away.

"Listen baby, there are some things I can't tell you in detail right now because you're just too young to understand. Just know I did what I thought was best. Marvin and I will always love you. But, your father is in the picture now and he wants to get to know you. So please, Justine, don't blame him for something he wasn't aware of. I think you should give him a chance."

I waited for Justine to say something but she kept quiet. I decided to leave her alone with her thoughts. Eventually, she'd come around. Sometimes life can bring you pain. Better she learned now.

Chapter 23

My head continued to buzz that night from the day's drama. It was like an emotional roller coaster with its highs and lows. But there was more to come. I expected Marvin to call me at any minute. He usually called around eight o'clock at night to get the daily news from Justine or me while on the road. I had a lot to report. I waited to tell Marvin last about Lewis' return because I didn't know how he'd react. One last showdown was all I could handle today.

The phone rang. I knew it was him. I let it ring two more times to collect my thoughts.

"Hello," I said, sitting up in bed.

"Hey baby, how's everything?"

"Everything's fine," I replied, sweetly. "Are you on your way?"

"Yeah, I should be there in another thirty minutes."

"Okay." I sighed loudly.

"What was that for?" he asked.

"I've got some news. Guess who's back in town?"

"Who?" he asked, sounding curious.

"Well, Justine's biological father."

I made sure not to say daddy on purpose, because I didn't want to hurt his feelings or offend him. After all, Marvin played the role of Justine's dad for the majority of her life. For better or for worse, he put his time in. Without delay, I went on to tell him about Stephanie and Lewis' chance encounter in the mall and that's how all of this started.

"So what does he want?" Marvin bluntly asked with an attitude.

"He wants to meet his daughter. Surely, you knew this day would actually come?"

"But after all these years, Toni?" His tone got nastier. "No letters. No phone calls. No nothing! And now he wants to meet her. I don't know about this, Toni."

I closed my eyes and felt every pounding nerve in my head. I knew this situation would come back to bite me in the ass. I lowered the phone to take a quick break and rub my temples.

"Toni! Toni, are you there?" I heard him say.

I raised the phone back to my ear.

"Marvin, you knew from the start I didn't have any contact with Justine's father. I told you I found out about my pregnancy long after he was out of my life. I couldn't find him. You said it didn't matter. You accepted Justine and me the way we were. Remember?"

Marvin must have recalled that very conversation we had the night he proposed to me on bent knee at the park, because he briefly got quiet and had nothing else scathing to say.

"Yeah, but don't forget," he said in a much calmer voice, "I'm still her father."

"Marvin, no one is challenging that, but this is about Justine. She deserves to know where she comes from and who her—"

"Just skip the lecture, Toni," he interrupted. "When are they going to meet?"

"Most likely this Saturday," I said, giving him an attitude back. "Lewis said he's only going to be here for another few days."

"Uh-huh," Marvin muttered under his breath. "Toni, you know I'll be heading to Maryland tomorrow morning, and I won't be back until Sunday night. You know this, right?"

"Yeah Marvin, I kinda expected that already," I said sarcastically.

"What the hell do you mean by that?" he pressed.

I didn't have time to question Marvin about his work schedule. A discussion about that would have to wait another day. I needed to get this father-daughter meeting all sorted out.

"Nothing," I replied.

"And how's Justine doing with all of this?"

"It's sinking in. That's all I can say."

"Well, don't push the girl," he said. "This is some heavy news for all of us."

Chapter 24

Marvin just could not get last night's conversation out of his head. By the tone of her voice, he got the inclination that Toni was very upset with him for working longer hours, and to make matters worse, her ex-lover was in town seeking to reclaim his daughter and maybe even Toni.

When heading out to work this morning, Toni barely had three phrases to say to him: Good morning, Have a good day, and Be safe. She seemed preoccupied and didn't even offer her daily kiss like she normally would. This got Marvin thinking as he drove down the long gray road: *Is she really that angry with me or was she just thinking about Lewis?*

During his lunch hour, Marvin made a detour to Concord Mills Mall in Charlotte, NC to even out the playing field and remind Toni who her man was. This year, he decided to make Toni's birthday unforgettable and go big. Marvin walked into Steinberg's jewelry store and bent over a counter of rings. They were all elegant and expensive looking, just what he needed to knock Toni's socks off.

"May I help you, sir?" said a polite white woman who appeared to be in her mid-fifties.

"Yes, I want to buy something nice for my wife. It's her birthday."

"Oh, I see. It's a last minute gift. That's no problem. I have plenty of pieces."

"No, it's not last minute," Marvin chuckled. "I didn't mean to imply her birthday is today. It's actually May 29. I still have over a week to find something good."

The woman nodded her head then revealed a smirk. "Wow! A guy who remembers his wife's birthday gift in advance, now that's impressive."

"Really, now why is that?" Marvin asked.

The woman tilted her nose down and looked up behind her glasses. "Mister, I've been working in this business for many years and from my observation, if a man takes his time and puts thought into selecting jewelry for a woman, then he must be really in love or he's in the doghouse."

The woman leaned into the counter. "So which one is your story?" She laughed.

"Let's just say I'm a man who loves his wife," Marvin replied, amused and smiling hard.

"Shoot." She sighed with disappointment. "That's what I thought. A good-looking man like you, a woman would have to be certifiably crazy to put you in a doghouse. Anyway, enough of my bad luck. Let's just get back to business. Which ring were you interested in seeing again?"

"That one." Marvin pointed while still chuckling inside from the woman's audacious flattery. "How much is it?"

"It's $200. But for you, darling, I'll sell it to you for $150."

"Sold," Marvin said.

The woman wrapped up the gift and rung him up. "Now you remember to stop by here the next time you're in the mall. I'd love to see your face again," the woman said, handing over the bag. She grinned wide, showing off the crow's feet around her eyes and the metal clasps from her upper partial. Marvin recoiled inside, thinking about the woman's serious intentions and offered a lighthearted question instead.

"Ma'am, are you trying to get me in trouble with my wife and put me in a doghouse?"

"No," she playfully answered while shrugging her shoulders. "But if you do find yourself in one, I'll bust you out. By the way, the name's Sherry."

Chapter 25

Saturday afternoon came around fast. The sun was blazing hot with no clouds in the sky for shade. Justine and I were on our way to meet her father at a pizzeria in Northgate shopping mall. For the past two days, Justine kept quiet and avoided eye contact with me. Obviously, she was still upset about the whole situation and maybe even angrier with me for concealing her father's identity for so long. Everybody told me to give her space. Give her time. And that's exactly what I did for her sake and mine.

I pulled into a parking space. Justine quickly got out of the car and shut the door. She walked ahead of me. Faster and faster she went without knowing exactly where she was going. "Justine," I shouted, "wait up." But she ignored me and kept on strutting. I understood the child was going through something, but that didn't give her right to disrespect her mother.

"Wait up, dammit! Wait up!" I yelled.

She finally stopped. I grabbed her arm and pulled her in close. "Justine, don't you make me slap your ass off in front of this mall." She still wouldn't look at me. The heat outside only agitated my nerves even more. I breathed in deeply to calm down. "Look, Justine," I said, talking to the side of her face. "You need to change your attitude. I am so sorry I never told you about Lewis before, but we are here now. Life is not fair! Do you think I haven't been hurt or disappointed?"

She turned around and gave me a blank stare. "Yes Mama, I definitely know you've been hurt before."

I ignored Justine's smart-alecky remark and rolled my eyes as I opened the mall's entrance door. "Come on Justine, let's just go."

We walked into the pizzeria and Lewis was there waiting on us. He stood up looking sporty as usual wearing a high-top fad and another windbreaker suit. In his hands, he held a plastic bag and a red and white teddy bear.

"Hello," he said, excitedly. "You must be Justine." He pulled out a chair.

"Hi," she replied, flashing a fake smile and got seated.

"Ah, I'll just go sit somewhere and give you two some privacy," I said.

I headed for the back of the restaurant and sat in a booth. I watched them from afar interacting with each other. It brought a smile to my face. My child finally met her father, and I felt good about that. She no longer had to wonder and question who she was. All of the missing pieces from Justine's young life were now in place.

And as I sat there, I couldn't help but wonder how things would have turned out if Lewis and I had developed a real relationship and gotten married. Would we have a fairytale marriage and lived happily ever after traveling the world, or would we have a marriage filled with trials and tribulations like I've endured with Marvin? I laughed in my head, fantasizing about a love opportunity long gone by. Besides, Marvin gave me Adrian and I wouldn't exchange that gift for anything in the world.

Chapter 26

Lewis sat across the bistro table feeling a little nervous as he watched Justine reach into the small plastic bag. She pulled out a red and yellow swimming cap with the word *Champion* written on it.

"I hope you like it," he said, giving her the warmest smile. "Your mother told me you like to swim."

Justine nodded her head and returned a forced smile. "Thank you, Mr. Taylor, for the gifts. They're nice," she said, giving him brief eye contact.

"You're welcome, Justine. I'm glad you like them." Lewis glanced back at the menu on the wall. "So, are you hungry? Do you want a slice of pizza or something?"

"No thank you, Mr. Taylor. I already ate."

"Right, I'm not that hungry either."

Lewis noticed how somber and uncomfortable Justine appeared. He scanned his brain for something interesting to talk about, anything to lighten the mood and bring some joy to her face.

"I heard you like sports," he said in an upbeat tone. "Do you play basketball?"

"No, not really." She shook her head, still staring at the table. "Track is more my thing. I like to run."

She paused and then finally made real eye connection with Lewis. "I heard you're a basketball player. Is that really true?"

"Yep, that's true," he said. "I've been playing basketball professionally for almost twenty years. Now you know where you get your athleticism from." Lewis smiled again, hoping it would warm Justine up. But it didn't work.

"Are you rich?" she bluntly asked, showing no emotion.

"No." He chuckled and shook his head. "Far from it. But I do alright. Do you have any more straight-to-the-point questions for me? Go on and ask. I'm an open book, you know."

Lewis smiled hard, at first, but then relaxed his grin when Justine looked away.

"No sir, I don't have any more questions." Justine's attention was focused on the teddy bear. Then suddenly, she grabbed it and started stroking its fur. The teddy bear seemed to soothe her uneasiness in Lewis' presence. She completely stopped talking. The air quickly became stale from the unbearable silence.

Lewis began to search for something else to talk about but changed his mind. He knew Justine wasn't up for a conversation. What she needed was time. They both did to process such a big, sudden change in their lives.

"You know, Justine, I bet this is really awkward for you. Believe me; this is kind of hard for me too. I just found out only a few days ago that I have a smart, beautiful daughter who I'm now just meeting for the very first time. So let's just start out slow. No promises or expectations. Just one day at a time…. Deal?"

Lewis reached out his hand. That did it. That broke the ice. Justine finally cracked a small genuine smile. They shook hands.

"Deal," she replied.

Chapter 27

It was after 9:30 PM by the time Marvin returned home Sunday night. He crept around the bedroom probably thinking I was asleep. Quietly, he undressed then took a quick shower. When he emerged from the bathroom, I was sitting up in bed waiting on him and ready to talk. I knew if I didn't say what was on my mind that very moment, I would never sleep through the night.

"Hey, baby, how are you?" he asked, yawning and crawling into bed. His eyes were watery and his body seemed worn-out.

"I'm fine," I replied, watching him adjust his pillow and then turn away from me. "Marvin, I know you're dead tired, but we really need to talk."

"Oh, about what?" he asked.

"Your work schedule."

"My work schedule?"

Marvin gave me a backward glance then exhaled. "Right," he said, nodding his head and sitting up in the bed as though he expected this very same conversation to come up. I turned my head and looked him square in the eyes.

"Listen Marvin, I know you're working hard trying to make extra money for whatever reason, but sometimes I get lonely without you. I mean, it really feels like I only saw you a few times last month."

"Hold on, Toni," Marvin said, getting out of bed. "Let me stop you right there. What do you mean for whatever reason? The reasons should be obvious. Have you forgotten we have bills to pay? You said you wanted to buy a house and get away from renting. And, believe it or not, there are still some things in life I want to accomplish as well. But these things come at a cost."

"Baby, I understand all that," I said. "But you make it seem like we're strapped for cash. For the first time in a long time, we're okay. I just think you should take a little more time out for us and the family, especially with what's been going on with Justine."

"Toni, don't even throw that in my face because we both know Justine is resilient, and she will be just fine." Marvin leaned in front of the dresser and folded his arms over. "But, you know what, Toni. I'm curious. What exactly do you want me to do? When I didn't have a job you complained and now that I do, you're still complaining. Do you want me to quit my job? Is that it? Well, that's not happening."

"Marvin, please don't make me out to be the bad guy because you know I don't want you to quit your job," I said in an exhausted tone. "I just don't understand why you're gone so much. Why does your boss always have to single you out to make weekend deliveries? Doesn't he know you have a family and a life back at home?"

"Look, I don't know why he comes to me with these assignments. And you know what?" He shrugged. "Honestly, I don't care. Because, think about it Toni, it's extra money in my pocket. Actually, it's extra money in our pockets."

"Well, I am so glad to hear you're happy overachieving on your job and pleasing the boss," I scornfully said. "But you've forgotten something. What about me?"

"What do mean...what about you?" he mocked.

"Well, I am still your wife, aren't I? I have needs too." I started to get misty-eyed thinking about the last time he wrapped his arms around me or the last time he gave me a passionate kiss. It was nearly June, dammit, and we hadn't been intimate in over a month. Something was up because Marvin's sex drive was just as strong as mine. I'd had a paranoid thought that'd been nagging me for weeks. *He's cheating on me.*

"Marvin, tell me the truth. Is there someone else? Are you seeing another woman behind my back and that's the real reason why you're spending so much time on the road?"

"Oh, my god, woman," he instantly exclaimed with protruding eyes. "Now I'm sleeping with other women? Where do you get this stuff? I truly believe you're going to be the death of me." Marvin let out a big sigh and rolled his neck around. "Toni, I tell ya, can't nobody in this world keep a secret from you."

"What's that supposed to mean?" I said, looking mystified. Marvin chuckled as he walked over to pick up his duffel bag off the floor. He pulled out a box.

"This is one of the reasons why I've been working so hard." Marvin placed the small black box in my hand. My face lit up. "I wanted to give you this on your birthday next week. But I guess it's best to give it to you now so you can calm your nerves," he said, grinning.

I made a funny face at him before opening the box. I gasped, putting a hand on my chest. It was a white gold diamond-studded band.

"Marvin, I love it!" I cried. "Thank you, babe." I slid the ring on my finger and rocked my hand back and forth to watch the small stones sparkle in the light.

"This is gorgeous. Are you sure we can afford this?"

"Yes, Mrs. Jones. See what extra hours on the road can do? I'm glad you like it," he said, getting back into bed. "Now can I get some sleep?"

Marvin looked over at me and waited for my reply. I nodded then leaned in to plant a big kiss on his cheek. "Are you sure you want to go to sleep?" I asked, giving him a seductive wink.

"Toni, please. Not tonight," he said as he turned around and pulled the blanket up halfway over his face.

"Fine," I groaned, wanting very much to get laid. "You're off the hook tonight. But you owe me good, mister."

Marvin didn't respond. He was already knocked out. I rolled my eyes and sucked my teeth. "It's your loss, buddy," I said out loud. My shiny new ring caught my attention again. I beamed at its sight then got comfortable under the covers. *Marvin doesn't have to give me any,* I thought as I stuck my hand deep into my panties. For the next few minutes, I quietly pleasured myself until I fell asleep.

Chapter 28

In the middle of a steamy June night, I arrived at Stephanie's townhouse to the sight of flashing blue lights. I got a phone call from Thelma telling me Stephanie and *that* boy got into a fight and I should meet her over there ASAP. "Don't call Mama," she urged. "We don't need to scare her this time of night. We can handle this problem ourselves." I agreed with her. It was the last school night before summer break, after all, and I felt the same about waking up my kids and husband over this situation.

As I passed the police cruiser, I saw Tyrese with his head tilted back and eyes closed. Maybe he was thinking twice about what he had done. I walked in the door and saw Stephanie sitting on the steps giving a statement to a police officer and Thelma holding little Jalen, Stephanie's one-year-old son.

"What the hell is going on?" I asked. Stephanie looked away. Her red T-shirt was torn at the collar and the left side of her face had bruises. I walked up to Thelma.

"What happened? Why were they fighting?"

"Girl, I don't know." She sucked her teeth through twisted lips and rolled her eyes. "Something about a bill and Tyrese coming home late."

"Ms. Williams," I heard the officer say behind me, "even if you choose not to press charges, we've seen enough to arrest your boyfriend and put him in jail tonight. That should cool him off." The officer left.

"You didn't press charges?" I asked.

"No." She shook her head.

"Why not, Stephanie?" Thelma butted in.

"Tyrese and I are under a lot of stress," she explained, dabbing her eyes with the ends of her shirt. "He didn't mean to hit me. I just kept pushing him about money and coming in late."

Listening to Stephanie made me remember how I used to say the same thing starting out with Marvin. I didn't want this for my kid sister. I wanted better. If she had only finished college and moved away from Charleston, she wouldn't be dealing with these kinds of problems. The girl had everything to look forward to: a degree, a good paying job, and a better pool of men to choose from. How could Stephanie let go of those opportunities? How could she let herself get sprung over the first man to make her eyes roll back in her head and get knocked up by him?

"He didn't mean to hit you." Thelma scoffed. "If I had a dollar for every time someone in this family said that, I'd be rich."

I couldn't help but give Thelma a nasty glance. I knew her comment was directed mainly at me. But I let it slide. I was too tired to argue and too tired to knock her ass out.

"Look Thelma, I thank you for coming over to help me, but I can't listen to your lecture right now. I have a huge headache," Stephanie said with an attitude.

"Yeah, you have a headache because of that huge knot on your face," Thelma snapped back. Stephanie steamed over and grabbed Jalen.

"You know Thelma, you're not always right," Stephanie said, giving a vicious squint while rocking her child. "When Toni took Marvin back all those years ago, you said it would be the death of her. But look at them now—they're happy. And yes, Toni had some terrible times with her husband, but she hung in there and turned Marvin into a better man. He works every day, and they don't fight anymore. Well, I have the same hopes for Tyrese."

Thelma shook her head and laughed out loud. "Are you kidding me? Is that what you really believe? If that's the case, you're more naïve than I thought. Marvin may be on his best behavior for now. But just remember, sister, a snake will always be a snake. Don't be a fool, girl. No woman can ever change a man stuck in his ways."

Part Three

Chapter 29
Late Fall

On the open road, Marvin felt in control. He had a sense of independence again. And better, he didn't have a boss to look at every day. This was the kind of job he could deal with: nobody to bother him and no clock to punch. Franklin, his old CDL instructor, put in a good word for his best student and helped him get a regional trucking position with a mid-sized food brokerage company, which came along with full benefits.

Pick up and drop off. That's all he was required to do Monday through Friday on dedicated routes between South Carolina and Virginia. Just deliver high-end deli meats to grocery chains and distribution centers. The hours were long, sometimes up to twelve a day, but the pay was good. All other times on the road were spent on I-95 north. He took Friday or Saturday night detours to strip clubs, cheap motels, and on occasion even cheaper pussy. "What Toni doesn't know will never hurt her," he'd come to justify.

When he started out on the job, Marvin had no intentions of cheating on his wife. And although stories of infidelity seemed to circulate CB radios and truck stops like the newspaper, at the time, those things didn't pique his interests. Marvin's mind was on the money. But eventually, he'd learned a truck driver's life meant a lot of loneliness and repetition on the road. For several months, he held out. But like most truckers, he gave in to temptation. Ever since February, the nudie clubs became a way to dull the boredom and provide a distraction from his routine life.

But, despite his deceit, Marvin believed he loved his family and was a changed man. He worked steadily, paid bills, and hadn't hit his wife in years. After getting off the hook for nearly killing Toni, he made a promise for the better. But he still had demons. Marvin still liked the company of a young woman and the taste of liquor. He managed to keep the secrets from Toni for almost a year. If he wanted to, he could be home early some evenings to spend time with his family, but he chose to stay out on the streets, indulging his desires.

Now in his forties, Marvin no longer had ambition for hustling in a young man's game to launch a record label or open a club. Those random thoughts of going back into the barbershop business in another state had even stopped. His contentment in this world came from trucking and all the freedom it afforded. And tonight, Marvin was on a late

Friday night run to see his favorite girl perform at Club Rendezvous, a strip joint in Fayetteville, NC.

He told the wife he'd be late again coming in from Maryland and may have to stay overnight, one of his many cover stories. Tonight his girl would make him feel alive and forget everything: all his failures and disappointments in life. Later tonight, she would dance just for him and treat Marvin like a king.

Chapter 30

Angela seductively walked on stage expecting the usual treatment: a bunch of catcalls and wide eyed, ogling stares from men and even women. She was an exotic dancer and tonight's headliner. "Cameo's Candy," her theme song, was playing loudly in the background as she moved her curvy body precisely to every beat. She sashayed around, winding up her hips and shoulders, letting the audience get a good look at her red sequin bikini against her fair skin before peeling it off. Angela started at the top, rubbing her C-cup sized perky breasts and then ran her fingers straight down into her half-shaven snatch.

Sensually, she teased and mesmerized them with her coordinated twists and turns.

And for the finale, she laid on her back and spread eagle to let lustful spectators see her full pink lips in all of their glory. The crowd went wild. Hands with dangling bills went up everywhere. But Angela had her sight set straight ahead. She crawled to the edge of the stage and whipped her long dark hair back and forth in front of her face.

"Is Big Johnson ready for me?" she asked, brushing away her hair and smiling wickedly at Marvin. "Give me about thirty minutes." She winked. "I've gotta get my money."

Marvin grinned and watched intensely as Angela slithered away and worked the room. The sight of her tight young body in motion always turned him on and made *Big Johnson* throb in his pants. Her ass was like a bubble and her legs were long. She had it all: a stunning face to match the figure. Angela's looks were that damn good. Good enough even to be on the cover of a magazine or the silver screen.

Angela was the reason for those so-called special deliveries to Maryland for the last seven months. They were lies and excuses made to simply catch her shows. Wherever she performed, he'd follow and gladly shed fifty bucks off his paycheck just to stuff it down her G-string and get a couple private dances. He was hooked. Marvin had seen plenty strippers in his time, but Angela was different. She had something special. And ever since he first laid eyes on her, back in March, no other woman would do.

Marvin continued to gaze at Angela in deep thought as she collected her loot and tantalized the audience.

"Candy!" They shouted her stage name and waved to get her attention. Twice she looked back at Marvin. He already knew she enjoyed their alone time just as much as he did and would save the last dance for him. During their last session, Angela came while dry humping his crotch. It was real. He felt her tremble and afterward she revealed her real name...Angela Reese.

Marvin waited patiently for his turn with red roses to give. But now his mind was on much more than just a controlled lap dance. His loins boiled with lust. He wanted sex, and tonight he would make Angela an offer he knew she wouldn't refuse.

Chapter 31

About two hours later in a motel room, Marvin was finally getting what he wanted. A night with fine-ass Angela, one of the sexiest women he'd seen in a long time. It didn't take much convincing. Just a look and a whisper in her ear back at the club, and Angela agreed to leave with him without hesitancy. "I don't normally do this," she'd said, gazing innocently into his eyes. "But there's something about you I find so attractive."

For a while, Angela had been careful not to get personally involved with club patrons. Having only been in the business for about three years, it was a rule to live by. Many times she had heard other dancers complain to club owners and to each other about stalkers and aggressive clients. "Watch your back and keep it business!" others had warned her as she nervously went on stage for the first time. On one occasion, she actually witnessed a man jumping up on stage and throwing a girl over his shoulder. It took two big bouncers to tackle the man down, but not before he got the chance to cop a feel and lick her breast.

And yet Angela felt comfortable with Marvin. Maybe it was his charm and good looks. Maybe it was his respectful demeanor and willingness to follow instructions during a lap dance. Whatever the reason, she trusted him and had no problem breaking her rule tonight.

Angela emerged from the bathroom naked and looking stunning as usual. Marvin was lying on the bed waiting in full attention. She paused and looked at him with enticed eyes. Her nostrils flared, mouth watered, and skin tingled.

"Don't be afraid of Big Johnson," he softly teased while rubbing himself. "This is what you've been wanting, right?"

"Yes," she answered in a whisper, spellbound.

"Well, what are you waiting for? Come over here and get it," he commanded.

And just like that, Angela gave into her lustful urges and moved in quick like a tiger on the pounce. Several times she fantasized about having Marvin deep inside her. And now the fantasy was coming true.

They took turns giving each other oral pleasure, using their tongues and lips to explore the landscapes of their bodies. And after the foreplay ran its course, they tossed and turned like wild animals fucking in different positions. At the end Marvin couldn't believe how hard he came. Neither could Angela. It was everything they both dreamt it to be. Great sex…plain and simple.

"Here's my number," she said, dropping a piece of paper on the nightstand before leaving, "Call me when you're back in town."

Chapter 32

"Hey, Wanda!" I heard a woman call out across the parking lot as I loaded the car with grocery bags.

"Wanda, is that you?" she shouted out again, her voice getting closer behind me. This time I turned around and looked her direction. She was smiling and waving at me with a sense of certainty.

This woman must be mistaken, I thought as she walked up.

She pointed her finger at me and smiled. "You're Wanda Hamilton, right?"

I pulled back a little at first, but then it finally registered. I hadn't heard that name in over six years.

"It's me, Rachel Spencer from My Daughter's House," she said with excitement, as though the introduction alone would instantly make me recognize her, but it didn't. I searched my memory bank thoroughly for the name and face and still couldn't recall either.

"Well, the look on your face says it all. You don't have a clue as to who I am, do you?" she said, placing her hand on my arm. "But I remember you."

I stood there profoundly confused. I wasn't at that shelter very long. How could anyone remember me? *Who was this white woman?*

"You're right, Rachel," I said, feeling awkward. "I have to admit. I don't know who you are. Sorry." I smiled politely and shrugged my shoulders.

"That's fine." She sighed. "It was a long time ago. But I was your roommate. You know, the big girl with glasses and curly hair."

My eyes grew large as flashes of memories started to come back.

"Uh-ha, now you remember," she said, watching my reaction.

No wonder I couldn't place the woman's face. The last time I saw her, the girl looked to be over 300 pounds on a short 5'4 frame. And now she looked totally different. She was slim, attractive, well dressed, and seemed happy...very happy.

Rachel continued to reminisce. "I remember the night I arrived at that shelter. I was a very frightened, sad little girl who cried nonstop. But that's when you came over and held me and sang to me all night long until I fell asleep. Wanda,

I've never forgotten that or your beautiful voice. Don't you know every time I hear the song 'His Eye is on the Sparrow,' I think of you?"

I gripped Rachel's hand with gratitude and in full memory of that night. She was just a sheltered twenty-two-year-old kid struggling with self-esteem issues and an alcoholic older man for a husband. Her country backward-thinking, moonshine-drinking father pushed her into marriage too soon because of her size. "No other man is going to marry you. You best get 'em while he asking," he'd told her.

Now look at Rachel. The passing years had definitely been good to her.

"Oh, stop all this talk about me girl, look at you," I said. "You've lost so much weight. Your hair is straight and you're no longer wearing glasses. Chile, you look amazing!"

"Thank you, honey," she said, her head raised up a little and hands clutching her slender waist. "After I told that rat bastard husband of mine to get lost, I told my fat to do the same thing." She laughed out loud. "I've lost over 150 pounds, Wanda, and have kept it off for almost three and half years."

Her revelation instantly made my jaw drop wide enough to drive a truck right through my gaping mouth. "Well, don't hold back on your secret. How did you do it?"

"There's no secret. Just a little bit of everything really," she answered, then started counting on her fingers. "Let's see: jogging, running, swimming, eating right, and a lot of psychological sessions with my therapist."

"I'm speechless, Rachel. I don't know what else to say."

"Wanda, you don't have to say a thing. You've already done enough for me."

I wrinkled my brows. Her comment had me curious. "Really, how's that, Rachel?"

Rachel touched my arm again and gave me a serious look.

"You know, I wanted to thank you the morning after our talk, but you were still sleeping. And when I returned from counseling and my walk, you were already gone. I've always said if I ever saw you again, I would tell you what your encouragement meant to me. You told me I had to believe in myself and go after what I wanted because I had no children or anything holding me back. You said Ricky couldn't find another woman nice enough to marry him. He was the lucky one to have me, not the other way around."

I nodded my head, feeling humbled by her appreciation.

"I tell you Wanda, back then, my mind had been programmed to believe I was less than nothing. I didn't have one positive person in my life to talk to. But you, a perfect stranger, were so kind to me when no one else was—and that includes my damn self."

She smiled and squeezed my hand.

"Well, I took your advice and finished college. Now I work as a registered nurse over at St. Francis hospital. And guess what else? I'm also a volunteer counselor at a woman's shelter."

"Good for you," I said, giving her the warmest hug. "I'm glad you came out on top."

"And how about you, Wanda, did you ever get rid of your husband?" she asked wide-eyed and grinned expectantly.

"No not exactly, Rachel. My husband and I worked it out. We got counseling and now he's not the man he used to be. We're blessed."

I deliberately skipped the gory details of all the battles I had to go through to get to this point. There was no need to open old wounds. *But why did I lie about getting counseling or feel the need to justify or sugarcoat my decision to a woman I haven't seen in years?*

"Okay," Rachel said, her enthusiastic grin long faded away. "I'm glad to hear things worked out well for the both of you."

Rachel's vanishing lively energy was obvious. As I stood there and analyzed her body language, more questions and thoughts started to pop up in my mind: *Why did she stop smiling—was it because she felt embarrassed for assuming I got divorced? Did she not believe me when I said things were going very well with Marvin and me? Was she disappointed that I didn't leave my husband? I shouldn't even care what she thinks.*

"You know this is no coincidence us meeting up like this," she said, pulling out a business card from her wallet and writing a number on the back. "This is nothing but the good *Lord* at work." Rachel placed the card in my hand. "That's my home number on the back. Wanda, it was good seeing you again. Let's keep in touch."

She walked off and then turned around.

"I almost forgot…have a Happy Thanksgiving."

"Yeah, same to you."

I put the card in my purse knowing full well I wasn't going to call or pursue a relationship with her. I was truly happy for Rachel's accomplishments, but seeing her again only brought back painful memories I wanted to forget. The past needed to stay in the past. I didn't even bother telling her my real name.

Chapter 33

1990 came around with the country on the edge of war with Iraq and our economy slipping into a bad recession. But, the Williams family chose to keep a positive outlook for the New Year and new decade ahead. Mama kicked off New Year's Day celebrations right with upbeat music playing in the background and a massive spread on her dining room table: fried chicken and fish, red rice, okra soup, cornbread, assorted deserts…the works. It also featured her delicious collard greens and Hopping John—that would be field peas and rice cooked together. These were traditional Gullah side dishes eaten to bring in the New Year. The greens were for money and the Hopping John was for good luck. Every house in the low country would be serving up this combination during this time.

The family and some friends were standing around the table stacking food on their plates and then moving on to find places to sit nearby. This year, Justine agreed to spend the holidays with her father to meet new family members in Atlanta, Georgia. After Lewis got the paternity test results, he wasted no time introducing his new daughter to everyone. This would be their second road trip.

Marvin stayed home, avoiding my family as usual. But it was for the best; some wounds will never heal. "Bring me back a plate," he'd shouted half naked from the couch as Adrian and I walked out the front door. He had been working extra hours and was exhausted. He claimed the boss put him on Saturday runs twice a month indefinitely. Marvin kept saying the money was worth it, but I was seeing less of him and getting less loving in the bedroom. If I hadn't seen some money in the checking account or the oversized television in the living room, I'd think he was cheating on me.

"Toni, girl. I hear your daughter is off traveling with her rich father for the holidays," Charles jokingly shouted across the room.

"Boy, please," I said while smacking on banana pudding. "Lewis may have a little money, but he doesn't have it like that. Matter of fact, he told me he was looking for a coaching job."

"He's looking for a job. Sounds like you better get down to the courthouse fast and get those child support checks going before he runs out of money and splits," Charles said.

I chuckled at Charles' teasing and waved him off. "I'm not worried about that. As long as he keeps giving Justine her monthly change, I'm fine. And to answer your question about Miss Justine, she wanted to go. She was actually excited to go on a trip with her father."

"A man who wants to work and likes to go on trips? It sounds like this Lewis was the one that got away. Why didn't you try to become Mrs. Lewis, Toni?" Ms. Gertie asked.

We all laughed hysterically at Ms. Gertie's comment. She was serious about her question, but had no idea that her delivery of the question came across funny. She did this often. Her dry, shoot-from-the-hip talk always put us in stitches.

"Oh, no honey, Toni's not interested in becoming Mrs. Lewis Taylor," Thelma jumped in while we were still laughing. "She's going to do whatever it takes to hang on to that Mrs. Jones title even if it kills her." Thelma started laughing but everybody else stopped and stared at me.

"Who's Justine? Do I know this Justine?" Daddy hollered out of the blue while looking around confused. His mind was on a delay again. He now had full-blown Alzheimer's disease and basically struggled with everything: memories, conversation, and daily life.

"Charles, that's your grandchild," Mama said, snickering. "You know, one of Toni's children."

Everyone started affectionately chuckling again along with Mama, but I didn't. I kept my gaze right on Thelma. She really ticked me off with her comment. She wasn't trying to be light-hearted or humorous. No, that wasn't it. As usual, she was attempting to put me down and embarrass me in front of family and friends. I was tired of it and continued my wicked witch stare right before I gave her a good-ass reading.

"Thelma, you can go straight to hell," I said, making the room silent yet again.

"What did you say?" she replied with a sneering smirk.

"Oh, you heard what I said. All you do is criticize me. So what, I'm trying to stay married. Just because you walked out on your husband and children doesn't mean I'm ready to live your life of misery and loneliness. So tell me something, sister, since you're so quick to put a spotlight on my love life. Where is your man? Who are you sleeping with tonight? Maybe if you weren't so damn hateful, you could find somebody to love you."

Thelma shot up and pointed her finger at me. I hurt her. I could tell by her wet eyes and the sound of her whispery voice when she said, "You're right, Toni. I don't have a man. But at least when I go to bed, I go in peace. I don't have to worry about being terrorized in the middle of the night. Because never again will I ever allow myself to be some man's punching bag for the sake of having a man. And I will never allow a man to make me feel fear in my own house again."

Thelma rolled her slanted eyes and walked out of the room. I didn't care if I upset her; she deserved it. If you can dish it then you can take it. Besides, what I said was true. We all knew Thelma hadn't been in a relationship in years. And I strongly felt that was her main reason for taking her frustrations and unhappiness out on me.

Thelma chose to be alone. She could get a man. That wasn't the problem. Thelma was attractive, slim and had a professional look. Some even say she favored singer Anita Baker. But sometimes she could be a little too damn condescending and headstrong and no man wants that. If she were getting some loving, Thelma wouldn't be so bitterly grouchy and preoccupied with my household. After I happily poured salt on her open wound, my big sister didn't have another thing to say to me for the rest of the night.

Chapter 34

Justine enjoyed traveling and looking out at the changing scenery from the window of her father's 1987 black Mercedes Benz as they drove down the highway returning home from the holidays. The week had been filled with discovery for Justine. She visited a new state and got acquainted with new family members who resembled her and were over the moon to finally meet Lewis' baby girl. She also discovered how much she enjoyed spending time with her dad.

They had many things in common. With him, she felt at peace, safe and began to understand aspects of her own personality. It all made sense. Lewis was funny, mentally disciplined, and driven. He encouraged the need to set goals and save money to become financially self-sufficient, and those lessons appealed to Justine. She liked nice things and admired her father's comfortable, stable lifestyle. After all, she planned to live the same way.

Lewis caught a glimpse of Justine checking out her gold heart-shaped watch he gave her for Christmas. "Do you like it?" he asked.

"Yes, I love it! I've never had anything like this before," she said excitedly then smiled. "It matches the necklace you gave me for my thirteenth birthday."

"Well, I'm glad you like it, sweetheart, because you deserve the best...and always remember that." Lewis took delight in his daughter's happiness and wished he'd met her sooner. He appreciated their times together and thought Justine was an impressive, smart young lady with a good head on her shoulders. He could sense she had a destiny and would go far in life.

Lewis took another glance at Justine. She was already thirteen and would only be a little girl for a few more years. He regretted missing out on her childhood and felt unfairly deprived of her first steps, first day at school, and all those things that makes fatherhood worthwhile.

His parents told him he couldn't bring back the past, but there was still time to set things right for the present and future. "Justine is family and she must know that!" They came to an agreement. Lewis knew his relationship with Justine was just budding and nowhere near full bloom. But he wanted to take it to the next level and make it official and legal. *But how would she feel?* he thought and almost hesitated to ask.

"So Justine, can I talk to you about something very important?" he said cautiously.

"Okay, sure," she answered, giving him an intrigued look.

"I know we've only known each other for a short time, but you are my daughter and I love you very much. And I have to tell you the family flat out adores and loves you as well. So, how would you like to be a Taylor?"

"What do you mean?" she asked.

"I mean, I would like to change your last name to Taylor and make you my daughter, legally. I've already spoken to your mom, and she said it was up to you."

Justine was caught off guard with the question and felt clueless on how to respond. She had been Justine Williams all her life. That was her identity. That's how her friends and teachers knew her. What would they say? But then she thought about it. *Lewis is my father, not Marvin!* she declared in her head.

"Are you okay, Justine? Do you need more time to think it over? Honey, there's no rush," Lewis said, sounding deeply concerned and wondering if he'd made the proposition way too soon. He rapidly switched his attention between the road and his daughter while waiting for her response. "Justine, did you hear me? You can take as long as you want to decide."

"No, sir, I don't need any more time," she replied, showing off a confident smile. "I'm cool with it. Actually, I think Justine L. Taylor will have a nice ring to it. "

Chapter 35

Marvin kept an eagle eye on Pink Stiletto's front door from his rear view mirror. The strip club had just shut down and he was expecting Angela to walk out the building at any minute. It was a cold January night in Petersburg, Virginia, but Marvin didn't care. He hadn't seen or heard from his girl in almost four weeks and getting another chance to be with her was definitely worth the drive and braving the bone-chilling winter air.

Angela went away for the holidays. She said she desperately needed a break from her stripper's life and wanted to spend some time with family and old friends. "I don't know how long I'll be gone," she'd told him over the phone. "But, I'll make up something and leave a message on your job to let you know I'm back in town."

Time passed on and Marvin never got that call. As a matter of fact, when he dialed her telephone number, a recording said the line had been disconnected. But, on New Year's Day, he thought long and hard and remembered

Angela mentioning being booked as a feature act at this new gentlemen's club the first weekend in January.

The door opened wide and laughing women dispersed quickly toward their cars. Marvin got out of his truck in full winter gear holding a bag in his right hand and stood next to Angela's 1983 orange with black interior Ford Mustang GLX convertible.

"Angela," he called out, waving and smiling. She stopped her fast-paced stride and looked straight ahead in the distance with a squint.

"Do you know that man, Angela?" the extra-large bouncer shouted from the door.

Angela turned back. "Yeah, I know him. He's a friend of mine. I'm good, Jo-Jo. Thanks." She continued walking toward Marvin looking like a sexy ski-bunny wearing a pale pink jumper with a white fur hat and fur boots to match. A surprised yet curious expression etched itself on her face when she came close into view.

"I thought I saw you in the club tonight. What are you doing here, Marvin?"

He gave her an intense stare along with a crooked smile. "I know you said you would call, but I couldn't wait anymore. I had to see you," he said with certain coolness.

"Yeah, I'm sorry about that, Marvin. I meant to call you, but I've been so busy lately."

He nodded his head. "Why is your phone disconnected? Is everything alright?"

The question made Angela slightly uncomfortable. She looked off for a few seconds. "Everything is fine, Marvin," she finally answered. "I just moved out my apartment. I'm staying with a girlfriend right now to save money and figure out some things."

Her eyes drifted toward the bag. She smiled warmly. "Is that for me?"

"It sure is," Marvin said, handing over the bag.

Angela reached in and took out a card and a box of her favorite candy, assorted chocolate covered almonds.

"Aww! Thank you." She leaned in for a quick peck on the lips then gave a hug. "Marvin, you can be so sweet at times," she said, squeezing him tighter while sharing his body heat. "But you know those chocolates are only going to make me fat and lose my shape."

"Not a chance in hell." Marvin laughed and sneered at the possibility. "Well, go on, open up the card."

"Okay," Angela replied with a suspicious smirk. She tore through the envelope and then suddenly her face and voice went flat.

"Marvin, what is this?" she asked, pulling back. "There are two hundred-dollar bills in here. You know how I feel about you giving me large amounts of money outside of the club. I don't spend time with you for this." She raised the cash in his face. "I'm not a prostitute."

"Angela, sweetheart, you're taking this the wrong way," he said with light laughter. "I know you're not a prostitute. When I found out your phone was disconnected, I thought you may need some help. I'm giving you this out of friendship and admiration, that's all. If it makes you feel better, just think of it as a late Christmas gift." Marvin pulled her in close again and then started rubbing her back. "C'mon, sweetness, don't be mad."

Angela looked up into Marvin's eyes and nodded.

"That's my girl," he said, still caressing her back and arms. "Now that's all settled, may I please have a real kiss before I explode?"

Angela chuckled and flashed a naughty look. "Are you sure that's all you want?"

Chapter 36

Angela pumped hard and fast to bring them to a strong, satisfying finish. She fell off in exhaustion with sweat glistening all over her body.

"This will never get old," Marvin said, catching his breath.

"Well, nothing lasts forever." She snickered.

Marvin rolled over to spoon. "Don't say that," he whispered, gently kissing her neck and right shoulder. He snaked his hand underneath her arm and over her breast. The angel charm on her long necklace grazed the tips of his fingers. "Tell me about this necklace. You wear it all the time, even when you perform."

Angela turned around to face Marvin. "My mother gave it to me on my tenth birthday." She smiled. "She told me I was her little angel. That's why I never take it off." Suddenly, a look of sadness washed over her face.

"Hey, what's wrong?" Marvin asked.

"You know, my mother doesn't even know I strip for a living." Angela sighed and sat up in the bed. "I sat right across from her at Christmas dinner and lied to her face. She still believes me when I tell her I'm working a regular job, saving up money to finish college. But you know how it goes. It's easy to get caught up in this business. The money's that good."

Angela rested her hand on her forehead, thinking about the shame her lifestyle would bring to her church-going family. She started shaking her head. "Marvin, if my mother knew what I was doing, it would break her heart."

"Well, she doesn't have to find out, baby. Surely by now you've saved up some money and have it stashed away somewhere. You can just go back to school, pick up where you left off, and put all this stripping behind you. There are plenty of colleges nearby."

"Colleges nearby…. No, thank you." Angela scoffed. "Those same students, professors, and jocks are my clients. People I see all the time. What I need is a fresh start."

"A fresh start? What's that supposed to mean?" Marvin asked.

"It means I'm leaving. I'm moving to California to follow my dreams. You know, I did the college thing and it wasn't for me. I want to get into acting. That's what I want to do with my life."

Marvin sat up and gave Angela a worrisome gaze. "Great, be an actress. But why does that mean you have to leave? I heard there are movies being made in North Carolina all the time."

"It's not the same, Marvin." Angela walked over to her purse and fished out a cigarette. She lit up and exhaled. "I just need to start over. Don't you understand? I'm twenty-three years old. If I don't try now, then I never will."

"Darling, I know about chasing a dream. But aren't you making this decision too fast? California is a big, faraway place."

"No!" She shook her head. "That's the problem; I've been thinking about this for too long and not doing anything about it. I've got to take a chance. So my New Year's resolution is this: be out of this state by January 26."

Marvin walked over and pulled her in close. "Well, what about me? What about us?"

Angela shot him a puzzled look. "Marvin, what are you talking about?" She furrowed her brows with a chuckle. "There is no us. You're married with kids, remember?"

"Do you want me to leave them? Is that it? No problem." He shrugged. "I can leave them. I can move out to California with you and manage your career."

"Marvin, are you listening to yourself?" she said, giving him a serious look.

"Shh," he said, placing his fingers over her lips. "I know exactly what I'm saying, Angela. I'm falling in love with you. These past months have been the happiest I've had in years. We'd be good together. Don't tell me you haven't thought about it?"

Angela stepped back and mashed her cigarette into an ashtray. "Look, Marvin, I thought we were just having fun. You know nothing serious…just friends. I mean, I like you a lot. But I'm sorry; I'm not in love with you. I think we should end this right now." Angela pulled up her panties in a hurry and then scooped up her bra.

"Angela wait, don't do this. Please, just listen to me…just hear me out," he pleaded.

"Marvin, there's nothing to discuss," she said, fastening her bra. "You want much more from me than I can give you. My mind is already made up; I'm moving on."

Marvin reached for her arm. "So, you're gonna leave just like that? Just walk out? Who is he, Angela?" he asked through narrowed eyes.

"What!" Angela exclaimed.

"You heard me. This has nothing to do about you becoming an actress. You're fucking another man, aren't you? Does he have more money than me, is that what it is?"

"You know what, fuck you!" she snapped. "I'm not even going to answer that because we are over. Now let go of me." She jerked away.

Marvin walked over to his jeans and pulled out his wallet. "Is this what you want?!" he shouted as he threw a fistful of money at her.

"You bastard," she said, shaking her head and curling her lips. "I don't ever want to see you again."

Marvin stood there and processed Angela's words. He felt his frustrations mounting up. *No one leaves me* looped over and over in his head. And just like that, he lost it. He grabbed her arm again and squeezed it tightly.

"Let go of me, you crazy bastard!" she cried out.

Marvin slapped her hard and pushed her onto the bed. He began choking her. "*I* tell you when you get to leave. *I* do." The rage in him seemed to overpower his senses as if he were possessed. "If I can't be with you, nobody will."

Angela dug her nails deep into Marvin's wrist, trying desperately to break his strong hold, but it was useless. He continued to squeeze tighter and tighter until the lights faded away from her greenish-brown eyes. Angela was dead.

Marvin jumped back against the headboard and took several frantic breaths as though he just awoke from a hellish nightmare. His pulse raced, his pupils dilated, and sweat drizzled down his face and body. Everything went silent except for the sound of his heartbeat. He was in a state of shock. Marvin had never killed before. It was an accident, he told himself. He didn't mean to do it. He loved Angela. *Why couldn't she just listen?*

Marvin took a few minutes to calm down then leaned over to softly stroke the side of Angela's face. She was beautiful even in death. Reality started to sink in and made the next move clear. *I've got to get rid of the body.*

Chapter 37

Marvin waited until the dead of night to move Angela's body from the motel room. The time of night when people were long passed out from drugging, drinking, or screwing. He took precautions. He turned off all lights and even unscrewed the light bulb outside next to the front door before hoisting Angela over his shoulder. It felt like she weighed a ton, the heaviest he had ever remembered from all of their sex games and horseplaying. It seemed like it was taking an eternity to reach the back of his truck.

Marvin raised the door slowly, quietly, while his dead girlfriend lay in the shadows. Then he took another look around for prying eyes before hauling the body into the truck and rolling it up in plastic among the large crates filled with frozen meat. *So far, so good,* he thought, walking toward the rental office.

A cloud of cigarette smoke hit Marvin's face the moment he opened the door. A black forty-something night clerk flashed a flirty grin as Marvin began to check out. Her nicotine-stained teeth were magnified by the red lipstick she wore, which was outlined with black eyeliner. Marvin dropped the keys on the counter. Slowly, the woman scanned him up and down with a sexual overtone as she slid the rental keys her way. No doubt he was the best looking thing she'd seen come through the office in a long time, never mind the wedding band on his finger. But little did she know the handsome man had just committed murder and the body was only a few feet away all rolled up in the back of his trailer truck.

"I hope you don't be a stranger, sexy," the woman boldly said as she handed over the receipt. Marvin downplayed her advances: too old and too unattractive for his taste. He just nodded his head and gave her a polite smile as though he didn't hear a word she said. Besides, Marvin had a plan to think about. He convinced himself it would work.

Almost four hours of driving went by before Marvin found the right spot. It seemed secluded enough out there in the forest near a marsh where nobody ever visited except for wildlife. Dawn was fast approaching. He quickly unraveled the plastic and removed Angela's necklace and placed it in his pocket. He took a final look at Angela and swiped her fixated eyes shut. He began to stuff dry shrubs underneath her limbs and then doused her with gasoline.

He lit a match. The body went up in flames fast with the intensity to reduce an exotic beauty to a charred corpse in a matter of minutes. Marvin watched, barely blinking an eye, and became hypnotized as the fire burned through skin and hair. The more he stared, the darker his thoughts got: *Daddy was right, they never listen. They never stay. This was all Angela's fault. She was just like mother....*

Chapter 38
Jacksonboro, SC 1960

The sounds of laughter and a car door slamming made ten-year-old Marvin jump out of his sleep and run to his bedroom window. It was his mother coming home late again from a jook joint and getting out of a 1950s Coupe Deville. There was a man on the driver's side and two other giggling women in the back seat. "Sit tight. This won't take long," he heard his mother turn and say before going into the house.

Marvin nervously ran to the top of the stairs where his older sister was already sitting. They both knew their father had been cursing, chain smoking, and drinking all night long and waiting up to put a beating on their mother. It was after midnight, and he'd already warned his wayward wife about coming home late and, like a kettle on a hot stove, he simmered sitting on the couch ready to let his wife have it the moment she walked through the door.

"Lucille, do you know what time it is? What kind of married woman with children comes home this time of night?" he yelled in her face.

"The kind of woman who should of never married your ass in the first place," she hollered back. "Now step aside, Harold."

Harold didn't move. Lucille rolled her eyes and then bypassed her husband and headed straight for the bedroom closet where she started rummaging.

Lucille was a fearless big-boned woman with a temperament to match. A trait some say she inherited from her overly strict father. She ran away from home at the age of fifteen in search of freedom, showbiz, and a man who would accept her for who she was and would love her all of her days. Harold was that man. At least that's what she thought in the beginning.

He promised her the world. They would travel to towns, cities, and even state-to-state to promote her singing talent. But after they got married and quickly had their first child, Harold wanted a traditional wife. A good wife. The kind that cooked, cleaned, stayed home, and waited on him hand and foot.

Well, Lucille refused to live a life of maid service and a few years after Marvin was born, she wanted some of her life back and began to rebel. Lucille started up with the night scene again and didn't give a hoot about what Harold thought. Because even at the age of twenty-nine, she still felt the pull of her youth and liked to drink, party, and sing at the clubs, knowing fully well her independent thinking would cause violent brawls between her and her husband. But, she wasn't afraid of a fight; everybody knew Lucille Jones didn't take shit from no one and could handle her own. Lucille returned from the bedroom with two suitcases and a smile on her face knowing she really was going to do it this time.

"Where in the hell are you supposed to be going?" Harold asked.

Lucille dropped the suitcases and put her finger in his face. "You threatened me for the last time tonight, Harold. You said if I went out to the club, you'd change the locks on me. Well, do what you must, honey, because you can't change me, and I won't be controlled. I am nobody's dog to be trained."

"So you're gonna leave me and your children? Just like that, huh?"

"I'll send for them later," she said, bending over to pick up her luggage.

Harold became furious and hurled a heavy backslap across Lucille's face. She touched her cheek then snickered. And with her strong hand, she gripped Harold's jaw and pulled him in close, making sure he heard every word. "Nigga, that's the very last time you will ever hit me. Now, get your drunk-ass out my way!" she said, shoving Harold hard and making him tumble to the ground. She glared down at him for a second then scooped up her luggage.

Harold knew his wife meant business this time and hollered after her. "Wait a damn minute, Lucille!" Harold shouted, trying to get his balance while he watched his wife walk out the front door and out of his life. "Just listen to me. You can't leave me like this. Who's gonna tend to those chaps?"

Lucille ignored her husband, causing him to become even more infuriated.

"Fine, heifer, go ahead and leave me. But you ain't never gonna find a man who's willing to put up with yo' shit. You'll be back. I'll give it a month. You hear me…you no good, Jezebel. One month!" she heard in the background.

Marvin ran behind his mother. He heard everything from the stairs and agreed she was a horrible mother for staying out late and partying all the time. She was too different, not like the other mothers he knew.

"Mama!" he cried out, standing in the front yard in his blue and white pajamas. She stopped and turned around. Marvin looked at the women in the car, and the man in the front seat.

"I hate you! This is your fault," he said with tears dripping down his cheeks. "I don't care if you leave. And I don't want to live with you."

Lucille put her belongings in the car and got in. "Well, maybe you should stay here with your father."

Marvin watched the car pull off and barrel down the country dirt road in the dark. The hurt and abandonment he felt was overwhelming. His deep emotional wound made him keep his vow. Marvin never spoke to or saw his mother again.

Chapter 39

Marvin snapped out of his trance and shook off the memory of his mother. He noticed the fire getting low and poured one more round of gasoline on Angela's crackling body to make sure her identity would be lost forever. He tossed her purse, clothes, and tennis shoes in last and then walked off, not giving another thought about the so-called love of his life.

The sun shone bright in the morning sky. About a few hours later, somewhere in South Carolina, he ended up at a truck stop to shower and wash off his sins and the strong stench of gasoline. He let the water get hot—almost punishing hot—and scrubbed until his skin pruned.

As he walked out of the shower station, a chocolate pound cake in a glass case caught his attention in a connecting restaurant. He ordered a slice at the counter, sat down, and thought about the day's events. *Have I forgotten anything?* he asked himself. Then he remembered and put his hand into his pocket and pulled out Angela's necklace. It was foolish to keep it. He knew that, but couldn't bear the thought of not having something to remind him of her. She deserved to be remembered. That was the least he could do.

Marvin turned his head and made brief eye contact with a fellow truck driver sitting at the same counter on his far right side. They acknowledged each other with a nod and then went back to minding their own business. He was certain the man had been in the trucking field for a long time. The graying heavily bearded man had the same subdued, deep-thought look about him Marvin had seen on the faces of other old-timers before. He took another glance at the man's overgrown mask of fur and wondered what lurked beneath. He wondered what kind of secrets the hairy man carried from his years on the road...*because all truck drivers have secrets.*

The cake went down smoothly into his stomach. There were no sudden feelings of anxiety, paranoia, or fear. He felt safe. Marvin ordered another slice of cake to go. And then he headed home feeling confident he had just gotten away with murder.

Chapter 40

There was something definitely different about Marvin, but I just couldn't put my finger on it. On an early morning like this, I'd normally be getting ready for work and not cooking breakfast for the entire family. But Marvin was home again, surprisingly, for the third Saturday in a row. He's even been coming home a little earlier during the weekdays, making it possible to catch dinner with us.

I noticed a change in him. His body was present in the house, but his mind seemed to be somewhere else in deep thought. That was especially evident last night when we made love. Marvin felt cold and disconnected, like having sex with me was a chore for my sake instead of mutual enjoyment. Immediately after we finished, I asked him about the sudden change in his personality and work schedule. He gave me a short answer: "I'm just tired and work is good."

"So, no run to Maryland this weekend?" I asked as I set breakfast on the table.

"Nope." He shook his head and smiled. "I'll be here the whole weekend."

"It seems like your hours are being cut back. Are you sure everything is alright on the job? I don't know if I should be worried or relieved."

"There you go, Toni, overanalyzing again," he said, shaking his head. "Everything's fine. No need to worry. They're just spreading out the work. That's all. You'll be seeing a lot more of me. Isn't that what you wanted all along anyway, to have me home more?" Marvin looked up at me with a big-eyed grin.

"Yeah!" Adrian cheered. "Now, we can play football together."

"Sure. Why not, son? We can definitely start doing that."

Justine abruptly got up with her plate still full of food.

"Are you going to eat that?" I asked.

"No ma'am. I just suddenly lost my appetite," she replied. I picked up on Justine's body language and knew she had a little attitude this morning. For what reason was anybody's guess. I could never tell with her mood swings.

"Right," I said, sarcastically. "Well, we don't throw away food around here. So, go wrap that up and let those eggs and grits be your breakfast for tomorrow."

I turned to Marvin stunned.

"Who does she think she is? Eggs don't come free."

"A teenager," Marvin answered with a chuckle. "Look, don't let that get on your nerves. Besides, you two are somewhat alike anyway. You're both stubborn."

"Yeah, but I'm grown and her mother. That's the difference."

Marvin smiled as he jokingly waved me away. "Hey, forget about that. I want to ask you something. How would you like to take a little trip with me tomorrow?"

"Ooh, can I go?" Adrian shouted.

"No, son," Marvin said regretfully. "I need you to stay here with your sister. This is just for me and your mom. We can go somewhere another time, just me and you. Okay, bud?"

"Okay." Adrian pouted.

I threw Marvin a fast, curious look. "What are you up to, mister?"

"Just wear something warm." He winked.

On a chilly Sunday afternoon in February, Marvin took me on a short scenic ride to the coastal city of Beaufort, South Carolina in his truck. A treat for me, because I've never traveled in commercial tractor-trailer before, and I hadn't visited the area in years. The drive was romantic and relaxing with natural landscaping, marsh views and beautiful evergreen trees lining the main roads. Beaufort has always been one of the lowcounty's best-kept secrets.

After a fantastic seafood dinner, we ended up at a drive-in movie theater off Highway 51.

"Marvin, this was really a wonderful idea. I feel just like a teenager again on a date, but honey, I'm cold. Aren't you cold?"

"No, Toni, I'm fine." He sighed. "I told you to dress warm and all you brought is a thin jacket. Look behind your seat and put on my work coat. Do you see it?"

I nodded. "Yeah, I've got it." Marvin's coat was heavy and smelled like a mixture of cologne and sweat. But it was cozy.

"Are you warm enough?" he asked.

"I'm better, but my hands are still cold."

"Well, put your hands in the pockets."

I slid them inside and my right hand hit something. I pulled it out. It was a note with a number on it. It read: *Call Me. Angela.*

"Who's Angela?" I sharply asked.

Marvin grabbed the piece of paper, looking seemingly lost. He nodded his head then chuckled. "Oh, now I remember. This is old, Toni," he said, twisting his lips. She's a customer service manager at one of our warehouses in North Carolina. I had a problem with a missing pallet one time and she helped me locate it. It turned out someone in shipping made a huge mistake. The woman told me to call her direct line if it ever happened again. I guess I just forgot to take her number out my coat pocket." Marvin rolled down the window and tossed the balled up piece of paper into a nearby bush.

I kept staring at Marvin to let him know I still wasn't totally convinced. His story sounded reasonable, but he could have been lying straight through his teeth. Only God knew if he had any women out there on the road.

"Are you still cold?" he quickly asked. "Give me your hands."

Marvin nudged me over and blew his warm breath into my palms. Then he looked up at me and started kissing them. His eyes were frisky, causing me to melt my cold exterior in a split second. I smiled sweetly and then started to let go of all of my suspicions. I knew what was on his mind; I could hear his thoughts.

"Have you ever wanted to have sex in a truck?" he asked, sucking my fingers one by one.

"Never thought about it," I replied, breathing heavier and getting moist. "But there are people out there, Marvin." I said as I turned around and took a glance at the small number of cars parked in the twilight through the dirty window.

"Don't worry about them. They can't see us. Trust me," he assured as he guided my hand down his pants. From between his thighs I looked up and matched his sensual gaze.

His face was relaxed and body rousing with pleasure as I massaged his ample package.

"Are you warm yet?" he asked with his eyes slowly drifting closed.

"Yeah," I gigged, feeling heat everywhere.

My sexual appetite finally came to a peak when I saw Marvin's head throw back and mouth prop open. He let out a low raspy sound. Those tones and facial expressions triggered my saliva flow. I craved him and pulled out his firm cock and then fed on it right before mounting and riding it into the night, moaning loudly and not giving a damn about who saw or heard me.

Chapter 41

"Toni!" Paul shouted as I walked past his office. I stepped back and stuck my head in the door. He had a cheerful look on his brown middle-aged face as he sat behind his neatly arranged desk.

"Yes, sir," I promptly replied.

"Come on in." He waved his hand. "I've got an opportunity that just opened up, and I think you may be interested in hearing about it."

My ears perked up in curiosity as I hurried in and took a seat. He had my full attention.

"Okay, I'm listening."

"Well, I've got some interesting news. Larry unexpectedly resigned yesterday," he said.

"What!" I blurted out in shock.

Larry had been a successful air personality in Charleston for fifteen solid years. I used to listen to him spin records over the radio before heading to the discotechs on Friday nights. He used to get me pumped. And when I heard we would be working for the same radio station, I was excited. Larry's ratings were high and he seemed happy. I wondered why he left.

"Where did this come from all of a sudden?" I asked.

"I know," Paul said, shrugging his shoulders. "It was a surprise to me too. But there's nothing I can do to keep him here. He's already accepted a position with a large radio station in Philadelphia. There's no way we can match his new pay grade."

"Philadelphia," I said impressed and fully understanding Larry's resignation. There was also a time I too wanted to work and live in a big city. A bigger city meant a larger market, and a larger market always meant more money.

"Sounds like a nice opportunity. I wish him luck."

"Yeah, I do too. But the band must play on, as they say...and that brings me to you." He pointed his finger and grinned. "Toni, I think it's your time. How would you like to take over Larry's time slot and produce your very own morning show, five days a week?"

I gasped and gave Paul a protruding stare. "Really, five days a week?" I couldn't believe my ears. Finally, I had a platform on which to build my dreams.

"And of course, there's a pay raise with this position," Paul smiled. "Now, the company can't offer you a fancy big city salary, but I think it's an upgrade for you."

"Oh, I know that. But how much of a raise are you talking?" I asked with raised brows.

"Your new base salary will be $16,450 a year plus a higher percentage on every voice-over you produce from radio advertisements."

A big smile grew on my face. I was being offered seven thousand dollars more for a job that only required twenty hours a week on the air. It seemed like 1990 was looking to be my year to shine.

"Are you okay with that amount?" Paul asked.

"Are you kidding me?" I replied without hesitation. "I'll take it. When do I start?"

"Soon," Paul snickered. "Very soon."

"Thanks, Paul. I don't know what else to say."

After the meeting, I raced to the phone and told Mama the good news.

"Honey, your ship is finally coming in," she said.

The phone rang four times before Marvin woke up and answered it. I informed him about my promotion and pay raise. He sounded happy for me and said he would have something special for me when I returned home.

It took me several hours to run errands and meet up with Brenda after work. When I arrived home later that night, Marvin had dinner waiting for me. He cooked spaghetti with handmade meatballs, one of his best dishes.

"Good evening, Ms. Career Woman," he teased as he took off my coat and showed me to a seat at the table. "I'll be your waiter today."

I looked around. It was only the two of us in the room. I stopped him. "Ah, where are the kids, Marvin?" I asked.

"Oh, they're in their rooms. And yes, they've already been fed. Woman, I'm trying to do something nice for you. Can I serve you now?" He laughed.

I gave him a glance then nodded with an amused smile on my face.

"Good. Like I was saying, I'd like to serve you a great meal tonight, but before I do, I wanna give you something very special."

"And what's that?" I quickly looked up again, curious, and with a smirk.

"Well, close your eyes and you'll see," he instructed.

I felt something cool on my exposed cleavage.

"Now, open your eyes."

I looked down and saw a long necklace with an angel charm dangling between my breasts. I jumped up and walked over to the large mirror on the living room wall to get a better view up close. The chain didn't have a clasp and connected to the charm on both sides, making it easy to slip on or off over the head. But the charm was unique. I had never seen anything like it before. The silver angel was kneeling with praying hands and its wings looked like a butterfly's as it lay flat on my chest.

"Oh, Marvin, this is absolutely beautiful," I said, hugging him tightly and then kissing his lips. "Thank you, baby," I whispered in his ear.

"You're welcome," he replied, stroking my back. "This is just my way of saying congratulations, and I'm very proud of you. You deserve this."

My eyes started to well up with joy. It wasn't so long ago we had nothing but struggles, and now success appeared to be on the horizon. "This is really happening for us, isn't it, Marvin? All of these good things," I said, still in his embrace.

"We're going to make it, baby. I can feel it. It's just a matter of time until our dreams come true."

Chapter 42

Truck driving became dull and monotonous again. The lines on the road seemed to blur with every passing day hauling pallets of cold freight up and down the interstate. There was no amusement anymore, just loneliness. Only his thoughts, the radio, and some magazines kept him company. He said he wouldn't do it again, go to a strip joint. But he couldn't help it. He needed an outlet, a release from his frustrations and realities of life.

Marvin walked into Dusty's Kitty Club feeling confident and safe. It had been two months since the *accident*, as he preferred to call it. And still no sign of trouble. *Nobody knows me here*, he thought as he stood in the doorway and scanned the room.

The small nudie bar near the Virginia border had an older, honky-tonk atmosphere. Cigar smoke filled the air and country music played in the background. The building was almost empty with a few men outlining the stage watching tired-looking white women with sagging tits dance and swing around poles. This was not Marvin's scene...*a total disappointment.*

He looked over and saw the bar. It was 6:15 PM; his shift was over. "I might as well have a drink before heading home," he mumbled under his breath.

"What'll ya have?" asked the bartender. She chomped on chewing gum and wiped out a shot glass while waiting on his reply.

"Gin please," he said. The woman nodded and poured.

Marvin took the glass and swiveled on the stool to get another look at the girls. He shook his head and then finished off his gin. He'd seen better...much better.

He turned to the bartender again.

"I'll take another one."

The woman poured and slid the glass forward. "Anything else?" she asked as he tilted the glass to his mouth.

"No thank you," he replied, laying a ten-dollar bill on the bar. "Keep the change." The woman smiled hard, revealing every deep wrinkle that was etched into her over-tanned face.

Marvin stood up and glanced to the right. Something on the wall behind the bar caught his eye. He focused and took a startled breath.

"Do you know her?" the bartender asked. The flyer on the wall had a picture of Angela on it. It said: *Missing. Have you seen this woman?*

"No," he quickly answered, donning a fake smile. "She just looks like someone I knew long ago, that's all. For a second there, I actually thought it was her." Marvin tried hard not to give another look at the flyer but couldn't resist.

"Yeah, she is a pretty thing, isn't she?" said the bartender. "A woman came by here about a week ago and dropped off some flyers. She said her friend was a stripper in North Carolina and hasn't been seen or heard from in a couple of months."

The news made Marvin's head race with frantic thoughts and questions: *They found the body! Do the cops have any leads? Do they know about me?* It took all of his strength to keep his composure.

"Did the woman contact the police about her friend?" he asked, nodding his head and sounding like a normal concerned citizen.

"Yeah, but it didn't do no good," the bartender said. "If I remember right…something about no evidence of foul play. I told the woman her friend never worked here, but I'd be happy to hand out a few flyers."

The bartender grabbed a flyer and stretched out her arm. "Here, I only have one more left. Do you mind taking this and passing on the information? I sure hope they find her."

Marvin took the flyer and walked off, eager to get outside for fresh air. His heart pounded and the arteries in his neck tapped double time like a snare drum. It was still cold in early March with snow and ice on the ground from last night's storm. *Breathe!* he told himself in the frigid air as he climbed into his truck. Marvin drove off in shock with the flyer still clutched in his hand. He glanced at it again and then pushed on the gas pedal. It seemed like Angela was staring right at him with her haunting, judging eyes just waiting for him to get caught.

He crushed the paper and shoved it deep into his coat pocket. "*No evidence of foul play,*" the woman had said. Hearing that didn't give him any kind of relief. Marvin knew it was just a matter of time until someone found the body. The road was long and dark and solely illuminated by headlights as he plowed through the wintery mix. The darkness surrounded him and aided his mounting paranoid thoughts of loose ends.

"It was an accident!" he shouted, pressing down on the gas even more.

In a fit of rage, he went down the empty interstate fast. Then suddenly, he hit a patch of black ice and lost control. The truck swerved off the road onto the median and collided head on with a tree. Slumped over the steering wheel with blood drizzling from his forehead, Marvin was out.

Chapter 43

"Welcome back, Mr. Jones. You've got some kind of luck walking away from that accident with only a mild concussion," said a white middle-aged doctor standing next to Marvin, who lay on a hospital bed. The doctor chuckled. "I should take you to Atlantic City to play Blackjack with me instead of my girlfriend."

Marvin began to blink his eyelids rapidly while looking around the room. "Where am I?" he softly asked, trying to get his bearings.

"You're in an emergency room, Mr. Jones. You were in a bad accident."

"Accident?" Marvin repeated.

Then it all started to come back. A highway patrolman found him staggering on the side of the road near the crash site. "Are you okay, sir? Can you tell me your name and what happened?" he remembered the officer asking him. The last thing he recalled was looking at the patrolman and whispering, "Ice on the road." He figured he must have passed out seconds after that.

"How long have I been out?"

"About an hour and a half," the doctor answered. "After we got a MRI to make sure you weren't bleeding internally or had any brain damage, we patched you up and gave you some pain medication."

"What about my truck?" Marvin asked.

"Oh, I don't know too much about that. I just remember the police officer who came in with you saying your truck kissed a tree. Speaking of the reporting officer, he requested we take a blood sample from you for an alcohol analysis test. He claimed he smelled alcohol on your breath at the crash site and that gave him reasonable suspicion to ask for a blood alcohol count for a possible DUI charge."

"What! I wasn't drunk. I hit ice," Marvin said.

"Well, hold on, Mr. Jones. I got the report back from our in-house laboratory and have determined there is no evidence of alcohol impairment. In the state of Virginia, the legal BAC limit is .080 and your count was .027."

Marvin let out a sigh of relief. The last thing he needed was another case.

"Mr. Jones, I think you're going to be fine and can be released. If you get plenty of rest and take it easy for a few days, things should go back to normal. But if you experience worsening headaches, vomiting, slurred speech, confusion, or definitely an episode of seizures, return to the hospital right away. Is there anyone we can contact to pick you up, perhaps your wife?"

"Yes," Marvin nodded. "You can call my wife; her name is Toni Jones. But doctor, could you please leave out the part about the alcohol? Toni is a very inquisitive woman. I promised her I'd cut down on drinking and I don't want her to find out I had a drink tonight and get upset."

"Sure, your medical records are your private business. I'm not required to reveal anything you don't want to your wife. Take care, Mr. Jones."

Chapter 44

He had luck on his side. That's what the doctor told him three days ago. Now he was on his way to the boss' office hoping his luck hadn't run out. No doubt Mr. Crawford wanted to talk about the accident, but Marvin wasn't too worried. The crash wasn't his fault.

He knocked on the glass door twice. The boss looked up and waved him in. "Have a seat, Marvin," he said, using a serious tone. "I'm glad to see you're doing well."

Marvin nodded and smiled. "Thank you, sir."

"I'm going to get straight to the point," said Mr. Crawford. "We have to let you go."

Marvin gave his boss a puzzled look.

"I don't understand, sir."

"We can't afford to have you on the books anymore. You're too much of risk. Because of the accident, it's going to be expensive to insure you. And that's not all. The guys in service found an empty beer can in your truck."

Mr. Crawford paused and waited for a reaction. He got nothing; Marvin didn't say a word.

"So are you denying drinking on the job?" Mr. Crawford asked, annoyed by the silence.

"No, sir. I'm not denying anything. I did have an occasional drink, but it was never during my shift. It was after hours."

"Well, we have a zero alcohol policy when operating our property and you know that," he said sternly while giving Marvin a scolding look. "I don't care if you're making deliveries or you're on your way home. There's to be no alcohol in my trucks, period! You know, this is a real shame, Marvin. You came so highly recommended and for a while seemed reliable."

"Mr. Crawford, I am really truly sorry about what happened," Marvin anxiously said. "But I need this job. Is there any way you can give me another chance? I promise I won't ever disappoint you again."

"No," he said decisively and shook his head. "You should have thought of that before drinking beer in my truck. You can pick up your final check on your way out at the accounting window. Goodbye, Mr. Jones."

The walk down to the accounting office felt like a trip to the unemployment line. Marvin felt angry, embarrassed, and already misplaced. Trucking was his freedom, his outlet from the mundane world. *You stupid idiot, why did you leave that damn beer can in the truck?* He blamed himself. *Now, you're out of work. What the hell are you going to do?*

Marvin sat at the bus stop with his final check in hand thinking about how he would break the news to Toni. He lost his transportation and cushy job. What words could he possibly use to smooth over the fact that their comfortable lifestyle would have to come to an end for a short time or even longer? By the time he got home, Marvin would have figure out a way to tell his wife about the job lost. But he would never tell Toni the real reason he got fired was because of the alcohol found in his truck.

Chapter 45

Marvin gave me the news yesterday. I told him this was some bullshit! Absolute bullshit! How could they fire him for wrecking their truck on a hazardous road? He could have died out there. Marvin told me to calm down and let it go. He'd find another job. But, something didn't sound right to me. I wanted answers.

I met up with James Franklin at the trucking driving school during his lunch without telling Marvin. I sat in James' office and waited patiently while he finished up on a phone call. "I'll be with you in a moment," he said, covering one end of the phone with his hands.

I started scanning the room to kill time and noticed the certificates on walls and his degree from South Carolina State University. It was obvious James did something with his life. And then his face caught my attention; he looked good with age. Better than what I remembered in high school. The acne was gone and from the multiple framed pictures on his bookshelf, he had a good-looking family as well.

We used to be good friends in high school. As I sat there, my mind went back to some of the fun times we had in the marching band. I was the loud one and he was the shy type. We used to get along so well; such a shame we stopped talking after graduation.

He hung up the phone.

"Toni." He grinned. "What's going on? What can I do for you?"

"Well, James." I smiled. "I need your help again. It's Marvin. He's out of a job."

James gave what looked to be an expectant nod.

"Do you already know what's going on?" I asked curiously.

"Yes, I do," he answered. "News travels fast in this industry."

"Well, how could they fire him for something that was not his fault? He hydroplaned on ice, for God's sake! Please, just give me a second," I said, closing my eyes and taking in a deep breath to calm down and let go of my frustration.

"I'm sorry, James. I just get so upset thinking about what they did. It's just not fair. Listen, James, if there's anything you can do to help him find another job, I would really appreciate it."

James leaned forward.

"Toni, you've got to understand something. This is a business and Marvin cost that company money. They also found alcohol in his truck."

"Alcohol!" I exclaimed. I started to shake my head in denial. "No, that can't be right. I haven't seen Marvin take a drink in years."

James shrugged his shoulders. "That's what I've been told."

I looked away feeling like a fool because it all made sense now. There I was defending my husband, and I didn't know the half of why Marvin got fired.

"Look, Marvin is a liability," James said. "No one I know is going to hire him. So please, don't ever ask me to help your husband again. I've already taken a chance and put my name on the line for him. I've got a reputation as a trainer to uphold."

I looked up and nodded. "I understand, James. You've done enough, thanks."

I couldn't blame James for washing his hands of it all. He felt bad for me, though—I could see the pity he had for me in his eyes.

"Toni, you know, we go way back. So I feel I can be honest and direct with you," James said, sounding concerned.

"Okay, I'm listening," I said.

"Toni, it seems like every time Marvin gets into trouble, you run to his rescue."

"Well, he's my husband, James. That's what I'm supposed to do."

"And I understand that," James said, nodding. "But, in my opinion, Marvin created this problem all on his own, not the company. There's something else I want to point out, Toni. You were so shocked when I mentioned the alcohol they found in his truck. I think you need to ask yourself a hard question. Do you really know what's going on with your husband? If you didn't know about the alcohol, what else could he be hiding?"

Chapter 46

I left James' office overwhelmed with emotions: hurt, rage, betrayal. Marvin lied to me. He promised he wouldn't drink anymore and he didn't tell me the real reason he got fired. James was right; his question stayed with me all day. What else could Marvin be lying about?

"Mama," Justine shouted from the dining table. "Do you want me to set a place for Marvin?"

"No," I sharply replied. "I have no idea when that man's coming home."

Marvin was supposed to be out hunting for a job and following up on a lead. But only God knew what he was really up to. "Get Adrian for dinner," I told Justine.

We sat; we prayed and starting eating.

"I got a gold star for knowing how to spell, Mama. Just like last time," Adrian cheerfully said then grinned hard, showing off the gap between his two upper front teeth.

"That's good, baby," I said, barely cracking a smile.

"Mama, next week is spring break. Can we go swimming at Aunt Thelma's house?" Justine blurted out her question.

"I don't know, hun. We'll see," I said.

My mind was so stuck on Marvin that I couldn't interact with my own children. I told myself I wasn't angry. I just wanted to hear the truth from his mouth.

About fifteen minutes later, keys were jingling at the front door. Marvin walked in looking tired with his shirt unbuttoned at the top and his long sleeves rolled up. He sniffed.

"Something smells good," he said, sounding upbeat. "I sure am hungry."

Marvin fixed a plate and joined us at the table. The small talk with the kids was polite and over quick, then he dove into the pile of food.

"Toni, this pot roast is delicious," he said, taking a break from shoveling food into his mouth.

I didn't respond. All I could do was give a blank stare. He rolled his eyes, lifted up his glass, and finished off his drink in two big gulps. He wiped his mouth and looked at me again.

"Toni, what's wrong with you?"

"How was your day?" I asked instead, while looking at my half-eaten dinner and pushing food around my plate with a fork. "Did you find anything?"

"No, I did not find a job today," he replied, sounding suspicious. "Toni, what's with the cavalier expression on your face? I know something's bothering you."

I looked up and straight into Marvin's eyes.

"You're right," I said calmly. "Something is bothering me. Kids, please go to your rooms. I need to talk to your father."

The kids followed orders while Marvin went to the kitchen and poured more sweet tea. Justine walked off in silence but looked back with furled eyebrows, apparently concerned.

"Everything's okay, Justine," I said to her with a reassuring smile.

"What's this about?" Marvin asked.

"I'll tell you what this is about. This is about you lying to me."

Marvin put the glass down and walked closer to me. I stood up. "What have I lied about?" he asked, seemingly more curious than surprised.

"I saw James Franklin today. He told me the truth, the real reason why you were fired. When did you start drinking again, Marvin?"

Marvin stared at me like a deer in headlights for a few seconds and then rolled his eyes. Quietly, he came even closer and blocked me against the couch. I trembled a little but stood brave and held back my tears.

"I told you to leave it alone," he said harshly, putting his finger in my face. "You had no right to see James behind my back. I'm telling you I wasn't drunk. One drink didn't cause that accident. If it did, they would have arrested me."

"That's not the fucking point." I raised my voice. "Marvin, you lied to me. You promised you would never drink again."

"It wasn't an everyday thing, Toni!" he yelled back. "Did I ever come home drunk? Did you ever smell alcohol on me? Did you?"

I stayed silent watching his seething eyes grow. I hadn't seen this kind of anger with him in years. But I saw something else, something more than frustration and anger.

"Answer me, dammit!" he yelled louder.

The bass in his voice made me jump. "No," I answered, releasing a few tears. I turned my head and saw Justine in the doorway.

"Please, stop. Please," she begged, holding her chest and breathing rapidly.

"Everything's okay, honey," I said. "Marvin and I were just having a disagreement. Now, please, go back to your room, sweetheart."

Justine didn't move. She looked worried and stood there like a referee waiting on our next move. Marvin glanced at her and stepped back.

"Don't provoke me, Toni," he said. "You have no idea what I'm up against." He walked off, grabbed his keys, and headed for the door. And right before leaving, Marvin cocked back his fist and threw a punch into the dry wall.

Chapter 47

It took four days to hear the word *sorry* from Marvin's mouth. He apologized for losing his temper and blamed it on the stress of being unemployed. He called himself a fool. He regretted drinking in the truck and losing the best job he'd had in years. But, he really never expressed remorse for lying and breaking his promise to me.

But I chose to let the anger go and forgave him for everything: the lies and the job loss. I had to. It just seemed easier to keep the peace and my sanity. And yet, I still felt things were chilly between us, like we were living in separate worlds. We slept in the same bed, but there was no warmth or lovemaking. We just existed.

Justine also changed. She became quieter and more distant than ever before. Conversations between us were infrequent and short. And she avoided Marvin completely. In fact, I believe she despised him. The only time I saw a smile on the child's face was when Lewis called.

With the home life on the verge of a crisis, the radio station became my refuge and priority. I had no idea how long we'd be living on one income, so I knew my morning show needed to be a hit. But Marvin was trying hard to get back on his feet and find employment. I saw evidence of that when he broke down and wrote a passionate letter to the South Carolina Board of Barber Examiners for the restoration of his barber's license, but his appeal was revoked, stating his criminal record reflected a lack of moral character and handling sharp objects among the general public could pose a possible threat. I never understood that backward thinking. Marvin was fit and safe enough to drive a commercial truck, but not safe enough to cut and shampoo someone's hair in the great State of South Carolina.

Even after that disappointment, every day I'd watched Marvin get up early and head out into the streets searching for work. And although being jobless was his fault, I felt bad for him when he'd return home in the evenings looking defeated.

Chapter 48

On my last day of working the weekend shift, I met my replacement, Kenneth Moore. He was on time and waiting patiently behind the glass window until I got the chance to break for a commercial. Yesterday, Paul asked me to help Kenneth get adjusted to our computer system and work on promos in preparation for next week's transition. He said the kid was still somewhat green at the age of twenty-eight with only two years of radio experience, but had wonderful voice-over tapes and projected a lot of confidence.

I buzzed him in and got a closer look. Tall and dark with amazing eyes, the man was nothing but sexy. And his dreaded hair was pulled back into a ponytail and manicured all the way down to the roots. Polished shoes, ironed slacks, everything about his appearance was impressive and by the look of his left hand, he was single. *If I were only ten years younger!* I smiled while entertaining my dirty thoughts.

"Hello, I'm Kenneth," he said, snapping me out my daze. "It's nice to meet you." He extended his hand and showed off a handsome smile.

"Same here," I replied, gripping his hand. "Listen, just let me sign off and then we can talk and get acquainted properly."

He nodded, sat down, and crossed his long legs.

"We're back. And you have been listening to a very special edition of Toni's Midday Cafe on Foxy 100. And as you may already know, this is my last weekend broadcast and will be launching my own morning show right here on Foxy 100 starting Monday next week. I want to thank everyone for their support and prayers. So, for the final time, I'm signing off from Toni's Midday Café." I took the headphones off and placed them on the table.

"Wow! You really have an amazing radio voice," Kenneth said.

"Thanks. But I can't take all the credit. I inherited my talent from my father. He used to sing in a doo-wop band and host variety shows in the clubs back in the day. Besides, I heard you're not bad yourself."

Kenneth grinned then touched his chest. "I do okay, Mrs. Jones."

"Toni, just call me Toni. There'll be none of that formal stuff around here."

"I got you," he said with a chuckle.

"So, Kenneth, I also heard you used to work for a radio station in Columbia. What brings you all the way down to Chuck-town?"

"Let's see: food, family, and culture," he answered. "But I'm not just a DJ; I'm also a photographer. And what better place to shoot than Charleston? The city and people here are absolutely beautiful."

Kenneth leaned his head back, made a picture frame with his fingers, and raised it to focus on me. "Actually, has anyone ever told you that you have high cheekbones like women in Africa? They're amazing. Maybe I can photograph you someday?"

He lowered his hands and revealed a half-sided smile.

Was that a flirt? I silently asked myself. Paul was right. Not only did he possess confidence, Kenneth was bold.

"Boy, please," I blurted out, laughing and feeling somewhat embarrassed. "You sure know how to turn on the charm. I'm not worried about you. I bet you'll have your listening audience and everyone else around here eating from the palm of your hand by the end of this month."

Kenneth gave me a gracious smile and shrugged his shoulders. "If that's what you think, then I'm honored by the compliment."

"Yep, that's what I think. Now, let's get working on those promos."

Kenneth pulled out a notebook and started on a script while I gathered up my paperwork. I turned back to look at him…well-mannered and suave. I liked his energy and knew he'd be a great addition to our staff.

Oh, what the hell!

"Kenneth, let me get a rain check on that photo shoot."

Chapter 49

It was April again and old man winter finally decided to go away after an extended stay. But there was no change for Marvin. He was still unemployed and we were still just being cordial with each other. Mama told me to *let go and let God*. And that wasn't hard to do now that the show was doing well in ratings and taking up a lot of my time. But today was about Justine.

I was expecting her to arrive at any minute with her father. He was back in town and she spent the weekend with him. Lewis told me he had important news to share, but he wanted Justine to hear about it first.

I made her favorite Sunday dinner: macaroni and cheese with fried chicken wings. That was my subtle attempt to bring a little joy to her world. One month later, it seemed like Justine was still angry with me and Marvin for the blow-up. And I knew the moment she stepped back into this house, she would turn cold.

I looked out the kitchen window and saw Lewis' Mercedes pull up the driveway. Marvin and Adrian were in our bedroom watching television. I headed outside to greet them. Justine walked past me fast, looking upset.

"What's wrong?" I asked. She said nothing. I turned to Lewis. "Are you going to tell me what's going on?"

"It's not you. She's mad at me," he said, standing on the other side of the car.

"Then why is Justine angry with you, Lewis?"

"She's upset because I'm leaving. I've taken an assistive coaching job overseas."

"What!" I said, in shock. "Lewis, you just came into her life and now you're leaving."

"I know, Toni. But this is a chance of a lifetime. I've been asked to help coach the Spain team for the 1992 Olympic Games in Barcelona and that means I have to relocate for at least two years. I know that's a long time, but I can't pass up this financial opportunity."

I nodded my head. And although it was tough to hear for Justine's sake, I knew he was right. "Congratulations." That was all I could say.

"What's wrong with Justine? I can hear her in her bedroom crying," Marvin asked as he came out on the front porch. He looked over at Lewis and gave him a slight heads up. Lewis returned the gesture.

"It's alright, honey," I said, walking up to Marvin. I lowered my voice. "It's really nothing, babe. I'll explain everything. Please, just give us a few more minutes." Marvin took another glimpse at Lewis, nodded, and went back inside.

"Don't worry about Justine," I said, walking back to Lewis. "She's a tough kid."

"Yeah, I know. But it hurts me to disappoint her like this. Listen, maybe after I get settled, we can work on getting her a passport. Maybe she can visit during the summers."

"Yeah, we'll see. I know she'd like that. So, when are you leaving?"

"In a few weeks," he replied, nodding his head. Then suddenly he changed the subject to me. "So how are you holding up? Justine told me that Marvin lost his job last month. That's gotta be tough, right?"

His question caught me off guard, and I gave him a slightly surprised look. It never dawned on me that Justine would talk about our home life with Lewis. But he was her father.

"Well, Lewis, it could be worse. I just got a promotion at the station, so we're hanging in here. And Marvin will find something soon."

"Well, hey. Keep your head up and congratulations on the promotion."

"Thanks," I said.

"Okay then, Toni, I've got to run. Please, just let Justine know that I love her and everything will be alright. And I'll also try to send her something in the mail every month."

By the sound of Lewis' voice, he really seemed concerned about leaving his daughter behind. They met only a year ago, and I could already see the bond between the two of them. How lucky for Justine to have the love of a good father and apparently a good man.

I waved goodbye as Lewis backed up his car. It reminded me when I waved goodbye to him at the airport the morning after our fling so long ago. But this time, I knew he'd return. Not for me, but for Justine.

Chapter 50

He finally caught a break. "It's not what you know, but who you know," Marvin said with excitement while taking off his clothes and heading to the shower. "I really think this is the one, Toni."

It was a relief to hear Marvin sound so positive and full of hope again. He had a job interview this morning and apparently it went well. *Thank God for Scott!*

It was last week at a fuel station when Marvin ran into Scott, a truck driver he helped on the road with a flat tire several months back. He told the man his story, and Scott promised to pass on Marvin's information to the hiring supervisor on his job. Scott said this was a good time to apply because the company he worked for was growing fast and needed more experienced, reliable drivers who were ready to work.

"I'm happy for you, baby," I shouted, sitting on the edge of the bed.

Marvin stuck his head in the doorway and nodded while brushing his teeth.

"So, tell me about the job, hun."

He stepped out the bathroom drying his face and body. "It's a regional freight transportation company. They transport all kinds of goods for various companies."

"Regional?" I asked.

"Yes." He nodded. "They do business in the South Atlantic region. You know: the Carolinas, Georgia, and Florida."

"Sounds like longer hours on the road to me."

"Maybe." He shrugged. "But the job pays $7.25 an hour with benefits. And if we want to get to where we want to be, we need that kind of income. With our combined salaries, we can buy that bigger house we talked about."

Damn right! I said in my head, knowing I couldn't pay all the bills and save money all on my own. "So, when are they gonna tell you something?" I asked.

"The supervisor said I should hear back from him within a week. He was really impressed with my grades, Toni."

Marvin sounded so happy, but I couldn't get the obvious question out of my head. *Did you tell the man how you lost your last job?* It was like ignoring the big pink elephant in the room. But, I fought the urge off and decided not to change the mood.

"Well, I've got some news of my own." I smiled.

"Oh, and what's that?" he asked in a seductive way.

Marvin moved in front of me wearing only a towel. I looked up and saw something in him I hadn't seen in a long time. He was horny and rising. He touched the side of my face and gave me a lustful stare. I got hot. It felt like a huge heat wave had crashed up against my body.

"I'm hosting the Memorial Day concert," I said, breathing deeply as he lifted my shirt and bra over my head in one swoop.

Marvin lay on top of me with skin still damp from the shower and stuck his tongue into my mouth. It tasted like a hint of alcohol. But I wasn't sure. *Is that what he's doing when he's out all day looking for work, drinking? Or was that just mouthwash?*

He grabbed my left breast and all of those worrisome thoughts instantly stopped the moment he started sucking and pulling on my nipple. His intensity felt good. It had been three long months since Marvin touched me.

Quickly, he bent me over and slid in deep easily from my overflow. With a firm grip on my hips, he steadily pumped. The more he rammed into my flesh, the more I hollered in search of sexual ecstasy. I was loud but didn't care. The kids were at school.

Our eyes met when I turned over. Watching me fondle myself made him pump even harder...harder than I had ever remembered. But I wanted it and took it until we both popped. For the next few days, I repeated many times...*thank God for Scott!*

Chapter 51

Porsha Brooks waited patiently in the smoky hallway for her turn to speak with the owner of Club Rendezvous. One of the bouncers stopped her in the middle of questioning a stripper and told her she needed to see Mr. Leroy if she wanted information about one of the girls. Sneaking backstage and disturbing performers on the job was not allowed.

It had been three long months since Porsha heard from Angela. She had already visited several other strip clubs along Interstate 95 and from the brief conversations she'd had with Angela about her work life, the trail ended here.

She met Angela five years ago in Virginia at Norfolk State University where they were students. They became close friends as roommates and hung out all the time. But, after sophomore year, Angela became tired of college and got into stripping to financially pursue her acting career while Porsha went on to receive her bachelor's degree in art education.

Porsha remained in Virginia and Angela hopped between states for work. And even though their lives went in different directions, they had a bond and vowed to keep in touch with either a monthly phone call or an occasional visit.

The last time they spoke was on New Year's Day. Angela was ecstatic about moving to California this past winter, but when February came and went without a call, Porsha became concerned. To make matters worse, she no longer had a number for Angela nor did she know where or with whom she was living temporarily until the big move. It seemed like there were so many obstacles blocking Porsha from locating her friend. She didn't even have a way of contacting Angela's family.

But she knew in her heart something was very wrong. Angela would never leave the East Coast without giving Porsha details about the trip. Like how many hours it would take to drive to California and what were her plans for rest along the route. Especially since her car was older. Not only that, Angela would have called the moment she arrived in the Golden State, happy and overexcited to be starting anew.

From Porsha's point of view, all of it seemed too strange. And if passing out flyers at strip clubs between Virginia and North Carolina every other weekend and collecting information from this Leroy "Big-Boy" Jackson character helped her find Angela, then so be it.

The office door swung open and a tall overweight black man emerged.

"Sorry about making you wait, Porsha. I had a business call to take care of. So, they tell me you're looking for your friend Angela, or Candy as we used to call her around here."

"Yes, I haven't heard from her in about three months and that's unusual."

"Well, same here, sweetheart." He shrugged then reached for his half-smoked cigar. I haven't seen her in months either. She told me and some of the girls that she was ready to leave and was heading off to California. Matter of fact, she didn't even finish her last week of shows, and I'm still not too happy about that."

Leroy picked up the flyer and gave Porsha a skeptical look.

"And for some reason you think she's missing."

"Yes, Mr. Leroy, I do…."

"Hey! Hey, just call me Leroy. You make feel old with all that, *Mr* stuff." He smiled wide, appearing less intimidating.

"Okay, then, Leroy. I'm telling you, I know Angela. She wouldn't just vanish. And she definitely wouldn't just get in her car and go off driving across the country without calling me along the way. She's adventurous but not enough to do that trip totally by herself. It just doesn't make sense. Now, I know she was staying with some girl temporarily. Would you happen to know who that was?"

"Sure don't." Leroy chuckled. "Angela was a private person, especially when it came to her personal life. When she didn't show up here to do her last shows, I couldn't get anybody around here to tell me a thing. And when I tried calling the number I had on her, it was disconnected."

Porsha nodded her head knowingly because she ran into the same problem.

"Have you tried calling her people? Maybe she went home for a while."

Porsha ran her fingers through her shoulder-length hair then shook her head. "No, because I don't have their number," she answered.

Leroy seemed surprised. "You mean to tell me, you two are close, but you don't have her mother's phone number? Sounds like you may not know her as well as you think you do." He smirked.

"Look, I know Angela pretty well. It's just in the years that I've known her, she rarely talked about her family or went home. Besides, I've only met her parents once back in college. At least I do know they're from Tennessee."

"Well, let me tell you what I think," Leroy said. "I think Angela is in California right now shaking her ass off and making some money. If I were you, I wouldn't worry so much. I bet you'll hear from that girl in another month or so. But in the meantime, this is a business. And I can't have you in here passing out flyers and spooking my customers."

Porsha rolled her eyes and sighed.

"Listen," Leroy said in a sympathetic tone. "I feel ya. You're worried about your girl. But if you strongly believe something's happened to her, then just go to the police."

"Leroy, I've already done that," she said, sounding defeated. "I've been to three different police stations and after I told them my story, they all seemed disinterested. They basically said the same thing you just said—she's in California. At least they took my flyers."

"See, I told you."

Leroy leaned back in his black oversized chair and got a thought scanning Porsha's body up and down. He noticed she had a nice shape underneath her high-waist pants with suspenders. And if she took off her glasses and put on a little makeup, she could be cute. She was no Angela, but with the right G-string, maybe, she could even be sexy.

"Hey, Porsha, you're not so bad looking yourself. Have you ever thought about getting into the lucrative world of exotic dancing?"

Porsha stood up and gave Leroy a repulsed look knowing his middle-aged mind was undressing her with nasty thoughts roaming in his head. "Nope," she quickly answered. "I never learned how to dance anyway. Thank you for your time," she said then walked out of his office.

Back in the car, Porsha pulled out a list of strip clubs where she knew Angela had performed. There were a total of six written down and Club Rendezvous in Fayetteville, NC was the last one. She crossed out the last stop then put the paper back in her purse. She shook her head, started up the engine, and released a big sigh knowing her search was at a dead end. Porsha drove off hoping everyone was right. But still…Angela hadn't called.

Where in the hell are you, Angela?

Chapter 52

From the start, I had my doubts and knew that job opportunity Marvin got so excited about was a long shot. James Franklin had already given me a stiff warning. Once you get a negative trucking motor vehicle report on your employment history, you were blackballed. And getting another decent commercial job was next to impossible.

Marvin received that rejection letter about a week ago and, still, he was moping around and cursing the world for his bad luck. According to the letter, good grades and good work attendance weren't enough to trump bad references and a police record.

"The man is always going to keep me down. Why do I even try?" he griped almost every day. With Marvin, he was always the victim and everybody else was against him.

His pity party annoyed me. I suggested he put truck driving to the side and look for other types of work or maybe even go back to school. But, he scoffed at the idea as usual. Talking about how he wasn't cut out for a normal 9 to 5, but then later agreed when he heard about a car salesmen position over at Ford in North Charleston.

It was Saturday, Memorial Weekend 1990 and my day to shine as the host of Miki Howard's *Come Share My Love* concert, featuring David Peaston. I had on a black mini dress, a little number I picked out to show off my curves and long legs. My hair was crimped, eyebrows were arched, and face made up to perfection. I looked damn good. Even Marvin came out of his funky mood to give me a compliment and tag along.

"I want you to enjoy yourself, baby," I said to Marvin as we received our backstage passes. "Let's just forget about tomorrow and have fun tonight. Okay, love?" I kissed him and watched a small smile appear on his face. He looked good standing there dressed up in black slacks and a long-sleeved shirt with a circle red, yellow, and green African medallion around his neck. I touched his low cut tapered beard while looking heatedly into his eyes.

"Toni!" I heard a familiar voice call out from behind me. It was Kenneth coming from across the room. I leaned into Marvin.

"That's Kenneth, the new DJ on staff I told you about, honey."

"Toni, you look fantastic," Kenneth said with a wide-eyed reaction. This was the first time he'd ever seen me all dressed up and with makeup on. *I guess I still got it!* I teased in my head.

"Aw, thanks," I said, flashing a blushing grin. "By the way, this is my husband, Marvin."

Kenneth reached out for a handshake. "Hey, nice to meet you, man. Toni talks a lot about you."

Marvin nodded and shook his hand, but didn't say word.

"Well, they're ready for you," Kenneth said, not even fazed by my husband's ill manners. He just kept on smiling, apparently still amazed by my appearance.

I turned to Marvin and told him I had to go. He nodded his head again and walked off to the side of the stage to stand next to the oversized speakers. I could tell something was bothering him. He was standoffish.

"How's everybody feeling tonight?" I shouted into a microphone, across a large thunderous crowd. The lights were bright; the people cheered and I was on my game. This is how I always imagined it. Hosting a popular radio show combined with MCing live events. I knew it was just a matter of time until I became nationally syndicated.

I took a glimpse at Marvin to share the joy that was plastered all over my face. And there he was, raising a can of Budweiser to his mouth. He didn't even try to hide it this time and gave me a smug grin. My instinct was to confront him the moment I stepped off stage, but I didn't and walked right past him. Tonight was my night; I refused to make him the focus.

By the end of the show, I think Marvin had at least seven beers. But, I actually lost count by the time Miki got on stage. He staggered a little as we walked arm-in-arm back to the car after the show. The stench from his mouth almost brought me to tears. It was a mixture of alcohol and cigar smoke. Passing by, Kenneth saw me struggling and offered help.

"No," I responded politely. "I've got this."

Marvin reclined the car seat and then started to drift away. Watching him fall asleep tipsy unsettled my nerves. I couldn't keep my feelings inside.

"You promised me, Marvin," I said softly.

"What?" he groggily asked.

"You're drinking again. Are you doing this to hurt me?"

"Toni, you told me to have fun tonight. Isn't that what you asked me to do?"

"Don't use that as an excuse, Marvin." I elevated my voice. "You knew what I meant."

"Toni." He sighed. "Please stop telling me what to do. I'm a grown man."

He yawned, dozed off for a second, then started up again. "If I want to take a drink now and then, I will. Stop worrying so much. I know how to handle me. It's not like before."

Marvin turned away and fell completely asleep. He wasn't worried about his drinking, but I had every reason to be concerned. Things always went wrong when he drank. Unemployment and alcohol never mixed.

Chapter 53

Another rejection was all he needed to give up. The car salesman's position he applied for didn't come through like he'd hoped. No experience and limited openings were the excuses they hastily gave him over the telephone. "Fuck them!" he said, hanging up.

But he knew better. The advertisement said, "No experience required, on-the-job training available." This wasn't about the lack of sales experience. He was a hustler and could outsell anyone in the building if given the chance. No, this was about his police record. A record he obviously couldn't outrun. And to Marvin, it was just confirmation that nobody would hire him.

Why try?

He went to the bathroom to take a piss. He rinsed off his hands and took a glimpse of himself in the mirror. He looked old and felt even older. His graying hair and beard were knotted and hadn't been trimmed in days. And the fat around his waist hung over like a muffin top. *How did I get like this?* he asked himself, disgusted with life and his appearance. But he knew how and in that moment decided he didn't care.

Marvin went to the kitchen to get a few beers. The note on the refrigerator said: *Please don't forget to pick me up tonight at 8:30.* He remembered Toni was at the radio station covering the night shift for a co-worker. She left the car and caught a ride with a friend early this morning. Marvin was supposed to be job hunting and getting status checks on applications already sent, but it was 1:15 on a Friday afternoon. He wasn't going anywhere.

Marvin took down the note and threw it in the trash. *I've got time,* he thought. The first can of beer tasted good going down his throat into an empty stomach as he lounged on the couch watching television wearing nothing but boxers and socks. He flipped through the channels; a commercial for the Moja Art Festival week caught his attention. Then suddenly, Toni and Kenneth appeared on the screen. They were promoting an event they'd be hosting together.

That's the nigga from the concert, the muthafucka that disrespected me by staring at my wife!

Marvin threw back the second can of beer to calm his nerves.

Toni had been spending a lot of time at the station working on her show and other projects. He couldn't help but wonder if they had something going on behind the scenes. After all, Kenneth was a handsome, much younger man. Marvin seriously started to think about the possibility of a wild affair by the time he hit the third can.

When he was done gulping down the fourth and fifth, jealousy settled in. Marvin thought about his failures and compared them to Toni's recent successes. Her dreams were coming true while he was on the sideline with no idea of where his life was going. Several times he thought about leaving to start fresh with no obligations attached to him and maybe, down the road, find another woman, a quiet woman, who wouldn't harass him about drinking or keeping a job.

But Marvin knew there wasn't anyone better than Toni. Losing everything made him realize that fact. In his mind, they were soulmates, divided only by death. And *no woman*—not a girlfriend, Angela, or even his own mother had ever stood by his side and loved him like Toni. *If it's war you want, Kenneth, that's what you'll get.* His wife was worth the fight. After he took a couple of sips from the sixth can, he passed out into a deep sleep.

Chapter 54

Kenneth Moore continued to impress me the more we worked together on various projects. We had just covered the evening shift for a colleague who was attending the *Jack the Rapper* music convention in Atlanta, Georgia. And our collaboration went well just as expected.

We had a flow. Kenneth knew his music, old and new. His commentary was sharp, humorous, and witty. And, most important, he displayed good timing. In my eyes, Kenneth was the real deal, a natural talent on the air. For a guy with only a couple years of broadcasting experience, he held his own against a veteran radio personality like me.

My hunch was right. I asked Kenneth to co-host tonight to test our on-air compatibility. After taping the Moja commercial, I got the idea that he may be the perfect addition to my show, something like a sidekick. But I had to find out his aspirations in life.

I switched on a pre-recording until the next DJ took over and then started packing up my gear. The day had been long and I felt it in my muscles. I stood up to stretch out my waist and arms and then went on to rub the back of my neck.

"Sit down," Kenneth said. "Let me help you with that."

"Nah, I'm alright," I said, still trying to get the kinks out myself.

"Toni, don't be so stubborn," he said jokingly. "Seriously, I give great shoulder massages. Just sit down and let me try."

I sat down and gave in. He was right. His strong hands were like magic, as the tension in my body seemed to instantly melt away with every rub. *I could use this every week,* I thought, with my eyes closed and feeling light as air.

"Do you need a ride home, Toni? Or did you say your husband's coming to pick you up?"

His questions snapped me out of la-la land. I sat up in the chair and leaned over to see the clock: 8:54 PM. Marvin was late but I wasn't shocked.

"Yeah, he's supposed to here by now. I don't know where he is. But, don't let me keep you. I'll be alright. Besides, it's a Friday night. I'm sure you have something to do."

"No," he said. "Me and my girl aren't doing much tonight."

"You have a girlfriend?" I asked, surprised, only because he never mentioned her before. "I didn't know that. But then again, there's a lot about you I don't know."

"What do you mean by that?" he snickered, walking over to a chair. "I'm an open book. What do you want to know? C'mon, try me."

"Okay, here's a simple one," I said, facing him. "Do you have any children?"

"Yes. I have a six-year-old son. His name is Micah and he lives with his mother in Tucson, Arizona. That place is too hot for me." He chuckled.

"Oh, that's far, Kenneth." I winced at the thought. "Do you ever get to see him at all?"

"No, not really ever since Tracey got married to a military guy two years ago. But, it's alright. I plan on seeing little man later this summer."

I smiled and nodded.

"Is there anything else you wanna know about me?" he asked with a jovial smirk.

"Actually, there is something I'm curious about," I said. "What plans do you have for your radio career? Have you ever wanted to be on the national level like Walt 'Baby' Love?"

"I never really thought about that," he said. "I mean, I love to DJ, but I'm also passionate about photography. Right now, I'm living the best of both worlds." Kenneth sat down and rolled his chair closer to mine. "Is that what you want—to go national? Because I think you have the personality and talent to do it."

"Absolutely, Kenneth. It's always been my dream to reach the masses through a national radio talk show. I remember when I was a little girl I used to practice my stage voice in the mirror, just like my dad did. That was the only thing my father I had in common: our love for music and entertaining people."

"So, what's holding you back? You could have been out of here a long time ago."

Kenneth's blunt question shot straight to the core of me. It was as though it triggered an instant flashback to all of the disappointments, violence, and sacrifices I went through.

Those were the things that held you back, my mind answered.

"Trust me." I sighed. "If it were only that simple. I've got a husband and kids with a whole lot of responsibility. And then the next thing you know, it's over ten years later."

I shrugged my shoulders and gave a tight-lipped smile. I guess Kenneth saw right through my brave front because he came even closer to me and took my hand.

"Toni." He said my name with great gentleness. "I know I've only known you for a short time. But from where I'm looking, this place is too small for you and your talent. When I see you on stage, in front of a camera, or even with those headphones on, it's like you shine, lady. And I don't care what year it is. If it's a nationwide audience you want, then you need to go for it and give them hell."

A few tears slid down my cheek as I reached over to hug Kenneth. He was the missing piece I wasn't getting from my own husband over the past year: support, warmth, and friendship.

"How did you get so wise, so young?" I whispered in his ear.

"Living, Toni. I've done a lot of living," he whispered back.

Bang! Bang! Bang!

I heard at the window. It was Marvin snarling at the window while banging on the door. "Open this damn door!" he hollered. I hesitated to buzz him in because I knew he had the devil running through his veins.

"Open this door right now, dammit!" he hollered again.

"What's going on?" I heard Travis, the security guard, shouting down the hallway. Marvin kicked in the wooden door and headed straight for Kenneth.

"You've been fucking my wife, boy?" Marvin yelled, jacking Kenneth up by the collar.

"Man, get off me!" Kenneth pushed him away. Travis swooped in and pounced on Marvin right in the nick of time.

"What the hell is wrong with you, Marvin? There's nothing going on between Kenneth and me. You're acting crazy."

"I'm calling the cops," Travis said. His heavy body pinned Marvin to the ground while he handcuffed him.

"Get off me!" Marvin protested.

"No Travis, please don't call the cops on my husband. Please." I begged him.

Travis stared at me, contemplating his next move.

"What about you? Are you alright?" he asked, looking at Kenneth. Kenneth took a glimpse at me and saw the desperation on my face.

"Man, he's nothing," he said angrily.

"Toni, I won't call the police this time, but you better never bring him here again," Travis said, pulling Marvin off the floor easily like a little kid in suspenders.

"But you know I still have to report this incident, right? Look at the damages."

I nodded and took a look around. The door lock was broken, the window had a small crack, and a crate of records was scattered all over the ground. My eyes met Kenneth's. I was so embarrassed. *I'm sorry,* I silently mouthed and left the station in shame.

Chapter 55

As we drove home, Marvin just couldn't leave it alone. He kept ranting on and on about how he knew Kenneth and I were having an affair. I told him he had it wrong, but it seemed like his mind was set only on getting a confession out of me. I let him keep talking and hoped all his squawking would burn up the alcohol in his system and calm him down. He reeked of cigarette smoke and stale liquor. I leaned into the cracked window to catch some fresh air and clarity. The stars were bright. I said a silent prayer: *Please, God, don't let me lose my job.*

Marvin grabbed my arm.

"Are you listening to me?"

"Yes!" I shouted, snatching my arm away. "What do you want me to say?"

"I want the truth. You're fucking him, aren't you?"

"Marvin, why are you so jealous? How many times do I have to tell you? No! We're not having sex! Kenneth is twenty-eight years old with a young girlfriend at home. Why in the world would he want me? Are you hearing yourself?"

"Yeah, right, I've seen the way he's looked at you. Or maybe you want him." Marvin turned into our neighborhood like a maniac and missed the stop sign. Then he turned his attention away from the road and faced me.

"If nothing's going on, then why were you hugging up on him?"

"Marvin, you're scaring me. Slow down and get your eyes on the road."

"Answer my fucking question!" he ordered.

"You wanna know why I was hugging Kenneth? Fine! It was because he was giving me something you haven't in a very long time: love and support."

Marvin accelerated the car.

"This has got to stop, Marvin. Now, please, slow down!" I pleaded and cried.

I could see us getting dangerously closer and closer to the Dead End sign and beyond that, the woods and railroad tracks. I was afraid for my life and thought about my children. The blood in my body felt like it had drained away, breaking me out into a cold chill, and my eyes became wider than all of outside.

Right in front of me, I watched my husband change into a straight-up psycho. He took his hands off the steering wheel, pulled my arm, and started rambling.

"You ain't gonna leave me, Toni. You're mine; God gave you to me. If I have to die or fight for you, then I will."

"Leave you, Marvin?!" I hollered. "What are you talking about?"

As soon as I finished saying those words, I saw the headlights shining brightly on black bold letters. I screamed and gripped my seatbelt. Marvin slammed on the brakes, but it was too late. We had already crashed through the sign and were halfway into the woods.

Chapter 56

"It's my fault." That's what I told everyone: the police, my family and friends. The truth would have only made things much more complicated knowing Marvin crashed us right into a tree. And, by the grace of God, neither one of us was seriously hurt.

After getting over the initial shock and making sure we both were still alive and kicking, we got out of the car to assess the damages. As I looked at the wreckage I couldn't believe I had once again escaped death and my only ailment was a sprain right ankle from pressing down on the floor too hard, as if I had control of the brakes and could stop the car. Marvin walked away free with only a busted lower lip and a sore side.

The car was another story. The front was caved in and far beyond repair for the car's worth. Then suddenly, we heard voices shouting in the dark asking us if we were alright. Apparently, the crash was loud enough to wake up people in a nearby house. I turned toward the sounds and saw flashlights zig-zagging through the trees; they were getting closer to us.

"Hello. Are you alright? Can you hear me?" a man shouted from a distance.

Marvin turned quickly to me.

"Listen to me," Marvin whispered. "I want you to say you were driving, alright?"

"Excuse me!" I exclaimed, giving him a dirty look.

"You want me to take the blame for this shit? If you hadn't been acting like a crazy jealous fool, we wouldn't be in this mess right now."

Marvin blew out a long breath as though I did something wrong, like I was the one who slammed the car into the fucking tree.

"Toni, please, just do as I say," he anxiously begged. "I had a couple of drinks tonight."

"Just a couple?" I snapped.

"Okay, you're right," he admitted, holding his chest. "It was more than a couple. I'm sorry. I'm sorry about everything. But right now, I need you to say you were driving. Just tell them that you mistook the gas petal for the brake, and you lost control of the car. It's that simple. Do you understand?"

I stared at Marvin seething and contemplating what to do.

"Toni, we don't have much time, those people will be here any minute. Do you want to see me in jail? Well, do you?"

I couldn't believe I was here again covering up his shit. But, I knew if I didn't comply, the cops would have hauled his ass off to jail for DUI, and there would be nothing I could do about it. Lord knows he didn't need anything added to his police record.

"Fine," I said, pointing my finger. "But just know you caused all of these problems tonight. You're the one who totaled our only transportation. And you're the one who came on my job acting insane and causing chaos. Do you even care about that?"

The next morning, we told the kids what happened. Adrian was emotional as expected when he saw his mom and dad all bandaged up, but Justine walked away from her half-eaten breakfast seemingly unconcerned. But I knew she had suspicions. When I said the word *accident*, she immediately focused in on the dark bruise on my left arm and rolled her eyes. The bruises looked like finger marks and with Justine being the smart, observant one in the family, I could never get anything past her.

The police gave me a break, because I had a clean driving record and passed a sobriety test. The young cop believed my story and charged me only with a minor moving violation. "You've got the choice of going to court to contest the ticket or pay a small fine," he said. I chose the fine. The bed was where I stayed the rest of the day, thinking and praying.

Marvin got missing. The last words I heard from him were, "I'll get you another car as soon as I can."

Part Four

Chapter 57

Why me, Lord?! I screamed in my head as I limped out of the radio station on crutches. Paul told me it wasn't his call. He had absolutely nothing to do with it. The decision came down swift and directly from the station's owner. *My termination was immediate and final.*

"You really need to get your personal life in check," Paul scolded me like a disappointed teacher. "Because I've heard about your husband's violent ways long before this incident occurred. Why are you letting that man destroy everything you've worked so hard for? You're wasting your talents and opportunities. "

Paul's words hit hard like a kick to the stomach. Not just because he believed in and gave me a chance, it was because I knew he was right. And this job may have been my very last chance at realizing a longtime dream. *Who'd hire me? Where would I go?* There wasn't another black radio station for at least seventy miles over in Orangeburg, SC. It always seemed like the moment I got ahead, trouble came to push me back down. I glanced at my wedding ring.

Why was I still in love with trouble?

I slumped over Brenda's steering wheel crying, thinking about my career, Marvin, and money. *What money?* I was broke. I just agreed to have my last check forfeited to pay for studio damages and keeping that fool out of jail. Then I remembered the two freelance shows I had coming up. *Thank God!* I praised because, at this point, those gigs were my only source of income I had left. Money desperately needed to pay the upcoming rent and feed my family.

I sat up in the car seat and calmed myself. "What are you going to do, Toni?" I asked myself while I gazed into the rear view mirror. I looked bad…really bad. I looked extra tired with bags underneath my eyes and gray hairs peeking out of my scalp. Stress was obviously tearing me down and making me appear older than thirty-nine.

A half-smoked cigarette in the ashtray caught my attention. I promised I wouldn't smoke again. The doctor warned me. I pushed in the car lighter and lit up. *Fuck it!* I thought as I inhaled the cool, soothing nicotine. *Who keeps promises anyway?*

Chapter 58

I arrived home about an hour later to find Marvin in bed watching television on an early Monday morning. The sight of him lounging made my blood pressure rise all over again. *How can you search for a job lying in bed all day?* I said in my head, snatching off clothes and stumping around the bedroom. I could feel Marvin's eyes following me.

"What's wrong with you?" he asked sharply. I ignored him while trying hard to simmer down. This was one of those times I couldn't speak a word when angry.

"Toni, I asked you a question."

I wanted him to shut up. The sound of his belittling voice irritated every nerve in my body. Who was he to question me like a child? Deeply I breathed in. I closed my eyes, tilted my head back, and kept up the silent treatment until I was ready to talk. But then I heard him ask, "Why are you home anyway?"

That was it!

I turned around and gave him a fierce wide-eyed stare. "I got fired!" I said through tight lips. "That's why I'm home. You got me fired!"

Marvin bolted out of the bed and hovered within arm's length of my face. "What do you mean I got you fired?" he asked, using a sarcastic tone.

"Really Marvin, you've got to be either crazy or drunk to ask me a stupid-ass question like that. Just get out of my face," I said, pushing him away.

"You're trying me, Toni," he warned, straining his eyes and flaring his nostrils.

"What's that supposed to mean, Marvin? I yelled back with tears trickling down my cheeks. "What are you gonna do? What more can you do to me? I've got nothing!"

I hung my head low, feeling the heavy burden of worry and defeat crashing in on me. *How are we going to live? What am I going to do now?*

Marvin stepped forward. "Toni, I know you're upset," he softly said, then placed a hand on my shoulder. "But—"

Smack!

I slapped him hard. A sudden rage came over me the moment he touched my skin. I fixed my gaze on him and watched raw anger wash over his face. I knew it was coming; I'd seen that look before. Marvin quickly grabbed my arms and jacked me up against the dresser.

"Is this what you want?" he seethed, squeezing my arms tightly.

"You're hurting me!" I hollered.

"I saw my wife wrapped up in the arms of another man!" he exclaimed. "Now tell me, who the fuck would blame me for being pissed off?" He slapped my face, threw me onto the bed, and straddled my waist.

"Tell me!" he repeatedly demanded with every lash.

"Stop it!" I screamed, trying hard to fight back.

When Marvin finally tired out, I looked up into his damp strained eyes and felt my cheek. Whelps were forming and stung with every teardrop that trailed by.

"I'm tired, Marvin," I gathered the strength and courage to say. "I'm tired of fighting and living like this."

Marvin climbed off me and headed for the closet. He pulled out a large green duffel bag.

"You're tired!" he said, beginning to stuff his bag with clothes. "Well, I'm tired too. I'm tired of being treated like a child and wondering if my wife is fucking another man. You have no idea how hard it's been for me. No job. No prospects. And now I have to watch you spend more and more time down at that radio station with a younger man. So, if you're tired of me or if you don't love me anymore, then I should just leave."

I sat on the edge of the bed and listened to Marvin's bullshit. How could he question my love, my loyalty after all I've done for him? And after all I've tolerated? He couldn't name one damn person who'd supported him more. I remained silent while he packed knowing deep down, I didn't want him to go. But I needed peace of mind and space to be alone. Maybe this was for the best.

Chapter 59

Harold Jones grumpily peered at his son through an old, dirty screen door while balancing on a black walking cane. "I knew it," he said in a low husky voice as he unlatched the lock. He violently coughed twice then turned around and started shuffling his feet toward the couch to sit and retrieve his oxygen mask.

He was a thin, decrepit looking man at the age of sixty-six with a permanent frown on his light brown face. He had a medium-sized white afro and loved to wear his worn-out Budweiser trucker hat on his head every day. Harold lived alone. Ever since his second wife died on him, as he called it, eight years ago from complications of diabetes, he stayed mostly to himself with the exception of hobbling out a few times a week to play the numbers at the corner store or find a neighborhood prostitute willing to blow him off. Harold grew extra callous over time being widowed and learned to enjoy his solitude. He felt he didn't need anyone and stubbornly nursed his failing health with fried gizzards, pork rinds, beer, and an occasional cigarette.

Marvin closed the creaking screen door and stepped into the living room with his bag strapped across his back. "Hello, Dad," he said, sounding dismal.

"Don't you 'hello' me, boy," his father said, taking in a deep breath. "I told you not to go back to that woman. Now look atcha. You're a homeless grown man with his tail tucked between his legs. You're a crying shame. That's what you are."

Harold raised the oxygen mask to his face again and dragged in air while Marvin dropped his bag next to a shabby love seat and sat down. Marvin looked around. The room looked just like it did right before his stepmother Pearl passed away. Like his father, the musty house was stuck in a decaying time capsule. No cleaning had been done or any updates made. The ragged living room furniture had either holes in the fabric or brown stains. The paint on the wall had chips and there were spider webs and dust collecting everywhere.

"So how long are you staying?" Harold asked.

"I'm not sure. I just need time to get my head clear."

"Getcha head clear about what, boy?" He took in two breaths. "I'll tell ya whatcha need to do. You need to get out there and find yourself a good simple woman. Someone who wants to be home cooking and cleaning, she doesn't have to be pretty...pretty gets your ass in trouble."

For years Marvin's relationship with his father had been estranged. They would talk on the phone and look out for each other, but Marvin would seldom come to visit. There were just too many unpleasant memories to fight off. Harold provided his son with food and shelter but alienated his child from love and affection. He was strict on Marvin during his impressionable years and often criticized him. That's why Marvin left home at an early age. But he often wondered if his father's hardness toward him spawned from the hatred he had for his mother.

"I've already got a wife, Dad. I just needed to leave to let out steam. I'll get her back."

"Get her back!" Harold exclaimed, grabbing his mask and taking a hit. "You stupid fool. Don't you remember her family tried to get your ass locked up a few years ago? And now you're begging for more trouble. I told you not to marry that damn DJ girl. She's just like Lucille, always in the club singing and frolicking around."

"Hold on, Dad," Marvin said sharply. "You're talking about my wife, the mother of my only child. And she's nothing like Mother," he declared, giving his father a scowling stare.

Harold snatched up his mask and breathed in heavily with his eyes bulging. He caught his wind and started to stutter angrily. "Don't. Don't. Don't you sass me, boy, in my own house!" he said, lifting the mask once again for a quick fix. "I know what I'm talking about. I know an untrained bitch when I see one."

Marvin shot up and headed straight to the front door for a walk outside to cool off. His father's acid tongue never failed to make his blood boil and reminded him why he left home a long time ago. In a flash, an evil thought came across his mind. *You could do it again, Marvin. You could just snap the old bastard's feeble neck and finally put a muzzle on his goddamn mouth. The end!*

"Where in the hell are you going?" he heard his father ask behind him.

"To the store," he replied with his hand on the knob.

"Well, make yourself useful and bring me back a can of beer."

Chapter 60

On the last week of June, I found myself packing up and starting all over again. With no money coming in, I had to move on. Mrs. Fowler, the landlord, was sympathetic to my situation and allowed the lease to be broken without paying next month's rent. Apparently, she had a soft spot for single mothers.

"Keep the money," she said warmly over the telephone. "I remember what it was like being alone with a child to feed before I met my late husband."

I appreciated the old woman's help and dropped a thank-you card in the mailbox before pulling off in a blue 1980 Datsun sedan Charles Jr. had bought from a junk yard for $500 then fixed up for me. Somehow help seemed easier to come by when the family learned Marvin moved out.

Now, we were heading to the new house in Ladson, just a skip, hop, and a jump from the old neighborhood in Summerville. Mary Davis, a contact at the Charleston County Housing Authority, was able to get us a government-assisted house in a quiet subdivision located near good schools. I felt guilty for the many changes and uprooting the kids all over again. Adrian was going into the first grade in the coming fall, and Justine would be starting high school. But we needed assistance and at least I knew their education wouldn't suffer.

And as for Marvin, I hadn't seen or heard from him in weeks. Word on the street was he staying with his mean, salty-dog father. That was no concern of mine. Actually, I didn't even miss him as much as I thought I would. I enjoyed the peace and quiet and sleeping alone. Time long needed to get over my anger and focus on my priorities. But I knew his ass wasn't gone for good. He'd show his face soon enough. And when that day came, three big boxes of his stuff would be waiting for him in the garage.

I pulled into the driveway amazed. The yard looked nicer than it did when I drove by last week. The grass was freshly cut and hedges were trimmed. I never had a thing for gardening, but I could see myself wearing a floppy sun hat planting flowers here and there and mowing the lawn just to keep the yard work up.

I looked at the hardwood front door and imagined what was behind it. Up until now, I only had a description of the house's interior. According to Mrs. Davis, it was a very nice property that would go fast unless I moved on it. "You snooze, you lose with this one," she'd whimsically said over the telephone. I trusted her word and signed up blindly.

"This is our house?" I heard Adrian ask Justine in a whisper.

We got out of the car with bags in tow. Charles and some of his buddies weren't far behind with a truck filled with our furniture. "Well, kids, this is home," I said as I unlocked the door and pushed my way inside for the very first time.

"Ooh! Look, Justine," Adrian said excitedly. "The refrigerator has an ice maker." It didn't take much to impress a five-year-old, but a teenager was another story.

"That's nice," she replied nonchalantly, her arms folded over.

"Well, do you like the house, Justine?" I asked.

"It's nice," she quickly answered, then walked off saying, "Just hope we get to stay here."

I shifted my eyes away and let her comment roll off my back. Just for today. Today, we had too much to get done. But I knew she still had something against me. We barely spoke. She did her chores. She got good grades and never caused any problems. It was like Justine did everything almost perfectly so she could avoid her own mama.

"The backyard is huge!" Adrian shouted. "Mama, can we get a dog now?"

The boy had it right. The house was a dream compared to the older one we just left behind. Our new home came with three spacious bedrooms, brand new carpet throughout, updated kitchen appliances, and a fireplace in the living room. Even the master bedroom had its own full bathroom. *You really came through for us, Mary.* If it weren't for the housing program covering the rent and getting food stamps, I could never afford a place like this.

As I continued to look around and sort furniture in my head, memories of how Marvin and I used to live started to replay in my mind. Memories of a nice home and nice things; memories the children were way too young to remember. I bowed my head and raised my arms high to the ceiling to thank God for the blessing, because now my children had the opportunity to live in a beautiful home and not a run-down, cramped apartment in the projects.

Chapter 61

The mailman stood at the front door with a large package in hand. It was decorated with international stamps, and the name on it read: *Miss Justine Lynn Taylor* in bold black letters. It was from Lewis. The long-awaited mail she had been looking for since April had finally arrived. The same package she worried wouldn't get forwarded from our previous address. But it did. "Thank you," I told the man as I closed the door.

It was early August and not much had changed. I still didn't have a job or a single clue about what I was going to do with the rest of my life. My radio dreams were so shot to hell, I convinced myself to let them go just to keep sane. Something I thought I'd never do. But, the way I saw it, no ambition in life meant no disappointment. And I found that idea comforting like a warm blanket.

Some days I stayed in bed feeling numb, feeling sorry for myself and not wanting to face the world or even wash. And forget about applying for jobs. I gave up. I just got tired of being rejected from low-paying positions like a cashier or a waitress. But that's how living on Section 8 worked. I could have a job. But the moment my income crept back to the poverty line, financial assistance would stop–making me responsible for the rent or lose the property altogether. Forever stuck between the prospect of a low-income job and welfare. So I decided to play the game, take advantage, and not do too much. My kids were worth it and got the best part of the deal. They had a nice house to live in and were going to good schools. Besides, my life had no sense of direction. And if I had to give up free money to take on a normal 9 to 5, it was not going to be for a minimum wage job.

I walked into the living room where Justine was and handed over the package.

"What's this?" she asked.

"It's from your father."

Justine took the package and walked off down the hallway toward her bedroom. Apparently she wanted to open her mail in private and try to hide her emotions. But I knew better. Her typical cold demeanor was just a façade, because the moment I mentioned her father, I saw excitement flash across her eyes and face.

I waited a few minutes before entering her bedroom. Truth be told, I was hoping Lewis had sent some money and Justine would be willing to share. Things were that tight. So tight, I found myself visiting the bingo halls more at night, gambling and praying to God for luck. I played so much that the tips of two of my fingers became permanently stained green from a bingo marker.

"So, what did your father send?"

"This," she said, holding up a T-shirt with *1992 Olympics Barcelona* written on it. Whatever happiness she experienced was long gone by the time I got into the room.

"What's with the long face?" I asked. "You don't like the shirt?"

"It's okay," she said, straightforwardly. "He also sent me this."

Justine handed over a card. Inside was a check in the amount of $300. Now I understood the reason behind her sour look. I knew she was going to be stingy. *Time to put on my boxing gloves* rang in my head.

"This is a lot of money, Justine! I need you to give me half of this."

"Half?!" she snapped.

"Yes, half!" I returned the attitude. "And you better watch your tone, girl. How else are we going to pay the utility bills around here? You know I don't have a job right now."

"Yes, I know that, but I'm trying to save," she said.

"Trying to save for what, Justine?" I chuckled a little. "What bills could you possibly have at your age that are so pressing?"

"College," she replied, looking distressed. "I'm trying to save up for college."

"And this is why you're giving me an attitude? College? Child, that's more than four years away. I'm talking about issues that are affecting us in the here and now. And you're talking about college. Girl, when will you learn? Stop putting the weight of the world on your shoulders. You're only thirteen and a half years old."

I rolled my eyes and shook my head listening to her unnecessary worrying. "Stop being selfish, Justine. Put on your shoes and let's go cash this check."

"Selfish!" she repeated, giving me a shocked stare. "How can I be selfish when I always give you money, whether it comes from my weekend job or my father? And all you do is take it to bingo and gamble it all away. Just once I would like to keep my own money."

Justine folded her arms and let her pent-up tears stream down her face like a broken dam. I didn't care and gave her an angry gaze. Justine needed a serious reality check.

"You listen to me, Miss Little Rich Bitch! I go to that bingo hall to put food in your belly, to put clothes on your back, and to keep the lights on over your head."

"But you rarely win, Mama. It's just money going down the drain," she sobbed. "And I didn't ask to be born!"

"What did you say?" I yelled in a rage. Before I knew it, I slapped Justine right across the face, sending her tail straight to the floor.

"You ungrateful bitch!" I hollered, looking down at her. "I may not be the perfect mother, but I try. And as long as I am your mother and you live under my roof, you will respect me, young lady. Now get up and let's go."

Chapter 62

Justine had an escape plan as long as she could remember. Like a mantra, she repeated it over and over every day: *I can't wait to go to college. I can't wait to go to college.* For her, getting an education far away from home meant everything. Freedom from a toxic life and distance from a mother she'd come to resent for years.

She remembered it all: the good memories, but mainly the bad ones. The bad memories were strong. They lingered and hurt the most. Even at a young age, Justine remembered the fights, the loud arguments, and the constant moving around. And worst, she remembered the night her mother got stabbed. She saw the blood on the floor, heard the groans, and saw her stepfather hovering over her mother. No one ever asked her if she saw anything. No one knew how she found the courage to leave the closet and take a peek.

That night traumatized Justine deeply. She never told her mother about the nightmares or the anxiety she felt every time Marvin got angry or too close to her. *Why bother? Mama always takes him back. She'll always choose him first over me.* This was her firm belief. And although she still loved her mother in her own way, Justine felt her mother was selfish, irresponsible, weak-minded, and crazy to stay with Marvin. That's why she had a plan. She believed God gave her the wisdom and strength to save herself.

Step One: Get good grades.

Step Two: Stay out of trouble.

Step Three: Get into college by any means necessary. Never look back!

Justine came back from cashing her check and locked herself away in her bedroom. It was her sanctuary. A clean, organized space for her to think and get way from the chaos she couldn't control outside of her four walls. She went to her secret place underneath the bottom dresser drawer and pulled out an oversized envelope. She added $150 to the thick stack. Six hundred and twenty-seven dollars she counted in total. Money well saved over the years from everything and anything: father, job, birthdays, holidays, etc.

Justine learned to be resourceful, like getting a cash-paid summer weekend job at the flea market selling all kinds of memorabilia from Bart Simpson T-shirts to baseball caps. She refused to be broke or be a burden to her mother and vowed not to live a life of unnecessary struggle and pain.

She caught a glimpse of her bruised face in the mirror. "Don't you dare cry again," she whispered. Her left cheek and part of her lip were swollen. Mother had never hit her so hard. *If I could only talk to my father,* she angrily thought.

If Justine had her father's telephone number, she would beg him to let her live with him. She would tell him about everything. The violence, the struggles, and how her mother always took her money to gamble and in the past, give it to Marvin. But Justine knew better. She knew her father's busy schedule and location would keep him from saying yes. She didn't even have a passport. For now, Justine would have to suck it up and stick with to the original plan.

Chapter 63

An older dark green Oldsmobile I didn't recognize crept up into the driveway. I pulled back the curtains in the kitchen to get a better look. It was Marvin. I knew sooner or later I would have to face him. He knocked on the door and with hesitation, I opened it.

"What are you doing here, Marvin?"

"Well, that's a nice way to greet your husband." He grinned.

Marvin stood before me well groomed and with a box of chocolates and flowers in his hands. His beard was gone and his clothes were pressed off. He looked good.

"Are you gonna let me in, Toni?" he asked, smiling.

I gave him a blank stare for a few seconds knowing what was coming next. "I guess so," I replied. He came in the living room and took a look around.

"Toni, this is nice." He bobbed his head. "Looks like you're doing well."

I flashed him a shallow smile and folded my arms over. Then the room went silent, uncomfortably silent. I couldn't take it anymore. I wanted him to get to the point.

"Marvin, why are you here? And how did you find us?"

"C'mon Toni." He smiled again. "It wasn't hard to find you. Surely, you don't believe I'm going to be completely out of your life? We do have a son together."

"Fine," I said. "But since you're here, your clothes are packed up in the garage."

"C'mon, Toni. Don't be so cold. I'm here to see my boy, but I also want to talk to you."

"Talk to me?"

"Yes," he said, extending the box and bouquet of flowers to me. "These are for you."

I took the flowers already in a vase with water and placed it on the coffee table next to the candy. "So, go ahead, Marvin. Talk. But make it quick, because I've got things to do."

Marvin let out a breath and sat down on the couch. "Toni, I know things haven't been good between us, but I am here to man up and apologize for what I've done. In one night I fucked up everything you've worked so hard to achieve, and you don't know how much I regret that."

"Marvin." I stopped him. "You didn't just fuck up my job; you destroyed me. You destroyed my dreams."

Marvin came in closer and put his hand on my thigh. "Toni, I know I did. Just hear me out. I can't get your job back, but I want to spend the rest of my life making it up to you. No more jealousy issues. No more drinking. I'm totally devoted to you. Listen, I've been thinking. Why do we have to stay here? We can move to another state or town and find you a new radio station to work at. Your talent is bigger than Charleston. Didn't you tell me before you wanted to move to Atlanta…or was it Texas? "

Marvin paused and started gazing into my watery eyes. The thought of revitalizing my career and maybe even my family brought me to tears. I really gave up when I lost my job. It had been so long since I heard hopeful words that his positive outlook overwhelmed me.

"Look," he said, pulling a wad of money out of his pocket. "I've been working and saving. And I even have a car now. It's not brand spanking new, but it runs good. Toni, baby, I love you. There's nobody else out there for me. And I know you still love me too. So, please, let me come home. Let's start over."

Marvin started to rub my thigh while giving me a longing stare. He was right. I still loved him. He always had some sort of hold on me even through the worst of times. It would be such a lie to say I didn't miss him, especially at night. The night was when I missed him the most, lying alone in bed needing to be touched. No one satisfied me like

Marvin; he knew exactly how to please me. But could I trust him to keep his word this time?

"Daddy!" Adrian cried out, snapping me out of my erotic thoughts. "Where have you been? Are you home for good?"

"I don't know." Marvin shrugged. "You're going to have to ask your mother that. Now, come over here and give me a big hug and kiss. I've missed you, boy."

Watching Adrian's reaction only added to my stress. I had no idea what I was going to do.

"Hey, Mama…" Justine said and then suddenly stopped halfway down the hall. It was like she saw a ghost.

"What is he doing here?" she blurted out.

"Well, he's here to see us. And where's your manners, young lady? Aren't you going to say good morning?"

"Good morning, Justine," Marvin said. "How are you doing?"

Justine didn't answer. She just stood there like a deer in headlights.

"Justine, did you hear Marvin ask you a question?" I asked, walking toward her.

"It's alright, Toni. She's just surprised to see me. I've been gone for two months."

"Nah, that's not it," I turned around and said to Marvin. "You see, Justine has a chip on her shoulder. Her attitude has been getting really nasty lately, and she thinks she's grown enough to say whatever she wants. And it's pissing me off!" I returned my attention back to Justine and hovered close in her face.

"Are you going to answer my question or do I have to beat your ass this morning?"

"You're going to let him come back, aren't you?" she asked, shaking her head. "I knew it. I knew you would let him come back."

"What I decide to do in my house is none of your business. You don't run anything around here, little girl. I'm the mother."

"I know I don't run anything, Mama. But everything you do affects me. And I can't take it anymore. I just can't."

"Can't take what? What the hell do you have to worry about?"

Justine narrowed her wet eyes at me and took a deep breath like she was trying to muster up courage to say something. "Can't you see, Mama? He's going to kill you someday. If you take him back, you won't live to see the age of forty. I can't take this. I want to live with my father."

"You know, Justine," I said waving my finger in her face, "I'm just about tired of your disrespectful, grown-ass mouth."

"Toni, don't. Just leave it alone," I faintly heard Marvin say in the background.

"No Marvin, she needs to hear this," I said without taking my eyes off Justine. "If you want to leave, child, then go. But let me tell you about your father. He's shit. He might give you pretty things and a little bit of money, but he comes and goes. Tell me something: Can you contact your daddy right now? Do you even have a telephone number for him? Lewis cares only about Lewis. And eventually, he's gonna forget about you just like he forgot about me."

In that moment, I saw pure anger in my child's glazed-over eyes. Tears started to fall. She despised me.

"My father will never forget about me," she yelled. "And if you wanted me to have a better father, then you should have slept with a better man."

I couldn't believe what I heard. Anger surged through my body like electricity running through wires. Three times I hit her hard, hard enough to make her mouth bleed. She staggered a little, but regained her balance and stood firm looking like she wanted to hit me back.

"C'mon, bitch!" I dared her with my fist in position.

"No, Mama, please stop!" Adrian cried.

Justine touched her jaw and saw blood on her hand. She shook her head as tears shed and with a trembling voice said, "You can fight me, but you can't fight him. You two are just alike."

Her words instantly snatched me out of my wrath. I stepped back and took a look at the fear and busted lip on my child's face. I wasn't aware of my own strength. But I refused to apologize. How dare she disrespect Marvin and me? After all, he was the only father figure she knew before Lewis came into the picture.

"Justine, you will not understand the conviction of a wife to keep her husband until you get married. You're just too young to understand right now."

"No Mama, I will never understand, because I'm never going to be like you. I hate men! I hate him and I hate you!" Justine ran off to her bedroom sobbing.

"That's okay," I yelled down the hallway, "You don't have to like me. And if you live long enough to have children of your own, do better than me. That's what you do. Do better than me!"

Chapter 64

A temporary part-time job came along right on time to get me out the house. Justine and I were not on good terms and Marvin moving back in made the situation even worse. Tension was everywhere, and I needed a break.

Before allowing Marvin to come back, I took time to consider what Justine said. Was he really changed? Was he worth my family being upset with me again? But, it had been over a few weeks and he still seemed to be making an effort to doing right. And most importantly, the money he brought in from his salvage yard job paid the bills, and I didn't have to ask Miss Taylor for a damn thing.

"Excuse me, ma'am," I said, walking up to an older white woman passing by my booth in Walmart. "May I ask you some questions regarding the television shows you watch?"

And that's what I was doing these days. I took a job as a media researcher for Dyson Communications. The title sounded fancy but for $7.15 an hour, all I did was survey people to help the company calculate television ratings. The pay wasn't ideal, but at least I got to interact with the public.

"No, hun," the woman politely answered, "I really don't have time today."

I returned to my seat and took off my pumps to rub my aching feet. I still hadn't gotten used to standing around. Funny thing—although the position didn't pay much, the company expected employees to project a professional image at all times. And that meant looking like you were salaried and maybe had a company car.

"Wanda Hamilton! Is that you?"

I knew who it was before I looked up, Rachel Spencer. I forgot. I never told her my real name.

"I knew it was you," she said with a 100-watt smile. "Give me a hug, girl."

Rachel placed her thin arms around me and squeezed tightly for a few seconds then pulled away, still maintaining her signature bright smile.

"My goodness," she continued. "Don't you know it's been practically a year since I've seen you, and I'm still waiting on your phone call." Rachel wagged her finger at me and chuckled. "So, how's it going? I see you're working?"

"Yeah, I work here and things are going well. You still look good," I said, still amazed at Rachel's ability to maintain such a huge weight loss. And her short Demi Moore haircut really fit her oval-shape face.

"You know, Wanda, you crossed my mind the other day."

"Oh, really?" I said.

"Yes," she replied. "Do you remember me telling you that I volunteer at a women's shelter? Well, it's called Safe Haven, and they are in desperate need of volunteer peer counselors. These counselors are women who were once in abusive relationships but got help. And after taking a short training course, they come in to listen, share their personal stories, and maybe influence another woman in crisis along the way. Wanda, you've already been through counseling. I thought who better than you to take on one of those positions? But I didn't have your telephone number to reach you. And look, out to of the blue, here you are. See. I told you before, there are no coincidences."

"Yeah, well…." I sighed. "I hate to disappoint you, Rachel, but I don't think I can. I've got a lot going on in my life right now and I don't think I can inspire anyone."

Rachel gave me a displeased look and pulled a card out of her purse. "Wanda, don't give me a fast no. Please, just think about it. Here's my phone number. You're such a nurturer. I believe you could do so much good with these ladies and maybe you'll get something out of it too. Look sweetie, I've got to go. But, again, just think about it. And dang it, call me sometime."

After a hug and kiss on the cheek, Rachel quickly walked off and faded into the crowd. I took a glance at her business card and for some reason I didn't throw it away this time.

Chapter 65

Daddy lost his battle with Alzheimer on a dreary Wednesday morning. I remembered it rained long and hard. They said it was sudden but expected. But, for me, the news of his death was still a shock. It seemed like an era had abruptly ended. Before the disease took over, daddy had a personality that was larger than life and would make you foolishly believe he could live forever. But it really happened. Charles Tony Williams, the giant, had fallen.

There were more people at the repass than at the funeral. That was typical when it came to funerals around here. People will miss a long eulogy but never a free meal. The house was packed and alive with family and friends, the sounds of clinking pots and pans, laughter, and tossed-around stories. There were no outbursts of grief or tears flowing from anyone. Except for Stephanie; she took it hard.

At the funeral, she screamed, hollered, and draped herself over Daddy's casket as though she were in a Broadway play while everyone else calmly looked on. But we all understood Stephanie's reaction. After all, she was

Daddy's spoiled baby girl. Out of all of us, I saw her as the fortunate one. She had no painful childhood memories to deal with. Making it easier to grieve for a father you never knew in his fighting days.

Not everybody thought Charles Sr. was a bastard straight out of Charleston County. Actually, a lot of folks liked him for his charisma, talents, and sharp wit. But the man could be mean and had an explosive temper, and everyone knew about it. Just like everyone knew about the years of violence that plagued our home. Most of those who showed up to his funeral came to support Mama. We all knew she was the glue that kept this family together.

I started to maneuver through a crowd of black attire with polite gestures to others along the way to find Mama. It had been several hours since I'd last saw her pick up a fork to eat or take a breather. Last night, all she did was cook, clean, and worry about everybody else. I guess that was her way of mourning and keeping her head clear because, back at the church, I never saw her show any emotion or drop a single tear.

"Toni, are you going to see if Mama is ready to eat?" Thelma shouted behind me from the living room.

I turned around. "Yeah, that's what I'm trying to do right now."

Thelma and I had been back on speaking terms for several months but really came together the day Daddy passed away. We cried and forgave in each other's arms after viewing the body, realizing that life is short and death only cheats us from making peace by saying I'm sorry and I love you. Despite our life choices and differences, we were sisters first. I walked out of the kitchen into the dining room and ran into Sister Lula Mae. She pulled me aside.

"How are you holding up, honey?" she asked.

"I'm doing fine. How are you?"

"Oh, I am blessed, child. The Father woke me up this morning with praise in my heart. But, let me ask you something," she said with a curious expression and peering right into me. "How are your children and husband doing these days?"

"They're just fine, Sister Lu. Thank you for asking. Have you seen my mother?"

"Oh, yes. I just left her. She's in her bedroom." Sister Lula Mae placed her hand on my shoulder. "Now listen to me good, child. If you ever need me, don't ever hesitate to call. Because you know I'll be there. I'm going to pray for you."

"Yes ma'am," I said, flashing a half smile.

I knew she was talking about Marvin moving back in with me. No doubt Mama told her all of my business. That was the very reason why I asked Marvin to stay home. I'd rather deal with all of the judgmental stares, comments, and whispers on my own. I knocked on the door before entering. Mama was sitting on the edge of the bed looking at an old black and white photograph of her and Daddy.

"Mama, are you hungry? Would you like me to fix you a plate of something?"

"Oh no, baby." She smiled. "I'll get something later. Come over here and sit with me for a while." She placed the picture in my hand. It was the first time I had ever seen it. Mother looked beautiful and tiny in her V-neck summer dress and pinned up hair with a flower in it.

"Wow, Mama. You had it going on back then," I said.

"Yeah, that was taken a very long time ago. Maybe from the first or second year your father and I were married. We were so happy and in love during that time." Mama shook her head and sighed. "I wish we had more years like that."

For the first time in who knows when, Mama let her guard down and started crying softly. I reached my arms out to embrace her, feeling unsure about what to say. After all, I had my own confused sentiments toward Daddy. The entire day I felt somewhat numb and divided. My father was the person I loved, feared, and looked up to for musical inspiration, but I despised the way he treated Mama. Sometimes I wish I had the nerve to confront him back in the day or even when his health started to fail. During those sick years, I could have easily shared my feelings and not worry about him hauling off to hit me. And sure, I knew he wouldn't have been able to grasp or respond to anything I'd say but, at least, I would have vented my pain to his vacant, emotionless face. But, now, it's too late to say anything. I guess I never really stopped to think about him actually dying, and I never took the chance to properly say goodbye.

Mama pulled away and looked at me with sad eyes. "Toni, I'm alright. I'm not crying over your father. Right now, I'm just worried about you."

"About me? Why?" I asked, puzzled by her concern.

"I'm worried about that husband of yours killing you. Toni, why did you let Marvin move back in? Why would you do something so stupid like that?"

"Mama, please, I don't want to talk about this right now. Not today, okay?"

"Honey, you don't have to talk," she said softly, "Just listen to me because I don't want you to make the same mistake I did. I loved your father. And I will never regret the children we made together. But, if I had the chance to leave him, I would have taken it long ago."

I turned to Mama and gave her a surprised look.

"Yes, child. You seemed shocked, but it's the truth. You've got to understand something. Back in my time, women didn't have much support against abusive husbands. We were trained to take it for the sake of the marriage and the children. I couldn't leave. How would I support myself and feed my children? But, today, there's help out there. I just can't understand why you won't go after it."

Mama got up to put the picture in the drawer while I used my sleeve to dry my face. I'd never heard her speak so openly about her feelings and Daddy. She stood next to the dresser and continued to talk.

"Looking back on it all, I wasted a whole lot of years waiting on happiness and a peace of mind thinking your father was going change. But, he never did." Mama chuckled a little bit and shook her head.

"Seems kinda unfair when you think about it, doesn't it, Toni? He comes down with Alzheimer's disease and leaves this world not remembering a thing he did to me."

Our eyes met and we gave each other brief smiles. Mama shook her head again.

"Now, look at you girls. You've all been attacked by men and it's my fault. I've failed you all as a mother. Sometimes I think about the past when y'all used to watch me get beaten up and go through so much hell with your father. I wonder, did I teach you girls to do the same thing...just take it?"

"No Mama," I jumped in. "Please, don't punish yourself thinking like that. We are grown women. You didn't choose our men for us."

"Well, that may be the case, baby, but I'm sure I influenced y'all to stick it out. If there's anything useful you could learn from me, it's this: I lived under your father's violent hands for over thirty years. I had to endure so much with his constant mood swings and skirt chasing…. *My Lord.*" Mama waved her hand in the air as she glanced at the ceiling. She looked at me again.

"That doesn't have to be for you, Toni. *God* put it in my heart to tell you this. You are strong enough to make it on your own. And if you really need a man, wait on Him to put the right one in your path. No mother should ever have to see her child in a casket."

Chapter 66

Rachel seemed more baffled than shocked sitting across from me at the Meeting Street Diner in downtown Charleston. I just told her my real name. Her signature beaming smile was replaced with raised eyebrows and a serious stare.

"I'm sorry I lied to you, Rachel."

"That's what I don't get," she said, still looking confused. "Why lie about your name?"

"I guess embarrassment and too much pride," I answered. "I was embarrassed to be at My Daughter's House back then. And I was even more embarrassed to run into you last year when I knew things weren't so great at home. I'm not as strong as you think...."

I called up Rachel two days ago after having that heavy conversation with Mama. It had me really thinking. Was my marriage to Marvin worth saving and secondly, was it worth losing my daughter over? Justine and I were still not on speaking terms. At the funeral, she sat next to Thelma and barely made eye contact with me. She took care to be respectful and did what she was told. But there was no love or warmth from her. She seemed like an empty shell. I think moving Marvin back in the house made me lose Justine's trust forever.

In hindsight, maybe Mama was right. Maybe I did learn how to tolerate abuse from her. But, I'd never tell her that. She had too many regrets to live with already.

Like Mama said the other day, too many times she had to put up with Daddy's beatdowns. I can remember the smallest thing sending his temper soaring. Even when the bastard knew he was wrong. Just like that time when one of his side chicks boldly showed up at our house with a bowl of soup claiming she'd heard he was seriously sick with the flu. It was a lie, of course. Daddy was as healthy as an ox. And when he returned from the streets, Mama confronted him about the woman and threw that bowl of soup right at him. That night, Daddy whipped Mama so hard, she never asked about his women again.

I no longer wanted to waste my years on fights and lose the respect of my children. I knew what I had to do. But I couldn't do two hard things in the same week, bury my father, and give up the only man I'd loved for so long. Leaving Marvin would take time and that's why I called Rachel. I needed support and come clean about who I was.

"Wow, you are in a difficult position. But before we go any further, I've got a question for you," she said, grinning again. "Is there anything else you're hiding? I mean, you're not going to tell me you're really a man or something?" Rachel began to laugh out loud. It was catching and satisfying. I had no idea how badly I needed that comic relief to ease my tension.

"Listen, Toni." Rachel smiled saying my real name for the first time. "The name may be different, but the story remains the same, right?"

"Right," I answered.

"So all jokes aside, seriously, what's your plan for Marvin?"

I shrugged my shoulders. "I don't know. He's been on his best behavior, and we've been getting along. But deep down, I'm just waiting for him to snap."

"Well, why wait for him to snap? Get rid of his ass now!" she exclaimed.

"I know, Rachel. But it's much harder for me than you think. It's going to take some time to finally get him out my life."

"Toni, you don't have to tell me how hard it is. I've done this before, remember?" She sighed. "So anyway, this is what I think you should do. I think you should join a therapy group at Safe Haven. Let us help you find confidence about your decision to divorce your husband."

And there it was. Strange to hear someone else say it out loud. But there it was. I decided to divorce Marvin. And I wouldn't tell another soul for now.

"Toni!" Rachel called out, trying to break my trance. "Did you hear me? Are you going to participate?"

I blinked when her voice finally caught my attention. "Group therapy, I don't know about that." I shrugged. "I'm a very private person. And I have kids. Do I have to stay there to join?"

"No, woman. You don't have to live there to talk. All you need to do is show up and be honest. If it makes you feel better, don't give them your name. Just be honest with your story. So, C'mon, Toni. Are you going to do this or not?"

I looked at the intensity on Rachel's face and knew she wasn't taking no for an answer. Not after I told her my business.

"I'll try Rachel; I really will."

"That's all I'm asking, hun." She smiled then winked.

I gave Rachel a good look over. Seemingly, she had it all together with her appearance, career, and commitment to helping others. But she was still young at thirty, and no one can live life alone. I leaned in and couldn't resist.

"So, how's your love life these days?" I asked, curiously grinning.

Rachel appeared slightly stunned by the question and gave a half-smile like maybe I stepped over the line.

"I've been dating, but not much," she answered with a blasé attitude. "I'm taking my time. Besides, I've got my gym and my dog to keep me busy."

"Do you think you'll ever marry again?"

"I'm not sure." She shrugged. "But, I'll tell this much. After dealing with someone like Ricky, I've promised myself the next serious relationship I get into, he's got to be worthy. I mean something special for me to go back down that aisle."

"You are serious, aren't you?" I shook my head and chuckled at the same time.

Rachel folded her arms over. "Like a freakin' heart attack."

Chapter 67

He could never get used to it, that damn pungent smell lingering in the hallway at the coroner's office. Jack had been an experienced homicide detective in Clarendon County, South Carolina for twelve years, but the odors from chemicals and decomposing bodies almost always made his stomach churn at every visit. He walked in the morgue with his neck tie loosened and long sleeves rolled up. Jack appeared tired as if he'd just pulled an all-nighter with stubble on his face and ruffled hair. He grabbed a mask but applied a thin layer of menthol ointment first this time. The added stench of gasoline and ash filling the room was just too much to tolerate.

"Man, how can you stand the smell?" Jack asked, furrowing his brows and adjusting the masks around his nose.

The silver-haired coroner let out a hardy laugh as he walked over to the gurney. "I guess I'm immune to it," he said, gloving up with a smirk on his face. "If you've been doing this as long as I have, it becomes like a side effect of the job."

The coroner pulled back the sheet, and the room became still and serious. The badly decomposed body was torched and not visually identifiable. All physical traits such as eyes, skin, genitals, and hair were no longer distinctive due to high, accelerate-induced heat, environmental factors, and scavenging animals. This was a desecration by all sense of the word.

"Please tell me you've got something...anything," the detective asked, sounding disgusted and wondering who in the world would do some shit like this. By far, this was the worst burned victim he'd ever encountered in his career.

"Well, I can definitely tell you this is a woman based on the shape of the pelvic region. You see the female pelvic inlet is more oval than a male's. A male's pelvic region is...."

"Okay Doc, I've got the picture," Jack interrupted. "What about her age?"

"Oh, yes, her age," the coroner said, moving toward the counter and pointing to a set of dental x-rays on a view box.

"I took an x-ray of her jaw, and you see here? The bone levels around her teeth are high, not a lot of wear and tear. And look, her third molars—or wisdom teeth as people normally call them—are partially formed and haven't erupted yet. Based on these findings, I'm putting her between seventeen and twenty-five years of age. This was a very young woman. What a shame."

"What a shame is an understatement, Doctor. How long do you think she's been dead?"

The coroner shook his head. "I really can't say, Jack. The time of death is just too difficult to determine because of the body's condition. I have nothing to go on: Body temperature, rigor mortis, and post-mortem staining obviously cannot be assessed at this point. Maybe she's been dead several months—maybe even longer." He shrugged. "But I do know she was killed before she was burned. And under the circumstances, that's a blessing."

"What do you mean? How do you know this?" Jack asked.

"You see when a victim is being burned alive, a pugilistic position is taken. An example of this would be the clenching of a fist. With our victim, we have no clenching or any other defensive postures."

"So how do you think she died?"

"Well, I looked hard and found no signs of blunt trauma to the skull. But, I did find evidence of strangulation. Now, I can't definitively tell you if it were a manual or ligature strangulation. For that determination, I would need more intact skin or muscle tissue. But it's clear to me someone strangled this woman because her hyoid bone is fractured in two places."

"Right," the detective said, nodding his head. "So we know the *how*, but now we need to find out the *who* and the *why* as well as identify the woman lying on this table."

"And unfortunately, that's going to be a difficult task without having a separate set of dental x-rays for comparison. Even DNA testing isn't sophisticated enough to help out on this case," the coroner said. "So, how'd you find her again?"

"Can you believe this one? Two men fishing from the old 95 bridgeway over Lake Marion literally hooked her out of the water yesterday evening. Who knows where she was originally killed," Jack said, letting out a sigh of exasperation.

"Whatever trace evidence left behind was either washed away or destroyed by animals. The evidence just isn't here. So this is what we have to do. We're going to take the information we've collected and turn it over to the press and surrounding police departments. And since this murder happened so close to the border, I think we should also send a bulletin to the news outlets in North Carolina. You never know, maybe someone has already filed a missing persons report."

Jack took another glimpse of the body before leaving. He prayed someone would come forth and generate a lead.

"Whoever did this is a demented fuck and needs to be off the streets," he said, looking at the coroner. "We can't let this turn into a cold case."

Labor Day Week 1990

Chapter 68

As I left group therapy, I realized my life had come full circle. I was listening to different women tell the same stories I heard almost a decade ago at My Daughter's House. They were horrible testimonies of abuse by the hands of fathers, husbands, boyfriends, and even pimps. It appeared nothing really changes with time. There will always be an endless supply of cowardly men out to hurt, maim, and traumatize women.

I told Rachel I'd try. This was my second session, but I hadn't felt compelled to talk. Not because of embarrassment. I was older now and knew we all had something in common. We were all broken and had shared experiences of heartache and pain. I remained silent because I didn't have the worlds to express how I felt, which was strange considering I once made a living from talking to large audiences. But I'd never been good with telling people about my own personal struggles and private thoughts. I learned to keep those to myself a long time ago.

Tonight we had an interesting conversation with a clinical psychologist that made me think. The woman asked, "Why do you think we love so hard when 'love' is cruel and doesn't love us back?" Assuming she stressed the word *love* as a euphemism for men, the question triggered a firestorm of answers. Some said low self-esteem. And others shouted out stupidity and loneliness. But a woman sitting directly behind me caught everyone's attention when she said, "I suffer from a love sickness. That's my problem."

The woman explained that she always loved the idea of being in love and approached all of her relationships with a "never give up" attitude. And no matter how smart or confident a person she was within other areas of her life, she stayed with her extremely abusive husband because she sincerely believed he could be fixed.... And she would be the one to fix him.

Her words spoke to me, because I never saw myself as a weak, stupid woman with low self-esteem issues. Once upon a time, I used to be a rising star in a male-dominated broadcasting industry. The way I saw it, I just didn't like giving up on people I loved. Did that make me mentally ill? Did I fit that woman's description of someone being lovesick?

Maybe I have been so drunk in love with my husband I couldn't see reality through my impaired double vision. Maybe it was really time to let go of Marvin and deal with my own list of shortcomings? But how would I do it? It was something to think about on the drive back home.

Chapter 69

Toni came home late again. Marvin noticed it was the second time this week. She told everyone she joined a book club. It was the excuse she used to attend therapy sessions at the woman's shelter. She claimed the book club got her out of the house and gave her something to do since she stopped playing bingo. Reading and talking about books with other women stimulated her brain. But Marvin felt something was off about Toni. She seemed too quiet, too cold toward him.

Toni stood in front of the hanging mirror on the closet door in their bedroom. She began to undress, starting with her shirt then bra. Marvin walked up behind her, in the mood, and cupped her warm breasts. Quickly, she pulled away.

"Not tonight, babe. I'm tired," she said.

Tired! he thought. *When has Toni ever been too tired for sex?* Marvin watched Toni go into the bathroom while questions swarmed his head: *Is she still attracted to me? Is she still in love with me? Did she start seeing another man while I was gone?*

Marvin wanted answers to all of those questions but decided not to ask. It was too soon. He had only been back in the house for a short time, and the last thing he wanted to do was argue with his wife.

"Marvin, could you please turn on the TV to channel five. The eleven o'clock news is on and I want to see it."

"It's on," he said with a slight attitude, still feeling the sting from being rejected.

"Could you turn the volume up as well so I can hear it?" she shouted from the bathroom.

"Sure, why not."

"We've got some breaking news we have been following from Clarendon County," the news anchor said. "Police officials stated that they have found a burnt body in Lake Marion along Interstate 95 this past Thursday."

"What?" Toni said. She walked out of the bathroom and planted herself in front of the television, stunned by what she heard.

"The police believe this is the body of a young woman between the ages of seventeen to twenty-five. Now, the police are still asking the public for help. If you have any information that can help identify this person, please contact the Clarendon Police Department. Updates will be reported as they are made available."

"My God." Toni winced. "What kind of person could burn a woman and dump her in the lake like that? Marvin, are you listening to this?"

Like a deer in headlights, Marvin was too paralyzed to answer her question. His heart raced and his palms began to clam up. *It's her. I know it's got to be her,* he said to himself. *They'll give me life for this.*

"Marvin, did you hear me?" she asked, looking closely at her husband's face. "Are you okay? You don't look so good."

Toni's repeated concerns were ignored and sounded faint to Marvin in the background. He saw her lips move but his ears couldn't process a word.

He needed an out. It felt like the room was getting smaller and smaller by the second. Then suddenly he blinked and sprung up from his wide-eyed trance, nearly knocking Toni over. His actions were manic as he stumbled around trying to get his clothes and shoes on in a hurry.

"I can't deal with this shit here," Marvin said lowly underneath his hyperventilating breath as he bolted out the front door, heading for his car.

Fuck, I need to think…I need to think! Shit! I need a drink!

Chapter 70

Marvin returned home in the middle of the night, beating the sun by two hours or so. I waited up for him not to get an explanation for his actions but to let him know I was done. The moment he walked in the living room I could smell the scent of alcohol all over him. There were no words that could describe my feelings. It was far beyond anger; it was pure exhaustion.

He walked up to me looking guilty. I wasn't surprised. The way he ran out here like a headless chicken, I knew whatever set him off would lead him straight to a bar. That's why I packed up his shit so he could leave tonight.

"Thought you stopped drinking," I said, staring directly into his eyes.

"Toni, please, let's not do this right now."

"Well, if not now, then when because I'm tired of this merry-go-round. You run out of here like a maniac and then you come back drenched in alcohol. Is this supposed to be your big change, Marvin? Well, you can keep your change!"

Marvin looked right through me as if he had something more pressing on his mind. He had been drinking, but I could tell he wasn't drunk and understood every word I said.

"Toni, I'm in a lot of trouble. More than you could possibly image," he said, sounding desperate.

"Marvin, that's none of my concern. I've got children to raise. So whatever trouble you're in, I want no part of it." I walked behind the couch, grabbed his duffel bag, and tossed it at his feet. I stood there with my mind made up and arms folded over.

"What's this?" he asked.

"I've given you and this marriage multiple chances to succeed," I said without hesitation or a single tear in my eyes. I felt strong and good about my decision. "I need you to leave right now. You can get your other stuff later."

When those words came out my mouth, I suddenly felt free. Like a heavy old burden had been lifted off me, and I could breathe.

"I'm telling you that I'm in trouble and you're throwing me out?" He raised his voice.

"I can't help you, Marvin."

"You can't help me, hah." He started to seethe. "You can't help me!" And then he lost it. Marvin punched me in the face and then threw me to the ground with a hard kick to my side. This time his force felt different. Marvin was furious and out of control.

"Stop it! You're hurting me! Why are you doing this to me?" I screamed.

Looking like something straight from Hell, his eyes became dark and empty when he replied, "Bitch. You don't tell me when to stop. I'll stop when I think you've had enough!"

I lay on the floor with blood dripping from my nose. He kicked me again.

"Please, stop!" I begged in agony.

While I tried crawling away, I prayed for relief and asked myself the same old questions in my head: *What in the world did I do to deserve this? Why have I put up with his shit for so long? Why won't he just leave?*

After all the fights, after all the cover-ups, and after putting my children's lives in jeopardy far too many times, the answer finally became clear. It took his last blow for me to see the truth flashing before me...we were both insane. He was crazy for beating me all these years, and I was just as crazy for staying with him and allowing it to happen. That woman and Thelma were right. I was lovesick. But, no matter what he did to me, it would end today.

"Mama, what's happening?" Justine hollered from the end of the hallway. I turned my head. "Go Justine. Go to your room and lock the door." It took all my strength to say it.

Marvin dragged me off the floor and pushed me up against the wall. He got in my face and put his arm underneath my chin. He pressed.

"I can't breathe," I managed to get out.

"I should have done this a long time ago," Marvin said through clenched teeth.

"Get off my mother!" Justine screamed with a cordless phone in her hand. "I've already called the police and they're on their way."

Justine flung her arm back and hurled the phone hard at Marvin. It struck his head with a loud thump. Instantly, he stepped back, and I dropped to the floor. I moved my hand over my throat and sucked in air for life. There was a burning sensation in my chest when I inhaled.

"So, now you're going to hit your father?" he said, holding his head and looking shocked. "Your mother is right; you are disrespectful." He started to walk toward Justine. Quickly, she moved to the other side of the living room, trying to keep a safe distance.

"I'm not afraid of you and you're not my father," she shouted.

Adrian came out of his bedroom already sobbing and stood next me. "No, Daddy, stop," he cried out. But Marvin ignored his son and kept his attention on Justine.

"Bitch, look at what you've done!" he said, assessing his fingers after touching his head again. "I'm bleeding. I should have whipped your ass a long time ago too."

Marvin took off his belt and blocked Justine into a corner. Tears were gushing down her face but she held her ground and did not whimper. Not one sound.

I used the couch to pull myself up. Then I saw Marvin spring back his hand. Fright made me run. Even with crippling pain, I used some kind of superhuman strength to move in fast. And just when he threw his arm forward, I caught it and stood in front of Justine.

"Not my daughter, you bastard!" I told him with blood trickling from my busted lip. "Hit me, but you will never touch my child." I pushed him away. "Now, get out! The cops will be here any minute. And you know you don't want to go back to jail!"

Marvin took a step forward but I didn't blink or flinch.

"Get out!" I screamed again then glared at him through my one un-swollen eye. "We're over!"

Marvin turned away, picked up his bag, and left the house without a single word. The moment the door shut, I ran to lock it. I came back and Justine was sitting on the couch with a vacant expression on her face. I sat down next to her and called over Adrian. I held them and rocked back and forth.

Now I understood Justine's anger and fear. I betrayed her. A mother is supposed to protect her children. But I invited the devil back into our home and made my kids live in Hell.

"I'm sorry, y'all. I'm so, so sorry. Please, forgive me," I whispered with my eyes closed as tears rolled down my face, trying hard to ignore my physical pain.

Justine wrapped her arms around me and for the first time in a long time, she hugged me back.

Chapter 71

Many hours later, I found myself settling in at the Safe Haven shelter. Rachel and the police officer strongly advised me to pack up a few things and leave home immediately just in case Marvin returned. Earlier at the hospital, they put me through a lot of testing and a female officer took photographs of my face, stomach, and other areas of my body.

They told me I was a walking miracle. I survived the attack with no concussion or internal bleeding. But I had deep muscle contusions, bruised ribs, and a broken nose. After the doctor manually realigned the bones and cartilage in my nose, he put me on prescription grade Ibuprofen and told me to get plenty bed rest and try icing.

This time around I didn't hesitate to press charges. I wanted to see Marvin behind bars and far away from my children. The police department assured me the restraining order would be fast tracked and processed within forty-eight hours. But they needed to catch and serve Marvin.

"I'm proud of you, Mama." That's what Justine said to me. It felt good to hear her say that. But I was more proud of her. She was my hero the way she stood up to Marvin. And right there in the hospital, I made her a promise. I told her I would follow through this time and make sure Marvin pays for what he'd done.

It was Monday afternoon and I was more than tired and so were the kids. Three-thirty felt more like ten-thirty. Rachel put us up in a nice room with two queen-sized beds. I kissed my children and told them everything would be alright. Afterward I slipped underneath the covers and fell into an overdue deep sleep.

Tuesday morning, I awoke feeling rested but still sore and ready to wash the previous day away. I stepped out from the hot shower. The steam fogged up the bathroom mirror. I grabbed a dry washcloth and began wiping in circular motions. My reflection caught my attention. For the first time, I got a good look at my fresh bruises. I had a swollen face, a black eye, and dark purple marks all over my side and back. There were so many of them mixed in among my old scars. Something felt wrong in my mouth. I skimmed the edges of my teeth with my tongue and leaned into the mirror with a smile.

"Shit!" I exclaimed, shaking my head in disgust. My front upper left tooth was broken and noticeable when I talked.

I pulled back and finally scrutinized my naked body with a sense of honesty I hadn't taken in a very long time. I realized I was a horrible wreck. My body resembled a battered soldier coming in from the front lines with each bruise and scar telling different battle stories of war from my marriage. I stared at the mirror wondering how I survived them all. By the way I looked, I should have been in a morgue a long time ago.

They served breakfast at 8:00 AM and, for those who were interested, an early morning therapy session would be available at 10:30. Rachel recommended that I start talking. She said it would help release some of my frustrations and anxiety. I asked Justine to watch over her brother and let him play with the other kids in the backyard while I attended.

I sat down and looked around the room. It was almost empty, making me feel more at ease. Only two other women I recognized from last Thursday's meeting showed up. Rachel was counseling. I nodded and gave faint smiles to each member of the group as our eyes met.

"Good morning everyone," Rachel said. "Does anyone want to start off today? Get whatever you need off your chest?"

We all looked at each other and wondered which brave soul would go first. And then the young girl with a long slash across her left cheek raised her hand. I knew she couldn't be any more than twenty years old, but the healing laceration on her face made her appear older.

"I'd like to start," she said in a soft tone.

"Okay, Davina. Go ahead," Rachel said.

"I think I'm leaving today." Davina smiled. "I talked with my mother last night and she said Darnell stopped by with flowers and money to pay the rent. My mother felt he was really sorry this time and would never do anything that would put my life and our son's life in danger."

"Not in danger? Well, how'd you get that cut on your face?" the other woman blurted out and shook her head.

"That was an accident!" Davina snapped back.

I closed my eyes and tried to hold back the anguish I felt listening to the young girl, but I saw my image in her face. Her story was like mine: the cover-ups, the many excuses, the lies. I turned my head and could no longer remain silent.

"Don't do it, Davina," I said as tears rolled down my face. "I spent over ten years of my life with a man who beat me, tortured me, and turned my child against me."

Davina looked at me and gave me her full attention.

"At first, I didn't want to hear what other people had to say about him. And yet the warnings came anyway. They said he was violent and came from a violent family and that he would never be good for anyone. But I ignored them all because I was raised up in a violent home myself, and who better to understand him than me? I believed my unconditional love could heal him, help him. Make him the man I wanted him to be. But, I learned the hard way: you can't help a man who's sick. Do you know my husband almost killed me?"

I unbuttoned my shirt and exposed the long train-track scar that ran between my breasts. Davina's horrified eyes fixated on my scar as she touched her face.

"Yeah, he did this shit to me," I said, nodding while trying hard to fight back new tears. "He did this because of plain jealousy and nothing else. You see, I was being honored at a banquet for my contribution to black media. My husband saw City Councilman Lester Banks congratulate me with a hug and a kiss on the cheek. He knew Lester and I went way back as kids. And still, he concluded from Lester's small gesture that we were secretly having an affair. But that wasn't true.

"That night really got to my husband. It was too much to bear. Watching me get an award and Lester touching me made him furious and ill with jealousy. So he left the party without saying a word and decided to wait for me in the bushes at our home. And after a friend dropped me off, he jumped out, looked me straight in the eyes, and stabbed me. All I remember saying to him was—'God ain't dead.'"

I raised my hand to my chest and touched the rugged scars. That's when I started to sob and finally let everything go. The memory of pain and being on the brink of death soon rushed in and made me question my own mental state. *How could I stay with a man who did this to me? What's wrong with me?*

Rachel quickly scooted over with a box of tissue. "I had no idea. I never knew," she said.

"No one knew the truth, Rachel," I said, wiping my face. "I never told anyone until now."

"You see, Davina," I continued, "the man I loved left me with only one lung to breathe, and I covered up what he did to me for years. So, from one scarred woman to another, don't take him back. Don't let him tear your body and soul apart. Men like them never change, and we can't help or change them. No matter how hard you try."

Davina looked away and kept quiet. It wasn't clear if I made a breakthrough or not.

"I need some air," I said, leaving my seat and heading for the door. In the hallway, I took in two deep breaths and dried my face.

"Hey," Rachel said. "Are you okay?"

"Yeah." I nodded. "I'll be fine. I'm just glad to get that out. I've been holding on to that secret for years trying to protect Marvin."

"Well, you may not know it, but you did some good in there. I think Davina heard you loud and clear."

"Yeah, maybe so." I shrugged. "Listen Rachel, I need to go back to the house to pick up some things. The kids and I need more clothes, and I've got some money hidden in the closet I forgot to bring with me. Could you keep an eye out on the kids while I'm gone?"

"Toni, that's too dangerous right now," Rachel warned. "You know Marvin is still out there somewhere. Can't this wait another day or maybe until this weekend?"

"No, Rachel. I can't wait. I'm out of money and the kids still have to go to school. They've already missed school today, and I don't want them sacrificing any more days because of the mess I'm in. If anything, they need structure."

I knew Rachel began to see things my way when her worried, bug-eyed expression started to fade away. She put her hands on my shoulder.

"Alright, fine. But do something for me? I've got a bad feeling about this, Toni. Could you just give it one more day to see if they catch Marvin?"

Rachel gave me a pleading look.

"Okay, I'll wait until Wednesday."

"Good," she said. "And one last request, Ms. Brave She-Ra. When you go to the house, make sure it's in the morning when there's more daylight. Today would have been good for me to tag along but after I finish up here, I've got to head out to work and tomorrow I have the early morning shift."

"That's fine, Rachel," I said smilingly, trying to get her to relax. "If it will make you feel better, I'll go bright and early in the morning after I drop off the kids at school."

"Thank you," Rachel said with a sigh of relief.

"You're welcome. And don't worry about me, lady. Marvin is not stupid enough to go back home. Trust me. He's long gone and probably hiding out at one of his cousin's houses in the deep country. But, to calm your nerves. How about I'll call you at work immediately after I'm done?"

Chapter 72

September 3, 1990 would go down as one of the darkest Labor Days in Porsha's life. She knew her gut instincts were right. Angela was in trouble, in fact, she was dead and her badly burned body was positively identified through dental records Monday afternoon by the Clarendon County Coroner's Office.

Porsha lay on the hotel bed and watched the slowly turning ceiling fan, still exhausted from yesterday's emotional explosion. There was so much hollering. Her attempts to console herself and Angela's family members at the morgue seemed useless. She felt a lingering soreness in her throat and pain in her heart. The sleep she got last night did nothing for her. Porsha cried hard and stayed up half the night thinking about her friend's gruesome death and killer.

How could someone do that to her? she questioned in her mind over and over again.

The Fayetteville Police Department in North Carolina got a call from a woman who said she had a roommate that supposedly moved to California but left a lot of her stuff behind. At first the caller wasn't too concerned. She knew her roommate had been eager to get out West and just figured she'd return for her things after getting settled. But she saw the news piece on television about a burned woman being found in Lake Marion and got suspicious. The caller had a strange feeling there was a connection to her former roommate.

An investigator was dispatched to the tipster's apartment to look through Angela's personal belongings. There were clothes packed up in boxes, bagged toiletries, and makeup on top of the dresser as well as a framed photograph of the missing woman and a female friend situated nearby. The woman was definitely going somewhere but there wasn't anything found that would help contact her next of kin. The roommate had no idea about Angela's personal life or family. Their living arrangement was temporary, and they weren't close friends.

The investigator returned to the police department with Angela's picture in hand to compare it to other profiles of missing persons posted on the wall. That's when the investigator called Porsha. The same name the tipster reported matched the name on the flyer Porsha gave to the Fayetteville Police Department several months earlier. All they had was a hunch. A blueprint was coming together, but the lines were still blurry. They would need evidence from dental records to make a definite ID.

By the time the investigator used Porsha's limited information to track down Angela's family and send it over to the Clarendon County Sheriff's Department in South Carolina, Porsha was already on the road Saturday evening praying, crying the body wasn't Angela's. And by the time Sunday morning came around, the Reeses were in town with dental records feeling distraught—and worse, fearing the coroner's report. *But it was a match.*

Now, Angela's parents and brother were getting ready to head back to Memphis, Tennessee to mourn with other family members and friends and properly give Angela's soul to rest. They planned on cremating her body and have the memorial by the weekend. Earlier that morning, Mrs. Reese called Porsha's hotel room and thanked her again for being a good friend to Angela and not giving up on looking for her daughter. "You're an angel," Mrs. Reese said, whispery through her tears. "You will always have a place at my table."

Porsha hung up the phone with damp eyes experiencing conflicting emotions. She was relieved to get some partial closure for herself and Angela's family, but she was still angry as hell. Porsha desperately wanted to know: *Who murdered Angela?*

Chapter 73

He spent two nights in a homeless shelter. Nobody asked for an ID card or cared where he came from. All he knew the cops were after him, and he made a vow not to go back to jail. Now Marvin found himself in a bar on the seedy side of North Charleston drinking and trying to think his way out his troubles.

He needed to move on. That was clear. *But where?* he repeatedly asked in his head. After the first shot of gin, he scanned the room for a familiar face. When he didn't recognize anyone, he let out a sigh of relief. It was just a hole in the wall bar sprinkled with hopeless-looking people and cheap booze. He fit right in.

The loud television in the corner showing the five o'clock news caught his attention. "We've got an update on the burned victim discovered last week in Lake Marion," the news reporter said. "The Clarendon County Police Department has positively identified the woman as Angela Reese, a twenty-three-year-old woman from Memphis,

Tennessee who worked as an exotic dancer in Fayetteville, North Carolina."

Angela's picture popped up on screen.

"Ooh wee!" the bartender exclaimed. "That was one fine woman. Who in the hell would burn that? He must be crazy."

Marvin was no longer rattled by the news. He made peace with it and always understood it was just a matter of time until someone found her body. But the bartender's comment made him snicker knowing he already had Angela in so many ways the man could only fantasize about. Marvin closed his eyes. He knew all too well what it was like to be inside her, to taste the essence between her thighs, to kiss her supple mouth and long neck, which was adorned by her cherished angel charm necklace.

"The necklace!" He gasped loudly out of his daydream, causing people to turn and look his way. He dropped a five-dollar bill on the counter and rushed out of the bar. He just remembered. The one piece of evidence that could connect him to Angela was around Toni's neck. What an arrogant dick he was to give Toni that as a promotion gift.

The plan was simple: Get the necklace and get out of town.

Chapter 74

By Tuesday night, I finally got the chance to make some calls to let people know where I was and what had been going on. Brenda was mad as hell at me for not calling her sooner. "I could have met you at the hospital," she said, horrified, over the phone. But she forgave me and was glad I was getting help.

I called Mama next. The last time we spoke was on Sunday morning. I knew she probably called the house about a thousand times and became extremely worried when no one picked up the phone. When I talked to her, the information I gave was basic. I told her about the fight, Marvin's arrest warrant, and my whereabouts. But there was no need to tell her about my pain or describe the bruises that were all over my body.

I said I was serious this time. Marvin and I were over and there was no looking back.

"Good," she said with a light whimper and a sense of relief coming from her voice. "Sounds like you're ready to leave him, baby. Sounds like you've had enough."

After I hung up the telephone, I turned around and saw Adrian staring back at me with stressed, overflowing eyes. I raised my hands to my face and blew out a huge sigh. Unfortunately, he'd heard everything I said about his father. But he just turned six years old and needed to know the truth.

I moved over to Adrian with my arms wide open and held him tightly as he burst out into tears. The child wailed loudly, pressed up against my chest. The sounds of his deep groans were heart-wrenching to me as a mother. Who knew what amount of frustrations and anger lay beneath his young skin and for how long? Children see and remember everything. I know I did.

"Adrian," I said softly, kissing his head. "I need you to be a big boy and understand something. Your father and I will never be together again, but I will always love you. That will never change."

He looked up at me and through his sad expression replied, "I know, Mama."

"Mama, are you really going back to the house tomorrow?" Justine asked while standing behind me and ironing her clothes for school in the morning.

"Yes," I answered. "Are you okay with that?"

"No, not really," she replied. "That's why I asked because I don't have to go to school tomorrow. I can go with you instead so you won't be alone."

"No, Justine. That's not necessary. I don't want you getting anymore absents counted against you. Besides, I'll be fine. I'm just going to pick up some clothes and money I left in the bedroom. I have no idea how long we're going to be here and I need that money. Don't worry."

"Mama?"

"Yes, dear."

"Are we out of money?" Justine asked, sounding concerned.

"Yes, just about, but we'll be alright. Why do you ask?" Justine's question seemed peculiar. I turned around and gave her a curious look. "What's going on?"

"Well, Mama, if we need money, I have some. I've been saving for a long time. But if we need to get by, then it's yours. I can start over."

"How much money have you saved, Justine?"

"$600."

"That's a whole lot of money, girl. Are you sure?"

Justine nodded her head then gave a slight smile. "Yes, ma'am, I'm sure."

She appeared genuinely happy to help out during our time of hardship. I was proud and blessed to have her as a daughter. In that moment I felt certain whatever challenges our situation would bring, as a team, we would get through them together. I would pick up her money for safekeeping, but not spend it. She earned it and deserved to keep it. I looked at my hand and figured out exactly how to get some extra cash. After leaving the house tomorrow, I planned on taking all the jewelry Marvin gave me, including my wedding ring, and hock it at a pawnshop.

Chapter 75

From the driveway, the house looked dark and lifeless even in the bright morning sunlight. I had a goal and that was to get in and get out fast. With my senses alert, I cautiously turned the doorknob and walked in. I turned left and right; everything appeared safe.

I stopped by Justine's room first to collect some clothes and the money she had in her secret place. Then I went into my closet, pulled out my stash in the pocket of my old coat, and stuffed it down my oversized bag. And just when I was about to leave, I decided to check out Marvin's belongings to see if there was any money or anything we could use.

Quickly, I rummaged through the closet and came across a small lightweight lock box hidden behind a milk crate of old martial arts magazines. The lock seemed easy to pry open. So I went to the kitchen, got a pointy steak knife, and returned to the bedroom. I placed the box on the dresser and popped it open quickly as expected. Inside was Marvin's birth certificate, a gold watch, two $100 bills, and a folded wrinkle paper. Underneath the paper lay a switchblade knife with a black and silver handle. I pushed in the button. The sound of the blade ejecting made me gasp and toss it back into the box. I believe that was the same knife Marvin wielded in my face before stabbing me.

I took a deep breath and steadied my nerves. I looked over at the box again and for some reason the paper aroused my curiosity. I picked it up and unfolded it. It was a flyer for a missing woman. She was young and attractive. The flyer said her name was Angela Reese. I scanned the flyer and zoned in on her necklace. It looked just like mine. Then suddenly, a light bulb came on and my brain flashed back to the note I found in Marvin's coat pocket. I remembered the piece of paper having a phone number on it and read: *Call me. Angela.* I dropped the flyer and threw my hands over my mouth.

Is this the trouble he spoke of the other day? No, he's not that crazy.

"But why would he have this?" I questioned out loud.

"Find something interesting?" Marvin asked, standing behind me.

My heart sank the moment I heard his voice. I turned around stunned then quickly grabbed the steak knife off the dresser.

"Marvin, what are you doing here? How did you know I was here?"

"I've been watching and waiting," he simply replied, giving me a venomous stare.

"Well, there's warrant out for your arrest and people know where I am."

Marvin didn't respond but kept his focus on the knife.

"Did you know that woman in the flyer?" I asked nervously. "Did you have something to do with her disappearance?"

Marvin stepped forward.

"What are you going to do with that knife, Toni? Do you really have the guts to use that?" he calmly asked with a bone-chilling smirk.

The menacing look on his face pierced right through my soul and made my hands shake, but I needed to know. "Tell me, did you know that woman?"

Marvin continued to ignore my questions and took another step forward.

"Stop right there, dammit. Don't you dare take another step! Answer me, Marvin!" I screamed with watering eyes. "I want to know. Did you give me that woman's necklace?"

"You know what?" he said, shaking his head. "Angela was just like you. She had too much damn mouth...and now she doesn't. Just give me the necklace and that box, and you'll never have to see me again."

I glanced down at the charm in disbelief. "What do you mean she *was?*" I said, getting a sickening feeling in my stomach. Marvin gave me a blank stare. "Oh, you sick fuck. You killed that woman. Didn't you?"

Marvin moved in fast and tried to reach for my neck.

"Get away from me!" I shouted as I climbed over the bed to the other side of the room. "I can't believe I married you. You're crazy!"

I swung the knife when Marvin got closer to me but missed. He laughed. "You've got to do better than that if you're going to take me out." I took two more jabs and then finally sliced his left arm.

"You bitch!" He grunted then lunged forward in full force.

I raised the knife over my head, ready to penetrate deep, but he caught my arm and wrestled me to the floor. I couldn't move. He was on top of me with my arm pinned above my head. The knife was far out of reach.

"You're hurting me," I cried out, still feeling the pain from my bruised ribs.

Marvin snatched the necklace off my neck and leaned in close. "See that wasn't so hard. You always have to make things so difficult."

"Get off me, Marvin," I said, trying hard to pull away. "You've got what you came for. So why don't you just leave!"

"You really think I'm going to let you go when you know so much?" he said. "Besides, I told you long time ago nobody leaves me."

"What do you mean? What are you going to do?"

"What do you think?" he said slowly through pinched lips.

"No, Marvin, please. Please, don't kill me," I whimpered. "I'm your wife. I won't say anything. You know you can trust me."

"My wife, right," he scoffed. "Just the other day you kicked me to the curb. Now, you're my best friend all of a sudden. No, I can't trust you. You're not loyal to me anymore and I'm not loyal to you."

"But, Marvin, you can trust me," I tearfully said, trying to change his mind. "Haven't I always kept your secrets? Haven't I always had your back? Whatever happened between you and that woman I know couldn't have been your fault."

A look of anguish washed over Marvin's face. He broke down.

"I didn't mean to kill her, Toni. It was an accident; I promise you."

"I believe you," I said, staring up into his eyes. "I believe you."

Marvin looked away and then started shaking his head. "No, I can't trust you, and I'm not going back to jail. I'd rather take my own life than go back there."

"You don't have to do this!"

"Yes, I do," Marvin said, fixing his killer's gaze on me. "I'm in too deep. But before I say my final goodbye, I want to get me one more look at your beautiful face."

Marvin came in closer. "I'm going to miss your sexy eyes," he said as he kissed them both. "I'm also going to miss your luscious smile."

Marvin pressed his stale mouth against my quivering lips while his right hand glided over my neck and gripped it. I felt disgusted but kissed him back to distract him from seeing my fingers desperately try to reach for the knife.

Too far up! I panicked in my mind.

My frightened eyes filled with tears and my body started to shiver knowing my life could come to an end at any second. *Please God! Just a few more inches, that's all I need!* I screamed and pleaded in my head while we continued to kiss. I wanted to fight. I wanted to live. My spirit refused to let Marvin kill me again. Then it came to me. I did the only thing I could think of. I bit down on Marvin's bottom lip hard. So hard, I tasted his blood in my mouth. The pain caused a knee-jerk response, and he let go of my arm. Instantly, I pushed up to grab the knife and then plunged it deep into the side of his neck.

Marvin stumbled backward and landed sitting up against the dresser. He held his neck and gave me a long intense stare.

"I loved you," he managed to mutter and then pulled the serrated blade out of his neck.

I cringed in horror as he gasped for air while reaching out for me. Blood gushed everywhere. Then suddenly, his bloodshot, watering eyes became empty and fixed. It was over. The insanity was finally over.

Chapter 76

God must have a plan for me because I should be dead. At least that's what popped in my head when I saw the body bag passing the police cruiser I was sitting in. Everything around me seemed to be in slow motion and my thought process was on a delay. I knew I killed my husband but all I felt was numbness shielding my nerves instead of remorse.

An out-of-body experience or shock is what I've heard some people call this sensation. It was like I was floating. Sounds appeared faint and slurred in the background. I calmly watched and answered questions the best I could while coming to terms with what I had done.

The detective who interviewed me in the house had a familiar face. It took a few minutes to jog my memory, but I figured it out. It was Sergeant Wade Anderson, the same detective who investigated my stabbing case four years earlier. I knew he recognized me when he got into the car and gave me what appeared to be an inquisitive glance from the rear view mirror. But it wasn't a judgmental "I told you so" look, and he didn't make any chastising remarks. He just looked.

After I turned over the necklace for evidence and to back-up my story, the sergeant told me the grisly details of Angela Reese's death. It was sick. But I wasn't shocked. I didn't have the right to be. I'd discovered a long time ago just how disturbed Marvin really was the night he stabbed me. The night he meant for me to die.

Marvin's contempt for my life and our marriage ran deeper than I thought when I learned more about his affair with the stripper. Apparently, they had been seeing each other for months. According to Sergeant Anderson, the Clarendon County Sheriff's Department tracked down the woman's car from a recent abandoned vehicle report and found a diary inside.

They said the diary was detailed and had cataloged every dime he gave her, every gift bestowed, every time he crossed state lines to watch her perform, and even talked about their salacious sexual acts. The young woman described Marvin as a good lover but too intense and felt he may want more than just a casual friendship. In the last entry of the diary, she said she was moving to California in late January and her affair with Marvin would have to come to an end. With that information, investigators started to piece together a story and tentatively concluded that Marvin strangled Angela when she tried to end the relationship and leave him.

After listening to the detective talk about the affair, I found myself not having an ounce of animosity toward the woman. I actually felt sorry for her and saw her as a victim as much as I was. The poor girl had no idea who she was dealing with. If I wasn't so blind back then and had Marvin charged for stabbing me, maybe Angela Reese would be alive today. But I couldn't dwell on past regrets or misfortunes I couldn't change.

The car began to pull away from the house.

And even though I still felt disoriented, one thing became crystal clear as I headed to the police station to face possible charges. I completely understood it was my diseased mind all along that wouldn't allow me to leave Marvin and, essentially, kept me hostage in a life of conflict for years.

Obviously, Marvin had his problems, but so did I. From my experiences, I constructed an unhealthy concept of love. To me, love meant always being forgiving and to give it unconditionally with no expectations in return. But now I saw romantic love is supposed to be a 50-50 kind of love and something nurturing for the mind, body, and soul. Not abusive, selfish, jealous, and controlling. I never had real love from a man.

My revelation made me think hard about my children. I felt guilty about their upbringing. I inherited my mother's weakness and unconsciously copied her tolerance for abuse at all costs from my childhood. I didn't realize I had already set myself up for a mental illness that could spread to my children and cause permanent damage. I had deep concerns for them. How would they adjust after this? What would their love lives be like in the future? Would they grow up repeating what they saw or would they avoid my mistakes and break the cycle of violence?

Acknowledgments

I'd like to start off my acknowledgements with thanking God, of course. Without God, I wouldn't be able to dream, imagine, or persevere. To my parents, I am so grateful two dynamic personalities came together to produce the independent-thinking woman I have become. To my family and friends, thanks for your encouragement and believing in me. And to the friends and readers of the future, I can't wait to meet you. A special shout-out goes to Ms. Mary—thanks so much for your gentle push and being my number one fan. Finally, thanks to my editor—Kristen, Grady, the cover designer, Spotlight Photography, and Michael, the IT guy.

About the Author

Autumn J. Bright is the author of *Love Sick*, her debut novel. She resides in North Carolina, but is a native of Charleston, South Carolina and still considers the beautiful city home. Readers are welcome to learn more about Autumn and future works at her website www.autumnjbright.com.

If you enjoyed this debut work of fiction,

you won't want to miss out on

Autumn J. Bright's upcoming novel

Lovely

Please read on to get an early preview

Lovely

Part I
The Early Years

Prologue

IN the dead of an October night, a knock on the front door caused Dolores Duval to jump out of her sleep. "Joseph!" she whispered urgently while shaking her husband's arm. "Get up. Someone's at the door."

"What?" he responded, barely awake.

"Someone's at the door," she repeated louder.

Joseph turned around and gave his tired eyes a squint to focus in on the clock. He looked at his wife again. "Dolores, do you know what time it is? It's almost two o'clock in the morning. Ain't nobody out there. You probably just heard the wind knocking up against the porch. Now, please, honey, go back to sleep."

"Joseph, you go back to sleep," she snapped then reached for her housecoat draped over the chair. "I'm telling you I heard something, and I'm going to see what it is."

"Now, just hold on a minute," Joseph said, raising his voice a little. He rubbed his eyes then snatched his glasses off the nightstand. "There's no need to get snippy and bent out of shape about it. Just give me a second to put on my slippers. I'm coming."

The middle-aged couple approached the front door with caution and opened it to find a note wedged in between the screen door.

"What is it, Mama?" Irene asked, walking up from behind them. "Who's at the door?"

They suddenly heard a cry. Dolores gasped and pushed the door wider. And there on the porch, on a cool fall night, lay a baby all bundled up in a worn-out plastic laundry basket.

"Lord, have mercy!" Dolores shouted with wide terrified eyes. She quickly grabbed the baby and started rocking it in her arms. "Who in the world would leave an infant on the porch like this?" Dolores said, looking around into the darkness.

Irene picked up the note from off the ground. Her face went pale. "Mama," she said, with a sharp roll of her eyes at the paper. "It's from Corrine."

The look of disappointment washed over Dolores' face. It all seemed too familiar. She nodded then sighed. "Well, go ahead and read it," Dolores instructed.

Irene paused for a few moments, preparing her nerves for the load of crap she was about to read.

Dear Duval Family,

I don't know what to say. I guess I messed up again. After all these years, it seems I still can't get it together. I just can't handle children right now. Please give Lovely the same upbringing and love you've given Cynthia. They deserve so much, much more than I could ever give them. I hope you can forgive me.

Forever grateful,

Corrine

P.S.... I'm sorry, Irene.

Irene crushed the letter in her hand. She felt a surge of emotions running through her body: anger, hurt, and betrayal. But mainly shock. They were all shocked. It had been five years since they'd seen or heard from Corrine. It had been five years since Corrine begged Irene back in college while they were sophomore roommates to help with the first pregnancy. And it had been five long years since she broke her promise to be a part of Cynthia's life. Now, Corrine was back with the audacity to dump yet another child on their laps.

"Mama, we don't have to do this," Irene declared as she feverishly flipped through pages in the phone book. "We don't always have to save Corrine when she's in trouble. We need to call her family or social services. Who does she think we are, an orphanage?"

Irene shook her head as she moved next to phone. "Oh, no, she is not going to take advantage of us again. I'm tired of her."

"Now, wait a minute, Irene. Let's just think about this before you make any phone calls," Joseph said calmly as he sat on the couch next to his daughter. He took the phone out of her hand and hung it up.

"We all know Corrine is wrong," Joseph continued. "The first time, it was an accident. The second time, well, there's no excuse. But, we also know that family of hers isn't going to take this child in. We've already been down this road before."

Irene blew out a long sigh, knowing her father was right. She remembered how Corrine's parents were so strict and religious about almost everything. But, most of all, she remembered how they never gave one objection to Cynthia's adoption at the courthouse and still refuse to be involved in any aspect of her life today. "Children born out of wedlock are bastard children and seedlings of the devil," Irene once heard Corrine's mother say.

"Listen Dolores," Joseph said. "We gave Cynthia to your sister because she couldn't have any babies of her own. And now that Richard and Harriet are going through some tough times, there's no way they can afford another mouth to feed. So, I think we should adopt Lovely for ourselves. My point is this: She's got an older sister right across the street; it would be wrong of us to separate these girls. When you put everything else aside, y'all know I'm right."

Dolores stared at the baby. *Just a crying shame*, she thought to herself. The child had been on the earth for only a blink of an eye and was already facing problems that were none of her doing. And in that moment, the decision was made. The little girl would be raised as their own. Lovely was family.

Chapter 1

IT was just my luck! On the last day of school, I had to be sitting right smack in front of Winston Elementary's worst gang of misfits. The school bus couldn't get me home fast enough. Tasha Brown and her dim-witted friends were at it again, shooting nasty spitballs through straws at the back of my freshly pressed hair. Who knew stopping to say goodbye to my favorite teachers would land me a seat among a firing squad.

"Stop it Tasha! Stop it," I turned around and screamed. "If you don't stop it, I'll—"

"You'll what, Lovely? Tell your mama?" Tasha said with an attitude, shifting her neck from left to right and standing way too close to me.

And on cue, the kids at the back of the bus started oohing and laughing.

"But, oh, that's right," she continued loudly, smacking on a big wad of chewing gum. "You ain't got no mama. You were left on the porch by a stork in the middle of the night."

Everyone within earshot started laughing. This was my last day being a student at Winston Elementary. In the fall, I would be starting middle school and leaving Tasha behind, yet again, in the fourth grade. I got fed up with all her teasing and bullying over the years. This time she had it coming.

"Why don't you shut up you stupid, fat cow!" I yelled, shoving Tasha's bubble butt back into her seat. "I bet you can't even spell stork."

"Fight! Fight! Fight!" the kids egged on in chorus.

I wasn't sure I could give Tasha a good beatdown, but I gave my eyes a squint, put my deuces up anyway, and hoped for the best.

"Shut that noise up!" Ms. Gaston, the bus driver, hollered. "There will be no fighting on my bus today. Do y'all want me to pull over?"

Nobody wanted Ms. Gaston to stop the bus. She was like a mama and a daddy all rolled into one and had a goatee and mustache to prove it. And when she got to fussing, her voice was like a boom box and you could see all of her missing teeth. Only those pointy canines remained.

"Tasha, sit your tail down," she continued to regulate from the oversized rear view mirror.

"But I didn't do anything," Tasha hissed. "Lovely pushed me down."

Ms. Gaston hit the brakes and gave her famous *don't play with me* look.

"Yes, ma'am," Tasha quickly followed orders, folding her arms over, pouting and flaring her nostrils. The girl sitting next to Tasha gave her a slight smile.

"What are you gawking at?" Tasha snapped.

"Now, Lovely, come up here and sit behind me. Sit next to Jamal."

As I walked toward the front of the bus, I could hear Tasha mumble "Imma getcha good, Lovely" under her breath. But I wasn't afraid. Tasha lived too far away from my house to walk. Besides, that would be like exercise. And C.C. Johnson Middle School was about a twenty-five minute drive from Winston Elementary. I figured by the time Tasha graduated to middle school, I would be in high school. So, I ignored her stupid little threat.

I sat down next to Jamal as instructed. He was the new kid on the block, a fifth grader who lived three houses down from me. Rumor had it his father was serving a long-term jail sentence in upstate South Carolina for armed robbery, leaving Jamal, his mom and younger sister behind to fend for themselves, renting out the old Curtis house.

"Hi," he said, with a small smile.

Oh, wow! I said in my head. In all of the eight months of Jamal living in the neighborhood and us sharing the same bus stop, this was the first time he'd ever said anything to me. I mean, it didn't bother me he never spoke when I'd smile at him at the bus stop. I just figured he was the quiet-shy type who was too afraid to look people in the eyes or he wasn't raised with good manners.

"Hey," I replied, returning the same small smile.

"That was a pretty brave thing you did back there," he said. "Not too many people stand up to Tasha the way you did and keep their two front teeth." Jamal chuckled.

"Yeah, I'm not worried about Tasha," I said, rolling my eyes. "She's just a big ole dumb bully."

Jamal shook his head and flashed a bigger grin.

"You know, Jamal," I said with one eyebrow raised, "I think she's jealous of me. I can read and write and get good grades in school with no problems. But she's not too swift and has to repeat the same grade almost every year. Must be frustrating being almost twelve years old and still in elementary school." I turned and looked Jamal's way. "Don't you think?"

Jamal nodded rapidly as we smiled hard at each other. Then it began. He started up with that dang-on giggling, and I followed right behind him. His giggles were so contagious, we had to cup our mouths with our hands and lean over into the seat so no one could hear or see our laughter. We couldn't stop and laughed until we cried and our stomachs ached.

"You're funny, Lovely." Jamal caught his breath to speak. "And I like your name too."

"Hey, thanks," I managed to get out. Jamal seemed like a cool person. I started to wonder if he was going to C.C. Johnson in the fall. To be honest, having a friend at a brand new school would be a great relief. "So, what about you, Jamal, did you pass? Are you going to middle school next year?" I asked.

"Yeah, I'm going to the sixth grade."

"Well, good," I said. "We have something in common. Maybe now we can speak to each other at the bus stop sometimes?"

Jamal nodded while pushing his drooping glasses up his nose.

"Alright, Lovely, here's your stop," Ms. Gaston announced with the warmest tone. "Tell ya mama I said hello and you take care of yourself in school next year, ya hear?"

"Yes ma'am," I replied sweetly.

As the bus rolled away, I could see Tasha in the window waving her middle finger at me. She was like an irritating thorn I just plucked out of my big toe after running barefoot through an open field in the summer. I stuck my tongue out at her then looked over at Jamal. We burst into loud laughter again. Soon, the yellow elementary bus and Tasha Brown became distant fading images on the road.

Chapter 2

LIKE clockwork, Mama had been sitting on the front porch waiting for me to return home from school. And, as usual, her long salt and pepper hair was neatly tucked into a ball, and she had on one of her numerous oversized muumuus she loved to put on for cooking. Normally, Mama wore simple clothes and stayed away from anything flashy, but for some reason, she really enjoyed those multi-colored muumuu dresses. The busier the pattern, the more she seemed to like it.

The year was 1984 and as long as I'd known her, Mama had always been predictable. So predictable you could set your watch by her daily routine during the school week.

Breakfast = 7:30 AM

Mama sitting on the porch = 2:45 PM

Dinner on the table = 6:00 PM

The weekends and special times were no different. We went to church every Sunday and sat in the same spot and Mama always had freshly baked chocolate chip cookies ready for me on the last day of school. These days, at the age of sixty-five, Mama enjoyed being a retired librarian and a predictable homemaker.

"Who was that handsome boy you were walking with, Lovely?" she asked, smiling brightly as I walked up the driveway.

"Oh, that's Jamal Turner. You know the family that moved into Mr. Curtis' old house a few months ago."

"Oh, yes," she recalled. "That's that woman whose husband went to jail for stealing."

I was sure Mama got that piece of information from Mt. Moriah Baptist Church, which happened to be the place where most of the town's gossip got circulated. Mama never started gossip, but she definitely listened to it.

"I guess so." I shrugged my shoulders.

I never really paid any attention to rumors, especially since I had been the subject of gossip ever since the day I was born. My family never lied to me about my adoption. Knowing exactly how I came into this world gave me a tough skin at an early age.

"Such a shame that poor woman has to raise those kids on her own," Mama continued, still going on about the Turners. "What a pity…."

"Look, Mama, I made the honor roll again!" I blurted out, waving my report card in the air, hoping to change the subject. Mama didn't often judge people out loud, but she firmly believed that all children should have a mother and a father at home. There was only one problem: When she started talking about something that bugged her, she could go on and on.

"Oh, that's good, baby!" Mama hugged me and kissed my forehead. "I'm so proud of you. C'mon, let's go inside and get you some cookies." The smell of warm chocolate and tonight's dinner hit me the moment the door swung open.

"Did your friend pass as well?" Mama went on to ask.

"Yes ma'am," I answered, walking behind her. "He's going to the sixth grade too."

"Good, now you'll have someone your own age to talk to around here instead of you just clinging to Irene or reading in your bedroom all the time."

Mama had a point. I loved to read and could do it all day. Books took me to places that were fun and interesting. Not like around here in Willisburg, South Carolina. We lived out in the boonies among a few spaced-out houses on a country back road where a bunch of old people live. The only entertainment I got was from reading or catching fireflies in the yard during the summers. And when I really got bored, I'd just hang out with Irene.

"I really think you should try to make some friends at school next year. Maybe some girlfriends," Mama said. "You're growing up, Lovely, and you need to start developing some type of social life, but I think that boy Jamal will do you some good for now."

"Who's Jamal?" Irene asked, sitting in the kitchen eating my cookies.

"What are you doing here?" I asked instead. "I thought you were at work?"

"I took the day off. And don't change the subject, missy," she replied with raised eyebrows and a smirk on her face. "Who's Jamal? Is that your boyfriend?"

"No, Irene!" I wrinkled my nose at her like there was something funky in the air. "He's just a boy who lives down the street."

"Okay, okay. I'm just asking," she said teasingly. "Anyway, I like your outfit. You look cute today."

I twirled around to show off my pink and black polka-dot dress with black jelly shoes. Anything that had pink or red in it I liked. Those were my favorite colors. They looked good up against my dark skin—at least that's what Mama told me.

"Lovely, what are those white things in your hair?" Irene asked, interrupting my fashion show. "Girl, what were you doing today?" Irene brushed off the back of my dress. "Go look at yourself in the mirror."

Just when I thought I got rid of crazy Tasha, flashbacks from this afternoon came back to haunt me. "Don't even ask," I said, letting out a long sigh while walking away.

I stood in the bathroom mirror and shook spitballs out of my Shirley Temple curls. Mama always did a good job on my hair and kept it healthy and long, just like hers. She said the secret was a mixture of Shea butter and love. Whatever she used made me the envy of most girls at school and church. Maybe that's the reason I didn't have any female friends—well, except for Anika Douglas. Anika and I had been friends for as long as I could remember. We didn't go to school together, but we saw each other every Sunday at church. And she never seemed interested in my hair. Anika always kept hers in braids.

As I continued to fix myself up, I started to daydream about the up and coming school year. I felt excited because everything would be fresh and new: the school, the teachers, and now Jamal. It was just a couple of months until my new adventure began. I had a good feeling about C.C. Johnson Middle School.

82042153R00227

Made in the USA
Middletown, DE
31 July 2018